HEIR,
APPARENTLY

ALSO BY

KARA MCDOWELL

The Prince & The Apocalypse

This Might Get Awkward

One Way or Another

Just for Clicks

HEIR, APPARENTLY

A NOVEL

KARA McDOWELL

WEDNESDAY BOOKS
NEW YORK

First published in the United States by Wednesday Books, an imprint of St. Martin's Publishing Group

HEIR, APPARENTLY. Copyright © 2024 by Kara McDowell. All rights reserved. Printed in the United States of America. For information, address St. Martin's Publishing Group, 120 Broadway, New York, NY 10271.

www.wednesdaybooks.com

Designed by Devan Norman

The Library of Congress Cataloging-in-Publication Data is available upon request.

ISBN 978-1-250-87309-5 (trade paperback)
ISBN 978-1-250-87307-1 (hardcover)
ISBN 978-1-250-87308-8 (ebook)

Our books may be purchased in bulk for promotional, educational, or business use. Please contact your local bookseller or the Macmillan Corporate and Premium Sales Department at 1-800-221-7945, extension 5442, or by email at MacmillanSpecialMarkets@macmillan.com.

First Edition: 2024

10 9 8 7 6 5 4 3 2 1

TO SCOTT,

BECAUSE YOU DESERVE ONE OF THE GOOD ONES

HEIR,
APPARENTLY

PART I

CHAPTER 1

It turns out that the "too long; didn't read" version of the world almost ending in a fiery comet explosion is just the word "almost." It could have happened, but it didn't. Close but no cigar. The apocalypse-that-wasn't.

Life as we know it was *almost* completely different, and the weight of that "almost" is everything. Contrary to viral internet theories and speculation, reckoning with death *didn't* upend society, most of the population didn't quit their jobs to go off-grid or live in a van, and the economy didn't grind to a halt.

Which is good! But also . . . kind of weird?

The optimist in me wanted to buy into the *other* theories. The ones that thought humans would finally learn how to co-exist peacefully. No more gun violence, no more violation of basic human rights, and no more taking three weeks to respond to a text because you were lazy and then forgot.

We stared death in the face, and we lived to tell the tale. Call me naive, but I thought our new lease on life would mean something. When you're told you have eight days left to live and then defy the odds—shouldn't that change, like, *everything*?

Spoiler alert: it didn't.

On the outside, life looks the same as it always has. I'm at Wildcat Welcome Week at Northwestern University, and it's exactly what every college movie has prepared me for. Throngs of incoming freshmen have flooded the campus, with stars in their eyes and dreams of a new life filled with parties and booze, classes and friends, sex and freedom.

My life is on more or less the same trajectory it was when I landed in London back in June. Comet or not, I probably would have always been here, staring into the dark eyes of a stranger at a freshman orientation party thrown by an off-campus frat house. Classes don't start for a few more days, but college life has officially begun.

Despite what I once wanted to believe, this mediocre party is my real fate.

"What's your major?" the boy (Ethan?) asks as he fills my cup with foamy beer that I have no intention of drinking, while my phone buzzes endlessly in my pocket. I glance at the screen and have a quick internal meltdown before focusing back on the guy in front of me. He's a few inches taller than me, with light brown skin and shaggy black hair. He's thin but not lanky, and when he smiles nervously, I realize he's cute in a way that would have caught my attention, before.

I guess not *everything* is the same.

"Undeclared," I tell him, accepting the warm beer. "What's yours?"

He leans closer so I can hear him over the music. "Engineering."

"No hesitation! Nice!" I hold my hand up for a high five. He obliges with a laugh.

"I'm sure you'll figure it out," he says.

"That makes one of us." Sometimes I wonder if there aren't *too* many options at college. (In life!) I know for a fact that there are more than two dozen different engineering majors and minors.

"No plans?" he asks, the word "plans" pressing on my fight-or-flight instinct like a fresh bruise.

"None whatsoever," I confirm. It's a weird feeling; I went from being a girl with all the answers about her future to one who is utterly directionless. I don't even know what next week will bring, let alone what I want to do with the rest of my life. I briefly thought photography was the answer, but what if I'm wrong? What if I waste my second chance?

When the gaping black hole that is my future starts to scare me, I remind myself that fate had my back in Europe, and who am I to think I'm stronger than destiny? Life will work itself out. (*Right?*)

He smiles, so I smile back, to prove to myself that I am present, that I'm *not* thinking about the Google Alerts blowing up my phone. I let the silence settle between Ethan and me for a beat too long—and take that as my cue to leave. My eyes wander over Ethan's shoulder, searching for my best friend, Naomi, who's just as likely to be found in a corner reviewing her class schedule and texting her boyfriend as she is to be doing a keg stand and making plans to pledge a sorority. She's as social as she is ambitious, and these days I feel less and less like either. I open my mouth to say "See you around!" at the same time Ethan doubles down on our conversation.

"What'd you do during Comet Week?" he asks.

"Comet Week" is what everyone now calls those seven or eight days where we all thought we were going to die. I glance down at my drink and grimace, remembering the last time I got drunk (in a small Italian home, with a girl who hated my guts). The memory of that hangover—like everything from that week—feels painfully fresh. I take a small sip and shudder as I swallow.

"Nothing much," I lie. He stares at me expectantly. I need to try harder. "I dyed my hair. It was horrible."

"I like it."

I sigh, exhausted in my bones. He's nice, and I wish he weren't, because then I'd have a reason to leave. "It was worse before." I run my fingers through my hair. A few weeks ago, Naomi had dragged me to a salon. I was weirdly relieved when the stylist said the bleach had damaged my hair beyond repair and it needed more time to recover. She'd offered to tone my streaky red-orange locks, and I'd accepted, thinking that having something less stripey and more natural would make me feel like myself again. (It didn't. It looks pretty much the same—minus the stripes—and every time I look in the mirror, I hear a confused British accent say "What's a Gritty?" and I want to throw up.)

Ethan nods, probably expecting me to add something interesting to the conversation. Unfortunately for him, it'll be a long wait. The first few weeks after my trip, I felt like a shaken-up pop bottle—ready to burst with all the secrets I was holding. From having gone through so much but not being able to talk about any of it. From the knowledge that I looked more or less the same on the outside but inwardly felt like every one of my molecules had been rearranged. Almost three months later, I'm still not ready to talk about it, especially not with strangers.

"What about you?" I ask Ethan. I'm rusty, but I'm trying.

"My fam and I got matching tattoos." He pushes his sleeve up and shows off a big creepy creature that looks like the monster from *Stranger Things*. "No regrets!" he says, and once again I'm jealous of his certainty. My phone buzzes and I can't suppress my curiosity any longer; my eyes stray to the screen, desperate to open the newest alert.

"My mom won't stop texting me," I lie again.

"Nervous parents?" He nods sympathetically. "My mom said if I don't respond to her texts within an hour, she's going to call campus police."

The fizzy, restless feeling is back with a vengeance.

"Do you want to dance?" I shout over the music. Ethan nods enthusiastically, so we both ditch our drinks on a nearby table (I'm not coming back for mine) and I drag him onto the makeshift dance floor. I drape my arms across his shoulders, crossing them behind his neck. He rests his hands politely on my hips and we sway easily with the music.

"I'm glad I met you," he says, his lips inches away from my ear.

"Mm-hmm!" I respond, suddenly conscious of the unbearable heat in this room. His hand slips from my waist to my lower back. I make eye contact for the first time since we started dancing, and my heart sinks. I'm hip to hip with a guy who is cute and nice and not ridiculously off-limits, and all I feel is the hollow realization that I'd rather be anywhere else.

He leans in, his lips a breath from mine.

I jump out of his arms. "I can't. I, I—" I look around, hoping Naomi will swoop in and save me.

"Hey, it's fine." He raises his hands in the air as he steps back.

"I wish—" My voice cracks. My mind fills in the blank. *I wish I could forget this summer. I wish I could move on.*

"Do you have a boyfriend or something?"

Or something.

"I have to go." I push my way through the crowded dance floor and flee outside to the empty porch. The late-summer air fills my lungs as I sink onto the steps and drop my head into my shaky hands.

Why does this keep happening?

When I'm alone, all I want is to be with people. When I'm with people, all I want is to be alone. Nothing feels right, because *I* don't feel right.

With a glance to see if anyone is paying attention to me (they're not), I open the alerts for "Comet, dog." I felt like a stalker setting it up, but Comet is *my* dog, and there's nothing wrong with wanting to keep tabs on him. The problem is, I get sent way too many articles. I should have thought about that before naming my dog after the biggest global event of this century.

My inbox is now filled with unopened articles that mention Comet, which means he must have made a public appearance today. I pick the first one and open it. A video is embedded at the top of the article, and I'm surprised to read that it was filmed in Canada. I suck in a breath. *Is it possible*— I cut myself off before I can follow that thought to its natural conclusion and press play.

The video follows a procession of black vehicles, focusing on a Bentley as it pulls up to a curb filled with people waiting behind a line of steel crowd-control barricades. The car door opens, and Comet bounds out first, tugging my heart across the border. He waits patiently next to the open door, and my stomach twists in miserable anticipation. A moment later, the new king Theodore Geoffrey Edward George steps out, one hand holding Comet's leash, the other raised to the crowd. Every time I see him (when I'm checking in on Comet, obviously) I'm surprised to see that his hair is still the same shade of brown he got from a box of drugstore dye.

If I cared enough to read into things like this, I'd wonder whether he's also haunted by memories of this summer.

I study the figure on my screen, taking stock. I'm always measuring the boy I see in photos against the one I knew in real life, and today he looks startlingly like the Theo who kissed me on a beach in Greece. He has an effortless smile, a perfectly tailored navy suit that makes him look slightly older than his nineteen years, and an air of easygoing importance. He looks handsome and charming and loose. More notably, he looks *happy*.

It knocks the wind out of me.

The headline reads KING THEO DESPERATE TO IMPRESS, but I don't agree. He's surrounded by guards as he approaches the Canadian prime minister. They shake hands, pose for a picture, exchange smiles and pleasant greetings, and Theo looks like a fucking natural. He was born and bred for this exact moment: charming the crowd, acting as a familiar face in times of change and uncertainty, and reminding all the royal watchers out there why they've obsessively followed his family's every move for generations. The Commonwealth may be in upheaval following the untimely death of the Queen and the almost-apocalypse, but some traditions are constant. Steadfast. Unshakable. Less than two weeks before his coronation, Theo's presence is a reminder of that.

That's what I see, anyway. My knowledge of the royal family consists mostly of what I learned when Theo and I spent a week together on a mad dash across Europe, and the stories he told me *then*—of a boy trapped in a life he couldn't stand—hardly fit with what I'm seeing *now*. He looks *destined,* not stuck, and his future is clear as day. I feel a hot stab of envy.

I lean in, my nose inches away from the screen, trying to get a better look at his expression. Theo glances at the camera and grins like he wasn't thrust into a life he was dreading, like his mom didn't just die of an undetected heart defect.

My stomach drops.

Once upon a time, somewhere between a storm on a ferry in the Mediterranean and a flight home to Chicago, I thought I knew what made him smile. But maybe I was wrong.

Back in June, when a comet was on course to hit Earth and end life as we know it, Theo was on the run from his obligations. He was willing to give up his life to avoid becoming king, but by the time I found out that he was sacrificing his spot in his family's cometproof bunker, it was too late. I was already halfway in love with him (or so I thought) and I couldn't let him keep running. I sent him straight into the waiting handcuffs of the royal security detail, and I assumed he'd hold it against me for the rest of his life.

But maybe he likes being king more than either of us expected. Maybe now that he's the one in charge, he no longer feels like the monarchy is antiquated and unfair.

While I'm pondering his unpredictable feelings, I can't help but wonder how he feels about being my *husband*.

("Husband"! Every time I even *think* the word, my brain short-circuits like an American blow-dryer in a London outlet.)

I drop my face into my hands as laughter and music float out onto the porch. All around me, all summer long, it's felt like everyone has moved on from Comet Week. Like everyone else is focused on the *almost* of it all—but thanks to a very real piece of paper hiding under my mattress, my Comet Week choices have followed me home across the Atlantic in a way that feels more permanent even than Ethan's Demogorgon tattoo.

I've gone through the motions of getting ready for this school year: I registered for classes. I completed the online checklist the school sent out. (At my sister Brooke's insistence.) I bought a shower caddy and a microwave from Target. I'm going through the motions of becoming a college freshman and moving on with my life, but it hasn't been enough. I can't move on or forget or breathe a sigh of relief because of what "almost" happened. I dream about sinking boats and missed trains and stolen dogs, waking up each night in a cold sweat, my heart bruising my rib cage with every beat.

"Wren!" The front door slams behind me and I turn to see Naomi in her platform sneakers, a miniskirt, a crop top, and spiky space buns. "I've been looking everywhere for you!" She sits next to me and inhales deeply. "Does it smell like rain or am I getting my hopes up for nothing?" Naomi is obsessed with the weather and already has her future as a TV meteorologist all mapped out.

I miss that feeling.

"It's usually the second one," I say in a hollow voice.

She frowns. "What's wrong?"

I waver. She knows about Theo, but she doesn't know the full truth about the marriage certificate under my bed. "It's nothing," I say eventually, because I don't want to kill her back-to-school buzz.

"We're leaving." She drags me into a standing position, and when I try to protest, she cuts me off. "I was ready to go anyway. Got your pepper spray?" She palms the small bottle of pepper spray attached to her key ring. I have a matching one—a gift from her mom. Naomi pops open the case to her AirPods and hands me the left one. "Do we need 'sad girl music' or 'F-U music' for the ride home?"

I don't know if it's the ride-or-die look in her eyes or the videos on my phone or the knowledge that Theo and I are on the same continent again, but the pressurized fizz in my blood finally pops.

"What's on the 'I've made a big mistake' playlist?" I ask.

"Whatever happened, we can fix it," she says immediately.

I rub my hands over my face. "Not without a divorce lawyer," I mumble.

Her eyebrows furrow. "I don't think I heard you right."

I don't blame her for being skeptical. It *is* hard to believe without the proof. I take a deep breath, ready to spill the secret that I've been keeping all summer. "I have something I need to show you."

CHAPTER 2

Any remaining expectations I had for my first week at college quickly fall apart when I walk back into my parents' home before 11:00 P.M. I am *not* cool or fun or wild—I am accidentally married and missing my dog.

"Home already?" Brooke asks from the couch as Naomi and I dash upstairs after taking the train from campus. We always talked about going to college together like best friends on a TV show, so at least one thing I wanted came true. (For the sake of our friendship, we *won't* be roommates.)

I ignore my sister and shut the door firmly behind us. Naomi sits on my bed, which is now stripped of my favorite Squishmallows and my fuzzy blanket. After moving into my dorm at the start of the week, all that's left in my high school bedroom are my old sheets and a half-empty closet. I didn't expect to be back so soon, but my blood is buzzing with familiar excitement as I turn to Naomi and take a deep breath.

The first glimmer of a plan is coming together in my mind, and it feels good.

"You're freaking me out," Naomi says. "Are you pregnant?"

"Definitely not."

"Is it your parents?"

This throws me off. "No. Wait—what about my parents?"

"Are they finally, you know—"

Oh. "Getting a divorce? No. I don't think so. They're in therapy. They go on dates now."

"Then why do you look like your dog got hit by a car?" She sees something in my expression that makes her jaw drop. "Is Wally okay? *Did* he run away?"

"No. Stop guessing! Your guessing sucks."

"Then tell me already!"

"I want to get out of town before school starts," I announce. "Let's take a road trip."

She raises an eyebrow. "We meet with our peer advisers tomorrow!" To her, our peer advisers might as well be the dean of admissions.

"We can meet with them on Monday, and I promise we'll be home before classes start."

She narrows her eyes. "Where do you want to go?"

"Toronto."

"Why?"

"My dog is in Toronto."

She scrunches her nose in confusion. "Am I drunk, or did you just tell me that Wally didn't run away?"

"He didn't. Wally's fine. I'm talking about the dog I rescued in Europe."

She holds her hands up. "Back up. I only drank half a beer, but none of this makes sense. I thought Theo had Comet."

"He does."

Her mouth splits into a knowing grin. "Theo's in Canada?" she squeals.

"And he's not alone." I show Naomi the articles and videos I looked at earlier, pausing on a shot of Theo, his seventeen-year-old sister, Victoria, and his eighteen-year-old brother, Henry, strolling through the park with Comet on a leash. My heart pangs at the sight of my bulky yellow Lab, with his floppy ears and goofy face. When I found Comet abandoned at a gas station in France, Theo didn't even *want* to bring him with us. "He's mine. End of story."

"Theo or the dog?"

"The dog, obviously," I scoff.

She narrows her eyes in disbelief. "You want to take a spontaneous trip to Canada less than four days before college starts and you expect me to believe it has nothing to do with your royal boyfriend?"

"He's not my boyfriend!"

"Sorry. I meant fake husband."

When I first got home, I told Naomi about the amazing Greek family who'd rescued Theo and me after we'd jumped off a ferry. They'd believed we were engaged and would only agree to take us to Theo's family compound in Santorini if we got married first. I'd explained to Naomi how I'd convinced Theo to marry me under the assumption that he'd sign his fake name on the marriage certificate, that the wedding wouldn't be legal, and (most importantly) that we'd be dead in a few days anyway.

That's not what happened.

"If I show you something—do you promise to keep it a secret?" I ask.

Her expression turns serious. "Of course."

"Get up." I nudge her off my bed and kneel next to it. I lift one corner of the mattress and reach for the piece of paper that's been haunting me all summer. I'd hoped moving out of this room would help me forget about it, but I couldn't even make it a full week before it drew me back like a magnet.

"This was mailed to me." I hand the paper to Naomi and sit on the edge of my bed, chewing my lip while I wait for her reaction.

It's been weeks since the marriage certificate bearing the names *Wren Wheeler* and *Theodore Geoffrey Edward George* mysteriously showed up in my mailbox with no return address. I've studied that paper every day since, as if staring at the messy script will make it make sense.

Theo didn't even want to marry me at first! Knowing our marriage wasn't real was the only way he would agree to it. I don't understand why he would protest so much, nearly leave me at the altar, and then sign his real name.

Naomi looks at me with wide eyes. "Are you—" She cuts herself off and looks back down at the paper. "Does this mean—" She glances at it one more time before collapsing onto the bed, howling with laughter. "Are you married to the literal king of England?" Tears gather at the corners of her eyes.

"I don't know! But thank you for laughing at my misery." I moan and pull a Squishmallow over my face.

She yanks the stuffed squirrel out of my hands and hits me in the face with it. "Ah yes, the absolute misery of being married to the hottest, richest, most eligible bachelor on the planet. How will you possibly survive?"

"It's not like that."

"It's exactly like that. You're the queen! Of a whole damn country! Mazel!"

"I don't think they let random eighteen-year-old Americans *be the queen*."

"Maybe not, but you're going to be famous, at the very least. Imagine the followers you'd get if you casually dropped this online."

"Not to mention stalkers and death threats. Some of those royal watchers are unhinged." I raise an accusatory eyebrow at her. Naomi used to be a royal fanatic. Not the kind who would stalk anyone, but definitely the kind who would swoon over every picture in the tabloids. Of course, that was before she got together with her boyfriend, Levi, whom she's obsessed with, and before Theo and I got into this . . . *situation*.

"Okay, okay, but hear me out—imagine how much money the royal family would give you to keep quiet."

"I'm not going to blackmail my hu— *Theo*."

She shrieks gleefully. "You almost said 'husband'! *I knew it!* You love him! You're his American queen! Alexa, play Taylor Swift's 'King of My Heart.'"

"First of all, I don't love him. Second, I don't want to be 'the queen.' Third, he doesn't want anything to do with me!" The pathetic truth is, I tried repeatedly to call the palace and leave a message for Theo after his mom died and got nothing but silence in return. If he wanted to contact me, he would. He knows my name, where I live, and where I'm going to school. He has every resource in the world for tracking me down.

"That certificate says otherwise," Naomi counters.

I sigh and scrub my hands through my hair. There was a time when I thought that Theo and I were in love—shortly after we signed this paper—but that was just a rush of adrenaline and hormones. I fell in love with the moment and mistook it for being in love with *him*. The truth is, I trusted him with my life, and he kept secrets and lied to me and almost left me alone to die in Greece. "I don't want to be the queen of anything. I just want my dog back so I can unsubscribe from royal news and move on with my life."

"Who sent it to you?"

"I don't know."

"Was it him?"

"*I don't know!*"

She rolls to the edge of the bed and reaches for my phone, which one of us has accidentally kicked across the floor. She swipes through the pictures of Theo and his siblings. "Canada, huh?"

I nod.

"If I email my peer adviser and tell her I won't be in town tomorrow, she might be willing to set up a time to meet next week." She mulls this over for a moment before leveling me with an accusatory stare. "I suppose you have a full itinerary and master plan for how we'll find him and pull this off?"

"Would you believe me if I say no?"

She pretends to gasp, as if I haven't been acting out of character all summer. "Who are you and what have you done with my best friend?"

"The only itinerary we need is his, which is conveniently posted under the 'Future Engagements' section of the royal family's website."

Theo and his siblings are visiting High Park tomorrow to tour the zoo and gardens. It's not as detailed a plan as I'd like, but it's more than I've had since June, and for now it's enough. I need to find Theo, get my dog back, and figure out if this marriage is even real. "As for how we'll maneuver around his bodyguards and royal entourage to get close enough to actually speak to him . . . I don't know yet."

She grins. "I trust you to figure it out. You always do."

"And I trust *you* to summon some of that positive energy and convince your mom to let us use her car." I smile hopefully.

She crosses her fingers on her left hand and starts texting with the right. "On it. When do we want to leave?"

I jump off the bed and open the door to my room. "Ten minutes ago." It's about an eight-hour drive to Toronto, and we need to get on the road if we're going to meet Theo at the park in the morning.

Naomi grimaces as her phone lights up with a new message. "My mom needs the car tomorrow."

"What about Levi?"

"He sold his to help pay for tuition last week."

I groan.

"You know what this means," Naomi says.

I do *not* want to involve my family in any of this, but at this point, we're out of options. "Fine. I'll ask Brooke, but we're going to need a good cover story."

"Now this sounds interesting," a voice behind me says. I whirl around to see Brooke standing in the open doorway, her arms crossed over her chest. She arches an eyebrow. "Ask me what?"

CHAPTER 3

*G*ood luck and text me when you're ready to leave," Naomi says, squeezing around Brooke and me as she dashes into the hall.

"Coward!" I yell to her retreating back. She didn't even help me think of a good lie.

Brooke waits patiently for an answer. My sister is an inch shorter than I am, her brown hair an exact match for my natural color (RIP). She has curtain bangs that she cut herself late one night over the sink while watching a tutorial online. She calls them her "crisis bangs."

"Hey, sis," I say, aiming for nonchalance. I regret it immediately. We never call each other "sis." "Your hair looks really good tonight."

She blows her bangs out of her face with an exaggerated eye roll. "You need my car, don't you?"

"Yes."

"Where are you going?" she asks, with the kind of smile that says she's reveling in having the upper hand.

"Naomi's house."

"Try again, this time with the truth."

"Campus?" I lie, and I do it badly.

"I can't cover for you with Mom and Dad unless I know *what* I'm covering up. Besides, we're friends now, remember. I'm not going to rat you out."

Brooke and I *are* friends now, or at least on our way. Our relationship is one thing that actually *was* changed by the world almost ending.

I sigh, acutely aware of every minute ticking by. Now that I have a plan, I don't want to wait. "I'm going to Toronto with Naomi. Just for a day or two." Because she's still blocking my path, I haphazardly throw clothes that weren't cute enough to bring to school into an empty backpack.

"Why?" she demands.

"What does it matter? I don't even live here anymore." I reach into the back of my closet and retrieve the Polaroid I keep hidden in there. I shouldn't have left it here when I moved out— not unless I want to risk someone finding it.

"It matters because you want to use my car."

"Is that a no?"

"It depends. Can I come?"

I blink up at her in surprise. "Why would you want to?"

She shrugs. "I'm bored." Before the comet, she was hell-bent on following in Mom's footsteps and was enrolled in law school. Now she's deferred her acceptance for a year while she *finds herself*. I don't know why she thought it was a good idea to give up her settled future for the hazy unknown, and I don't know what she thinks she's going to find in Canada with us, but there's no time to argue with her.

"Fine." I sigh. "Grab your passport and meet me outside."

Ten minutes later, Naomi crosses the street with a bag slung over her shoulder and an excited pep in her step as I lean against the front of Brooke's Camry. "You got the car!"

"Sort of."

She opens the passenger door and freezes when she sees my sister behind the wheel. Naomi turns slowly to me, a wide, fake smile frozen in place. "Why is she here?"

"Nice to see you too!" Brooke quips.

Naomi shuts the door. "Does she know about Theo?"

"No, and I'm not planning to tell her either, so don't be weird."

"No promises!" Naomi opens the rear door this time and scoots into the back seat while I take the passenger seat. "I'm surprised you don't have anything better to do this weekend than hang out with us," she says to Brooke as she buckles her seat belt. "Shouldn't you be getting ready to start law school? It's not too late to change your mind and stay here."

"I'm not starting law school," Brooke says with forced composure as she starts the car and pulls out of our driveway.

"Oh, sorry! I thought you got in." Naomi smiles brightly. I turn around and Naomi winks, because old habits die hard and she spent the last several years disliking Brooke in the name of our friendship. Brooke's knuckles turn white on the steering wheel.

I groan inwardly. At this rate, it's going to be a very long drive.

I lean my head against the window and pretend to doze off until the steady hum of the car finally lulls me to sleep for real, and I wake up a few hours later as we're crossing the Detroit River and approaching the Canadian border. We present our passports to the border agent, and she asks a series of questions about what we're bringing with us, and whether we have fire-arms ("No"), fireworks ("No"), fresh produce ("No"), or live animals ("Not yet").

Brooke rears her head back in surprise at my answer. "What does that mean?"

I lean across the console. "If I acquire a dog in Canada, will I be allowed to bring him into the US?"

I can *feel* Brooke's mind spinning as she tries to figure out what I'm up to.

"If the dog is microchipped and has had its vaccines, bringing him over the border shouldn't be a problem," the agent says.

Fingers crossed the royals took care of that. "Sounds great! Thank you." I sink back into my seat as Brooke stares at me.

"We're here so you can 'acquire' a dog?" she asks incredulously.

I need to think of a believable lie, but my mind is a blinking cursor at the start of a homework assignment I don't want to do. I've got nothing.

"That's right." Naomi saves me by chiming in from the back seat. "Wren saw an adorable chocolate Lab online and she just *had* to adopt it."

"Like there aren't enough dogs that need adopting in Chicago?"

"This one's special," Naomi says, sticking her face between my seat and Brooke's. "He has beautiful brown hair and blue eyes—"

"Blue eyes?" Brooke asks.

I throw my shoe over my shoulder to shut Naomi up. "She doesn't know what she's talking about."

A few hours later (including one stop for gas and one stop for vegan breakfast sandwiches from Odd Burger), we're in down-town Toronto. I direct my sister toward High Park, where we're lucky to snag free street parking. Brooke parallel parks like an expert (of course) and gets out quickly, telling us she needs to stretch her legs after the long drive. I grab my backpack and go to open the car door when Naomi puts her hand out.

"Wait!" She leans into the front seat and pulls my door shut again. "Do you want to change first?" she asks. "Or, I don't know, brush your teeth?"

"Comet won't care what I look like."

"You're so unserious," Naomi huffs. "Quit living in denial and at least wipe the mascara from under your eyes." She hands me makeup-remover wipes, which I use to clean up last night's leftover smudges. Then she starts passing out one product after another, including a bottle of nail polish.

"I don't need to do all of this," I insist.

"You want to show him what he's missing," Naomi says matter-of-factly. She hasn't said his name, but we both know she's not talking about the dog. "I'll keep Brooke busy while you get ready." She shuts the car door firmly behind her, leaving me alone with all the thoughts I don't want to have.

"Don't get too close—Brooke bites!" I yell through the window. Naomi gives me the finger. Despite what she believes, I'm *not* doing this for Theo. Not for the reasons she thinks, anyway. I don't need him to miss me.

I glance down at my outfit. Sweatpants and an old Evanston Animal Rescue T-shirt that I cut into a crop top, an inch of my stomach showing above the band on my sweats, and a ring on a chain around my neck, hidden beneath my shirt. I can't bring myself to change. Not if doing so would signal to Naomi that I still have feelings for Theo, because I don't.

Naomi frowns when I climb out of the car. She looks at me from head to toe, taking in my third-day hair, baggy crop top, and Crocs. "At least your face looks pretty," she sighs.

Just the confidence boost a girl needs before seeing her estranged husband. I give her two sarcastic thumbs-up.

My already waning optimism falls even further as we approach the park, where guards are blocking the entrance. Brooke surveys them for a bone-chilling ten seconds before she spins in a slow circle, absorbing our surroundings. I clock the exact moment she notices the crowd-control barriers lining the street and streams of people walking by, craning their necks to see through the tree-lined fence, phones at the ready. All we need now is for the royal procession to drive by, flags flying from the roof of the Bentley.

"What's going on? Are we even allowed to be here? And this park looks huge. Where are we supposed to meet the dog?"

Brooke's rapid-fire line of questioning leaves me tongue-tied. "I, um, I—"

"There's a dog park. That might be a good place to start," Naomi says, leaping to my rescue again.

"Wren—what's going on? Do you have an appointment to meet this dog or not?" Brooke asks.

"Technically?"

She rubs her eyes with a heavy sigh. "I should be memorizing a course syllabus right now, color-coding my notebooks," she says wistfully.

"Hey, look—" Naomi points to a crepe restaurant down the street. "Why don't you get breakfast while Wren and I explore the park?"

"Fine. I am starving," Brooke concedes. "Can we please do something fun after you get the dog, though? I was hoping this trip would take my mind off school, not make me wish for it." She mutters the last sentence more to herself than Naomi or me.

"Anything you want," I tell her, though now that I've seen the security measures in place, I've lost all faith that I'll ever get Comet back. When she's out of earshot, I turn to Naomi. "This is the worst idea I've ever had. I'm tempted to call the whole thing off."

"We did not drive all this way just to give up so easily. Do you want Comet back or not?"

"Obviously."

"Do you want to yell at the king of England for maybe marrying you and then leaving you alone in Greece and *then* ghosting you when the world didn't end?"

"It sounds bad when you say it like that."

"Wren." Naomi puts her hand on my arm, holding eye contact for several excruciating seconds. It makes it a lot harder to pretend away my feelings. "It sounds bad because it *was* bad. As much as I joke about it because you're living my royal dreams of falling in love with the prince-turned-king, I can't imagine what you've been through, and I'm sorry that he broke your heart."

"I broke his first," I admit, blinking tears out of my eyes. I lied and turned him in to the authorities. I watched his own bodyguards handcuff him and drag him out of my life. And given the choice, I'd do it again.

Naomi links her arm through mine. "As your best friend, it's my prerogative to hate him, no matter what you did first. Now, let's find him so you can give him a piece of your mind before absconding with his dog."

I'd be lying if I said I hadn't lain awake night after night, imagining what I'd finally say if I saw Theo. But I never settled on the right words to explain how much I miss him, and how I'm glad he seems happy but also shocked that he could be, and how I'm sad that our week together turned out to be so easily erased from history and his life.

Maybe when I see him today, the right words will finally come.

Naomi leads me down the shaded sidewalk, away from the guards and the largest concentration of crowds, until we find another, smaller entrance. We enter High Park and the noise from the crowds and cars is muffled by dense trees. Naomi finds a park map and traces the path toward the off-leash dog park with her finger. My nerves wind tighter as we pass the greenhouse and then the zoo, and I hold my breath as we enter the dog park.

We stop cold and Naomi looks around skeptically. "I'm sorry, I just can't picture them here."

The dog park is a small patch of sand with a couple of picnic tables and benches scattered throughout, and not a member of the royal family in sight.

"Should we wait?" I ask uncertainly.

"They are not doing a royal photo op here," Naomi says, gesturing to a large pile of dog poop. "Let's double back, there's nothing on the north side except a sports complex."

We turn around and follow the paved path to an elaborate circular garden with a maple-leaf-shaped flower bed at its center. "Okay, Canada, that's very on-brand," I say, ignoring the familiar itch to take a picture of the trees on the banks of a rippling pond. After the comet didn't hit, I thought I wanted to keep memories of everything, but if this rescue mission is unsuccessful, I won't want any record of this temporary insanity. "That has to be a good sign." I point to the crowd-control barriers lining the walk-way.

Naomi has her phone out. "Wikipedia says that Theo's grandmother opened this garden in the 1950s. Maybe he'll re-peat history."

I'm immediately annoyed with myself for not doing any re-search. "I need a minute." I pace around the garden, trying to summon whatever magic I had in Europe that got Theo and me out of so many impossible situations.

I used to be the girl with plans A, B, C, and D—backup plans for my backup plans—but now? My brain is a ghost town. As hard as I try, I can't think of a single way to track down and steal the most famous dog in the world.

"I'm broken," I tell Naomi when I've completed my lap around the maple leaf. She's sitting on a bench, and I glance over her shoulder at her phone, where she's watching another orientation video for school I haven't seen. (Northwestern emails us approximately three dozen times per day. It's impossible to keep up.)

"What's wrong?" she asks, shutting off the video and giving me her full attention.

"I don't know how to do this anymore."

"Did you *ever* know how to steal a dog?"

"I don't know how to think on my feet. My brain feels like a sieve, everything is sliding through. I—"

The atmosphere in the park shifts; a hush falls over the crowd, followed by a buzz that travels like a flame on gasoline. Our gazes fly to the far entrance of the garden. A group of men in black suits is ushering spectators to either side of the walk-way.

"Is that . . ." Naomi trails off as she grabs my forearm and squeezes, her nails biting my skin. She doesn't need to finish the sentence. Everyone in the vicinity knows what's happening.

The royal family is approaching.

CHAPTER 4

The first time I met Theo, I had no idea who he was. Once I figured it out, I didn't particularly care. Three months that feel like a lifetime later, I'm just another one of his intense royal-watcher fanatics.

I stop breathing.

"I can't see anything," I say as more and more people flow into the garden. Naomi and I stand on our bench to get a better look as my stomach tightens with familiar anticipation. I tell myself it doesn't mean anything that my blood hums at the thought of him.

"Those are the royal protection officers," Naomi explains, although for once, she doesn't need to. I summoned men just like them to Santorini to handcuff Theo and drag him away. "I wonder if Major Winston is here," she says. She sees my bewildered look and explains, "He was one of the Queen's bodyguards before her death."

"How do you know that?"

"He's kind of famous. You really don't know who he is? He's

younger than the rest of them. Twenty-fiveish, I think? Hot. Biceps for days?"

"Not ringing any bells." The garden continues to fill as film crews, photographers, and a mob of overly excited weirdos anticipate the arrival of the royal family. "Who are all these people?" I demand. Flickers of contempt burn in my chest as I clock the tremor of excitement swirling around us. "The royals are just *people,* not zoo animals."

"Pot, meet kettle." Naomi motions from us to the crowd.

"We're not gawking; we're here for a dog heist," I remind Naomi as a cheer erupts from the crowd. I catch a glimpse of dark blond hair. The princess has arrived.

"This is their first royal walkabout since the Queen died," Naomi whispers.

"Their first *what*?"

"Walkabout. It's when members of the royal family go outside to greet and shake hands with the public—they *walk about*."

"Does the King do walkabouts?" I ask, and I cannot believe the words that just came out of my mouth. It's such a silly sentence, made even sillier because the answer has the power to annihilate me.

"The Queen did," Naomi says. "But it's also possible that he has something else on his schedule and sent his sister out to connect with the public."

"Theo hates this kind of thing," I say, but I realize immediately how ridiculous I sound. Like I know anything about the person he is after losing a parent and ascending the throne.

I bite my lip to distract myself from the painful riot happening in my stomach. The sound of my own blood rushing in my ears is deafening, the thud of my own heart bruising.

So this is how I die. Not from a world-ending comet, but from the excruciating anticipation of waiting to see a boy. *When did I become so pathetic?* I hope whoever writes my obituary takes it easy on me.

I've only had a moment to prepare for my imminent demise when I see him: the yellow Labrador of my heart, the dog who never left my side until I put him on Theo's plane, the reason I drove eight hours through the night.

Comet darts around a guard as he sprints to catch a tennis ball thrown by Princess Victoria. He returns the ball to her side, his heavy tail thumping happily against her thighs, his big tongue lolling to the side of his mouth. She crouches to give him a scratch behind his ears before handing the ball to a young boy in the crowd. When he tosses the ball, Comet leaps to catch it.

"I hate to say it, but he looks happy," Naomi says.

"I know." It's a double-edged sword, because I want my dog to be happy (I'm not a monster), but I want him to be *happier* with me. (I'm not a saint, either.)

She leans her head on my shoulder. "I *really* hate to say this, but I don't think Theo's here."

I know that too; the ranks have closed around the garden entrances, and Theo's nowhere to be found. (He's probably doing something more important, like shining his crown or bedazzling his scepter.) My stomach bottoms out from a painful mixture of relief and regret. Seeing him again would have been fraught, but now I'm doomed to spend the rest of my life under a cloud of *what if.*

Naomi's expression is crestfallen. "I'm sorry."

I shrug as the knot in my throat expands, making it hard to say anything.

"Do you want to try to get closer to Comet?" she asks. When

I nod, she surveys the guards blocking all four garden exits. "I don't know how we're going to be able to sneak him out of here."

"We're not," I say, finally accepting the truth. There was never any plan that would have worked. What I did in Europe was the result of impossible circumstances. I don't have any power compared to the royal monarchy. "I'll just say hi and give him a hug and tell him I miss him."

"Is that enough?"

It's not, but it'll have to be. "You'll cause a distraction?" I ask.

"Of course. Too bad the weather couldn't help us out at all." She side-eyes the cloudless sky. (Naomi loathes sunshine. She calls it *uninspired*.) "We could use a little help from nature's distraction right about now."

"You are so weird. And thank you for doing this for me."

"Ride or die," she confirms, giving my hand a quick squeeze before we split up.

She approaches the crowd from the left and I walk a far arc out to the right. I unzip my backpack and retrieve a handful of Wally's favorite peanut butter dog treats. Comet is chasing a bird when Naomi lets out an earsplitting shriek. "Victoria! I love you!" She sounds completely unhinged, and several nearby guards turn their attention toward her. *Perfect*.

Victoria raises her hand in a hesitant wave as Naomi shoves her way to the front of the crowd. When Comet's about fifteen feet from me, I whistle. He stops running and cocks his head.

"Comet!" I kneel behind the crowd of spectators and toss a treat in his direction while Naomi causes a ruckus. Comet's head swivels toward me, and a new fear zips through my system: What if he doesn't remember me? Then I say his name again and he takes off like a shot, crossing the distance between us in seconds. He leaps into my arms, knocking me flat on my back and licking me straight across the face like every dog in those "soldier returning home" videos that make me cry until I'm dehydrated. I'm not returning from war or anything, but tears prick the corner of my eyes at our reunion anyway.

I don't want to leave him again.

I sit up, my hand firmly around Comet's collar, and glance around. His tail hammers my side with a dozen painful thuds. Behind us, not too far away, is a newly unmanned street entrance. "What do you think, boy?" I ask, wrapping an arm around his torso. "Can we make it?" He eats the treats I dropped on the grass, perfectly content to stay right here in my arms where he belongs.

Indecision tugs me in two directions, which isn't like me. If I have any chance at this, I need to run *now*. "Let's go," I say. "We'll meet Naomi back at the car."

I turn to see if I can catch her attention, just in time to watch in horror as a royal protection officer slaps a pair of handcuffs around her wrists and leads her away from the crowd.

CHAPTER 5

My best friend is getting arrested in a foreign country and it's all my fault.

"I'm sorry, buddy. I still love you, and I won't ever forget you." I kiss Comet on the head, shoo him back toward the royals, and move without thinking.

"Sorry, excuse me, I have to find my friend. Excuse me, oops, sorry!" I take advantage of Canadian politeness to quickly elbow my way to the front of the crowd and approach the nearest security officer. "Excuse me! Please, I need to talk to you!" He doesn't indicate that he can hear me, but there's no way he doesn't, even with the jostling crowd and a steel barrier between us. "That's my friend you have over there, she's not dangerous."

He turns his head, and his eyes flash with recognition. He grabs the radio at his belt and pulls it up to his mouth.

"You know me!" I shout. I wedge my way forward so I can lean over the barrier and get a better look at his face. He's white, with dark brown hair peppered with gray and a face that appears in my nightmares. "You were there in Santorini. Theo"—his eyes flash again—"*the King* knows me. You know he does. Ask him. Tell him that you're holding my best friend hostage—"

"She's not a hostage," he says in a monotone voice. "And stop shouting or you'll join her."

"Let her go."

He turns away.

"Let me talk to the King," I plead. No response. Fumbling, I yank open the zipper on my backpack and pull out the one thing that might give me an ounce of leverage in this situation.

I shove the marriage certificate under his nose for two seconds before wrenching it back.

He tries to snatch it from me and fails. "What was that?"

"Let me talk to the King, and I'll show it to you."

"I'm not daft. There's no way it's real," he says tightly.

"You wanna bet?" My fingertips have gone numb with nerves, but I stand my ground. His jaw clenches as he deliberates, but after a moment he shifts the crowd-control barrier to allow me through. Whispers and titters move through the crowd, but mostly everyone is too busy craning their necks and pushing up on their toes to get a glimpse or a photo of the princess, who is now obscured by the film crews.

He leans in to speak quickly and quietly. "Follow the path south to the sunken garden. His Majesty and Major Winston will meet you there. Do not bring anyone with you."

"But Naomi—"

"He's coming!" an emotional voice carries through the crowd. Several girls burst into tears as the attention of the group shifts away from the princess toward an oak-lined path on the opposite side of the garden, and for the first time since we said goodbye, my eyes land on Theodore Geoffrey Edward George.

The king of England. My maybe husband. The boy who broke my heart.

"—safe and looked after for ten minutes," the guard says.

"What did you say?" I pull my gaze from Theo.

"Your friend will be fine."

"How do I know you're telling the truth?"

His lips form a tight line. "What do you think we're going to do to her?"

I grit my teeth in frustration as my pulse pounds heavily. "Fine. I'll see you soon."

I slip away from the crowd and follow a sign down a path to the sunken garden, which is a cluster of low, rectangular fountains surrounded by shrubs. I lean over the edge of the water and stare at my wide-eyed reflection, wondering how the hell I ended up here. I search my pockets for a coin, hoping to wish my way out of this mess and spare Naomi from Canadian jail. Instead of money, I find a dog treat, a hair tie, and an empty gum wrapper. With a sigh, I reach my hand into the cold water and scrape a handful of coins off the bottom of the fountain.

"Whatever it takes," I mutter to myself.

"That's bad luck, you know."

My heart rate spikes at the British lilt, but when I turn around, it's just another guard. I'm startled by how handsome he is. This must be the one Naomi was talking about—Major Winston. "Where's Theo?"

"His Majesty will be here shortly. First, I need to confirm that you're not carrying any weapons, and then I need to see that certificate you're holding." He motions for me to hold my arms out so he can search me.

"That wasn't the deal!" I insist as he quickly pats me down.

"It's the only deal you're getting."

Despite how badly I've wanted to make the marriage certif-icate go away, handing it over is shockingly difficult, but I'm at the mercy of the guard. I relinquish my only bargaining chip with a huff. He silently pockets it before leaving me alone in the garden with a wet arm and a handful of bad luck.

I close my eyes and toss all the coins over my head. They land with an ominous splash.

"Blimey, Wheeler. You didn't have to resort to blackmail. If you wanted to see me so badly, you could have called."

Theo strolls toward me, one side of his mouth hitched in a lazy grin that pierces me with its familiarity. I try to take in all of him at once, but don't know what to focus on. He's still distress-ingly hot, for one thing. His hair is dark, though it's a bit shorter and less floppy than it was before. His eyes are alarmingly blue, still full of mischief. And even with all of that, there's something different about him that I can't quite place.

I'm so thunderstruck by his appearance that I barely register what he said. When my brain catches up enough to process his words, I realize another thing about him that hasn't changed at all. His ego is still big enough to fill the miles between our countries.

I roll my eyes, hoping I haven't been gaping at him for too long. "Ego check, *Your Highness*."

"On what grounds?"

"I'm only here because your bodyguards have my friend Naomi in custody. They need to let her go."

He suppresses a smile, clearly amused by this entire mess. "How'd she wind up in that predicament?"

General chaos, most likely. "She was causing a distraction. On my behalf." I cross my arms, annoyed that he doesn't look a fraction as flustered as I feel.

"Ahh." His eyes light up. "One of your classic plans?"

"No. I don't do that anymore."

"But you must have had a reason for being here today. Correct me if I'm wrong, but you don't even live in this country."

"Neither do you!"

He has the nerve to laugh. I glower at him, my frustration mounting. He's charming and carefree and gorgeous, with all the leverage in the world—and I'm in sweatpants and an old T-shirt, begging for a favor. I've never felt the gap in our respective *statuses* as much as I do now. "Let her go."

"Is that what you wished for?" He nods to the fountain.

"Wouldn't you like to know."

"I would." He takes a step closer. "Tell me why you're here."

I hold my ground. "I'm in Canada to rescue Comet."

The corners of his lips twitch. "Grand theft dog, Wheeler? Really?" I wonder if he's remembering the time that we dabbled in grand theft auto.

"Not theft. I can't steal what's already mine. I'm here to—"

"Rescue him. I heard you. Do you think he must have been miserable all this time, trapped in a palace with everything he could ever want at his beck and call?" His tone is balanced on a knife's edge, giving nothing away.

"That life is clearly suitable for some, but no, not for my dog."

He narrows his eyes for a moment, scrutinizing me in a way that makes me feel painfully transparent. He always had a way of doing that, and I hated it . . . right up until the moment I stopped feeling exposed and started feeling seen.

"Are you going to release Naomi or not?" I ask evenly.

"I already did, as soon as my guard told me what happened."

Oh. I soften at this revelation, unsure what to say and more than a little relieved that Naomi's life isn't about to be blown up—and that being king hasn't changed Theo completely. He takes another step toward me. *Have his eyelashes always been this long?*

Over his shoulder, I see Winston approaching. The marriage certificate is nowhere in sight. Theo must hear him too, because he lowers his voice and says, "We probably don't have much time. But it is *really* nice to see you, Wheeler." There he goes again, calling me "Wheeler." It sounds like *Wheel-a*. It's a far cry from when he used to call me "American girl."

"Can I please take Comet home with me?"

He grimaces and rubs the back of his neck with his hand. "Unfortunately, I can't agree to that."

"He's *mine*!"

"Your Majesty," the bodyguard interrupts. "It's time to go."

Theo looks at me, his expression filled with regret. "I *am* sorry, for what it's worth."

I wish I could tell if he's apologizing for Comet, or *everything* else. He turns to leave, and once again restless frustration burns inside me.

"So that's it?" I ask.

He freezes mid-step and turns, his face indecipherable. Once upon a time, I would have let him go, too scared to say how I really feel. If the world almost ending taught me anything, it's that I might not get another chance.

I lift my arms in an exaggerated shrug. "I came all this way for five minutes of banter and now you're *leaving*?"

He glances over at his guard and then back at me, a sad smile on his face. "I thought you came all this way for Comet?"

He's calling my bluff, and I can't keep lying to myself.

I exhale, dropping my arms to my sides without taking my eyes off his. "Ninety percent for Comet."

His eyes blaze, and for a split second, he looks tortured. And then he moves.

He closes the distance between us in a flash and wraps me in a hug. I pull him tight against my body and bury my face into his neck, fighting the urge to cry. All the times I thought about seeing him again, I didn't dare to imagine it would feel like coming home.

Unfortunately, it doesn't last.

CHAPTER 6

A man shouts. Arms push us back. I stumble, but Theo keeps me on my feet. I hear another shout, followed by a series of clicks. I glance up and am blinded by a camera flash. Theo swears and covers my face with his hands, tucking me behind him to shield me from the cameras as bodyguards try to pull us apart.

"Who's the bird?" a voice yells. I look up and squint against the flash.

"Ignore them," Theo says, forcing the words out through gritted teeth.

What happens next is a whirlwind. Winston ushers us quickly away as another guard appears out of nowhere and blocks the cameraman from getting closer. Theo grips my hand as we sprint down empty paths through the park, the sound of heavy footsteps trailing after us. When we finally get to an exit, a crowd is waiting on the sidewalk, screaming Theo's name. Winston opens the door to a black car and forces us inside.

"We're being followed," he tells the driver.

I turn and see two different cameramen on motorbikes right

behind our car. One of the bikes speeds up to draw even with the rear window and swerves, nearly hitting us. Our car jerks right to avoid a crash.

"Bloody hell," our driver shouts.

"Get down, now," Winston says. I flatten myself against the floor while Theo lies across the seats. My heart accelerates with the speed of the car as we weave in and out of traffic, Winston and the driver arguing about the best way to lose them.

The car makes a hard left turn and Theo braces his arm against the seat to stop himself from rolling on top of me. I press my hand to my mouth to keep from crying out as my eyes fill with tears.

"Slow down," he orders, his gaze locked on mine.

"We're perfectly safe—"

"You're scaring her," Theo says. "*Slow down.*"

The car decelerates slightly until Winston says, "Yellow light. Floor it."

"But sir—"

"Now," Winston says, his eyes glued to the back window.

Theo and I lock eyes. *I'm sorry,* he mouths silently as the car lurches forward. I close my eyes and brace myself for disaster when I feel Theo's hand grip mine. The car swerves sharply and Winston shouts.

I lie perfectly still and count the painful beats of my heart. For all the time I spent in Europe contemplating my death, disaster never felt quite so imminent.

There's nothing romantic about dying on a car floor in Toronto.

The car finally slows, and I pry my eyes open. Anger is radiating off Theo in waves. "Is it over?" I ask.

"We lost them," the driver confirms.

Theo sits up and buckles his seat belt, but I can't bring my-self to move. My muscles are frozen, my brain disconnected from any of my limbs. This is where I live now.

Winston cranes his neck to look at me with a frown. "It's safe to get up," the bodyguard says.

"Nothing about that was safe," Theo snaps at Winston be-fore looking back at me. "But please get up and put your seat belt on."

There's a desperate rasp to his voice that I can't ignore. I climb back into the seat next to him, and he grimaces as he watches me fasten my seat belt with trembling hands. "This is all my bloody fault," he says quietly, dragging a hand over his face.

"It's not your fault those people are leeches. I don't blame you."

"You should." His eyes are bleak before they shutter closed. "I'm going to ruin your life," he says, and now that we're inches apart in an enclosed space, I can smell a whiff of alcohol on his breath.

A shiver of fear zips up my spine; I can't help but believe him. Ten minutes in Theo's world, and my life has never felt so far out of my control.

I turn my attention to Winston. "Where's Naomi?"

"Your friend was released from custody on His Majesty's or-ders quite some time ago. We don't have her."

"I'll ask her, and you can drop me off wherever she is," I say. Winston plucks my phone out of my hand.

"Hey!"

"We can't let you out of our sight. Not with paparazzi roam-ing the streets."

"Seriously?" I whirl on Theo, my pulse hammering ten

times for every second he blinks at me with those devastating eyes. I press my lips together. "Find Naomi and bring her to the hotel," I tell Winston.

He regards me with mild scorn. "She's not our responsibility."

Theo loosens his tie with a heavy sigh. "She will be if she gets in an accident because she's being chased by paparazzi for her connection with Wren."

I release a shaky breath, unnerved by the idea of it. "Don't lose that ego now, Theo. I'm not the famous one in this car."

"Until those pictures of us get out," he says, just as another cameraman on a motorbike pulls even with the car. Our driver quickly changes lanes and Theo angles his body sideways so he's covering most of the window while I sink lower in my seat. "Listen to her, Winston, and bring Naomi to the hotel."

"And my sister," I quickly add.

Theo gives me a sidelong glance. "Brooke's here too?"

"Brought the whole gang!" I force a smile, worry gnawing a hole in my stomach.

Silence descends over us. Theo and I are side by side but not touching, his bodyguard scanning the road for cameras while fielding dozens of texts on his phone.

"What do we do when we get to the hotel?" I ask finally.

"We wait," Theo says tightly. "We have the entire floor booked, and I'll make sure you, Brooke, and Naomi are provided with a room."

"We won't need to stay the night, will we?" I ask, and I don't *love* the silence that follows. "Once the cameras are gone, and you've killed the story, we can go back home, *right*?"

"Of course," Theo says quickly, exchanging a look with

Winston that makes me worry I'm about to be held hostage by the British monarchy.

I groan and drop my head to my knees. "This place better have a swimming pool. A hot tub. And one of those waffle makers for breakfast in the morning."

I'm describing a Holiday Inn, but when the car finally pulls to a stop, I glance out the darkened windows to see a towering luxury hotel. Less "family vacation on a budget" and more "fanciest place I've ever seen in my life."

"I'm guessing that's a no on the waffle maker," I mutter as we enter the lobby and come face-to-face with crystal chandeliers and a massive wood-carved ceiling.

"You can order waffles from the kitchen," Theo says.

"But where's the fun in eating them if I didn't pour the batter from a paper Dixie cup and personally flip the waffle maker over?"

His lip twitches as he fights a smile. "I understand most of those words, but not the sentence."

"Don't worry about it; it's a middle-class thing," I say.

His shoulders slump. When Theo and I were stealing cars and hanging out on grungy bathroom floors, it was easy to pretend that we weren't so different. Now that I've seen the kind of hotel he's accustomed to staying in, it's harder to trick myself into believing we have anything in common.

He clears his throat. "This is the Fairmont Royal York. You're safe from pictures here. The staff aren't even allowed to carry phones. This is where my family stays whenever we tour Canada."

"Like when your grandma opened the maple-leaf park?" I ask.

He looks at me warily. "You know about that?"

"It has its own Wikipedia page, unlike my grandma's favorite pastime: yelling 'bad answer' at the TV whenever a *Family Feud* contestant says something stupid."

Winston stifles a laugh as Theo's cheeks redden, and I remember how much he hates talking about his family's legacy. "Where are the others?" he asks his bodyguard.

"Your sister is in a car about ten minutes out," Winston tells him. "I don't know about Wren's people."

"Find them and get her a key to the Gold Suite."

"I would prefer if you were not alone, sir." Winston's voice carries a note of warning.

Theo rolls his eyes. "I'm not alone. Wren is here, and as you might recall, she acted as my bodyguard across five countries."

Winston nods and turns on his heel to leave. Theo leads the way through the lobby to an elevator. "This is a private lift to our floor," he explains as we step inside. "No one else has access."

The doors slide shut behind us, and the energy in the elevator abruptly shifts. Now that the crisis has passed, it's awkward again. He hesitates, looking like he wants to say something, but then leans against the wall and tips his head back.

"So . . ." I smile, trying to make this less weird. (Impossible.) "The world didn't end."

"Didn't it?" he says, so quietly I might have imagined it.

Something is lodged in my throat. "How have you been?"

"Never better," he deadpans. It's nice to know I'm not the only one freaked out by this situation.

"It's weird for me, too—"

"Obviously." He scrubs both hands through his hair and fixes me with a hard stare. "I've basically just kidnapped you, and you probably hate me for it."

"Oh." I have the sinking realization that we are not having the same conversation. He's talking about what just happened on the street, when I was talking about our reunion. *Mortifying*.

"The British press is vile, the absolute scum of the earth. If and when those pictures *do* get released, we need to have our ducks in a row before sending you back to the States. Make sure we have a cover story—"

"Can't we just tell them we met during the apocalypse, and now—"

Theo raises his eyebrows in question. "And now?"

I pull my shoulders back in surprise. I will not be the first one to address whatever is or isn't going on between us. "*And now* I'm here so you can return my dog!" I say, which doesn't get a response from Theo. That's fine. I'll keep trying. He's going to owe me after all this is over. The elevator doors glide open to reveal a long hallway. "So those guys with the cameras were British press?" I ask, remembering the one who called me "the bird."

"Some of them, yes. Others are local. Bloody wankers are usually better behaved than that on tour." We walk down the hall to a room that Theo swipes open with a key. He holds the door open for me as I walk into an impressive suite adorned with lavish furniture. I drag my foot across the hardwood.

"You probably don't need a black light for this floor," I muse, remembering Theo's horror when I told him about the time the carpet in my family's budget-core hotel room lit up like a neon sign in Vegas.

"No semen-covered duvets either," he says as he releases the door. It swings shut with an ominous click.

My cheeks flush. "A shame," I say dryly. I'm trying to play it cool but I'm emotionally vibrating with an intensity that could shatter glass.

Theo shrugs out of his jacket and rolls up the sleeves on his shirt as he peeks through the hotel curtains and swears under his breath.

"It's chockablock out there," he mutters, which is hilarious. The word, not the situation. He disappears into another room. "Wanna drink?" he calls through the open doorway.

"No, thanks."

He returns to the room with a beer and takes a drink before collapsing onto one of the sofas in front of the empty fireplace. "You may as well take a seat," he says. "There's nothing for us to do but wait."

"Wait for what?"

"Someone to tell us what to do."

"Aren't *you* the guy in charge here?"

He winces.

I suddenly remember what had to happen to make him the guy in charge, and if possible, I feel even worse. "I'm really sorry about your mom." He drops his head, but I can't stop myself. "I felt horrible when I heard the news. I wish I could have told you that." I stop short of bringing up the number of times I tried to contact him. This isn't about me, and I don't want to make him feel guilty for moving on.

He clears his throat and stands. "Actually, there's something I have to check on. If you'll, um, excuse me, I'll be right back." He dashes from the room like it's on fire and I'm the one holding the match.

I flop dramatically over the edge of the elegant sofa and pull a pillow over my face. I can't believe he said *If you'll excuse me*. Like I'm his royal grandmother or a teacher he's scared of. *UGH*. The formality is devastating. I let the pillow drop to the floor, Theo's *If you'll excuse me* playing on a humiliating loop in my brain.

"If *you'll* excuse *me*, I'd like to get the hell out of here," I say in a bad British accent.

"Don't let me stop you," an unfamiliar voice replies out of nowhere, startling me.

I scream, sit up, and nearly choke on my own breath.

Standing in front of me, in basketball shorts and no shirt, is Prince Henry.

CHAPTER 7

Thanks to a healthy dose of internet stalking, I know that the sweaty, half-naked boy in front of me is Theo's younger brother, Henry. If I hadn't seen pictures of him with Theo, I wouldn't have guessed that they're related, thanks to Henry's dark curly hair, dark eyes, and the dimple on his right cheek. I can't see the dimple now, though, because he's frowning at me, his bare skin glistening as he uses a balled-up shirt to wipe the sweat off his face.

"This is the moment where you tell me who you are and beg me not to call security," he says.

I'm surprised by his threat, because Theo would *never*. "I'm Wren."

He stares at me blankly, which is the soul-crushing moment I realize Theo hasn't told his brother anything about me.

"Go ahead and call Winston if you have to," I say defensively.

Henry's dark eyes flash at my casual mention of Theo's bodyguard. "Does my brother know that you're here?"

I bristle at the question. "He's the one who brought me here."

Henry blinks at me wordlessly before checking his phone. He turns his back to make a call and lets out a frustrated grunt when no one picks up. "I'm not trying to be rude, but Theo couldn't be arsed to tell me that he'd be having visitors."

I hold my hands up. "I'm kind of a surprise."

Henry snorts with laughter. Theo didn't talk much about his brother, except to say that Henry would make a better monarch, but I know the basics from the internet. Henry Alexander Philip James is eighteen years old. His birthday is in January, he goes to school in Scotland, and he's allergic to shellfish. He's not de-pressed. (As far as I know.) He's cute. (It runs in the family.) And he's just some guy. (As in, nothing about him screams *should-have-been-king*.)

Henry pushes his curls out of his eyes. "So, *why* are you here?"

I'm tempted to explain the situation with the paparazzi before I remember that Theo said we needed to get our story straight. I shrug. "You'll have to ask the King."

"Are you the girl from the train-station video?" He narrows his eyes at my orange hair with suspicion, and it seems like a good time to change the subject.

"I didn't see you at the park this morning."

He rolls his eyes. "You wouldn't have, as I was uninvited."

"Why?"

"You'll have to ask the King," he says with a wink, clearly pleased with himself. I'm struggling with how to respond when the door bangs open.

Comet barges in first, turns three circles on the rug in front of the fireplace, and then flops down on his belly. Victoria is next, and she stops short when she sees me. She has a small frame and hair that looks dark blond or light brown, depending on the light.

Her eyes narrow at the sight of me. "You're the girl in the pictures."

"Guilty," I say.

"What pictures?" Henry asks.

Theo enters the suite behind her, his expression stormy. "I tried to kill the story, but they didn't even give us a chance."

"Are we surprised?" Victoria's low voice drips with sarcasm.

Theo surveys his sister with a furrowed brow. "Did you get out of the park okay? Did the paps follow you? Do you need to eat?"

"What pictures?" Henry asks again as he crosses the room to join his siblings.

Victoria waves away Theo's concern and addresses Henry instead. "I'll show you." She stretches out on the rug, her head resting on Comet's belly; Henry and Theo crowd around her phone.

There's a quick knock at the door and Winston pops his head in. "Ms. Wheeler, your sister and friend are here. I've directed them to the Gold Suite, however—"

"Wren!" Brooke elbows her way past Winston and into the room, glaring daggers at me. "What is going on? Who in the fu—" She sees half the royal family and her words die in her throat.

Silence reverberates through the room.

"Hey, Brooke," the King says, grinning widely. "Fancy a cuppa?"

Brooke goes slack-jawed at being personally addressed by Theo. "Apologies, Your Majesty," she says, sinking into a quick curtsy. I'm shocked she knows how to do that.

"Take a cue from your sister—there's no need to curtsy in here," Theo says.

"Speak for yourself," Victoria says without looking up from her phone. "Maybe I want the Americans to curtsy for me."

"Good luck with that. If there's one thing I know about Wren, it's that she doesn't give a shit about my title, and she will *never* curtsy." He winks at me, charm oozing off him again. "That's why we're friends." He tips back another drink.

And with that, I've officially run out of the mental capacity for this conversation. "I'm going to leave."

Theo steps toward me. "I can show you to your room."

"I'll find it."

"It's right next door."

"Easy enough. Knock on the wall three times when I'm allowed to leave." I whistle for Comet to follow me.

He stands, forcing Victoria off his stomach, and trots to my side, licking my hand once to say hello. "Can I bring him to my room?"

Theo's eyes dart to his sister. She frowns. "I guess technically he's yours," Victoria says begrudgingly.

"Technically, he is! Thank you for remembering." I push Brooke between the shoulder blades, steering her out of the room.

"Teenagers," Winston mutters under his breath as he returns my phone on our way out of the suite.

The door next to Theo's is already open, and Naomi is standing with her arms crossed in the open doorway. She frowns, clearly annoyed at having missed out on meeting Theo. I lock the door behind the three of us and scan our room. (Nicer than a Holiday Inn, but not as nice as Theo's room.) Brooke and Comet eye each other as he sniffs her from toe to butt.

"This is the dog?"

"That's him."

"His eyes aren't blue."

I slant her a look. "It wasn't about the dog."

"No shit, Wren! I was scared out of my mind! Naomi shows up in some James Bond car outside the crepe restaurant and insists I get in! I thought we were being *Taken*!"

"Okay, relax!" I hold up a hand. "No one is being abducted. We're here *temporarily* because some paparazzi took pictures of Theo and me. They're already online."

Naomi whips out her phone and starts scrolling. "'Teen King High on Love in Toronto's High Park'!" She screams in delight. "It says that he was caught snogging a mysterious redhead while he was supposed to be on royal tour. Oooh, it sounds like he might be in trouble."

"'Snogging'?" I shriek, snatching the phone to scroll through the rest of the pictures. "All we did was hug. That's a stretch!"

"'Redhead' is a stretch," Naomi muses.

"Will someone please explain to me what is going on?" Brooke demands, and it's a reminder that Theo's not the only one who's been keeping secrets from his siblings.

"Don't think you can put this one off any longer," Naomi says, kicking off her shoes and sinking onto one of the beds, still scrolling.

When Theo and I were on the run in Europe, I'd told my family the bare minimum: that I'd met someone who owned a private plane and agreed to let me use it. Other than Naomi, no one knows that I spent Comet Week with Theo, despite a viral video of us from a train station that showed my blurry profile traveling with the runaway prince. I was worried someone from home would recognize me, but I didn't need to be. I had no connection to the royal family, and there was too much going on for anyone from Chicago to care who Prince Theo was spending his last days with. Brooke had even seen our marriage certificate and brushed it off as a joke.

"Do you remember when I told you that I met a boy in London?"

Brooke stares at me, dumbstruck for only a second as I watch her put the pieces together. "The private plane?"

"His."

"The boy in the Polaroid?"

"Him."

"The reason you've been in a funk all summer?"

Warmth rushes to my cheeks. I shrug sheepishly.

"Wren, you might have a problem," Naomi says, looking up from her phone with a worried expression.

"What now?"

"This website identified you as the girl in that train-station video. They also have your first and last name and know that you're an incoming freshman at Northwestern."

Brooke's eyes grow to the size of world-ending comets. She grabs my forearm and pins me in place. "Is that marriage certificate real?"

"I don't know," I admit.

"Wren!" She groans, raking her hands through her hair. "Mom is a lawyer! You didn't think to ask her to look into it?"

"I didn't want Mom and Dad to find out!"

"They'll know now."

Crap. Another thing to worry about.

"Where is it?" Brooke asks.

"Winston has it."

"Who?"

"The hot bodyguard!"

"I want to see it."

"It's probably in Theo's room. Go ahead and ask."

"I will!"

"Great! Do it!"

I stare at her expectantly. She doesn't move.

I'm shocked. I've never seen my big sister back down from anything. "Wait. Are you scared of him?"

Brooke scoffs. "Don't be ridiculous."

"Why'd you curtsy like that?"

She stands up, huffs across the room, and slams the bathroom door behind her, yelling "*It's protocol!*" through the closed door.

I flop backward on the bed. "That could have gone better."

Naomi pushes herself onto her elbow, propping her head up with her hand. "Do you want the good news or the bad?"

"Good, I guess?"

"You won't have to tell your parents about the wedding."

My stomach drops. "Why not?"

She winces. "The bad news is pretty bad," she says gently.

"Bloody hell!" A shout, followed by a long string of swear words, travels through the walls from Theo's room into ours. Fear prickles along my neck.

"Tell me."

Naomi hands over her phone. "I'm sorry, Wren."

Her phone is open to a gossip tabloid. I scroll through the headlines as my chest caves in.

Secret Wedding Disaster! Leaked Marriage Certificate Shocks Britain

King Theo Duped into Marrying Desperate American

Royal Crisis: American Wren Wheeler Reaches for the Throne!

CHAPTER 8

I s it possible I love-bombed Theo?"

I've spent the past two hours talking Mom and Dad off a ledge and reading wild conspiracy theories and fanfiction about my life, and I'm starting to spiral. My head is hanging upside down off the foot of the bed, and I feel like I might pass out.

"Stop reading the comments." Naomi nudges me with her foot. I slide off the bed and hit my head on the ground.

I'm too stressed to move. "Do you think I gaslit him?"

"Ugh, people will go out of their way to blame the girl every time," Brooke says.

There's a sharp knock on the door. Brooke answers it. A man in a suit looks past her to where I'm still lying in a pathetic heap on the floor. "We need you. Now."

Dread slithers up my spine. *My first royal summons.*

I'm led into one of Theo's sitting rooms and seated at a large oak table across from half a dozen people, with Theo directly across from me, and Henry next to him. (Wearing a shirt this time.) Naomi's surprised expression makes it clear that we *will* be discussing Henry after this meeting is over.

We're introduced to the royal communications secretary, a bald man named Richard Graves, as well as Theo's private secretary, a tour secretary, and a communications officer. Winston and another guard are standing at the back of the room, and on a laptop screen set up on the table is yet another stone-faced representative of the Firm.

When Theo talked about "the Firm" and their power over his life, I'd assumed most of that control stemmed from his mother and her wishes, and that once Theo was in charge, he could forge a different path.

Now that I'm sitting across from an entourage of people determined to tell me when and how I'm allowed to leave this hotel (or not), I'm realizing my thought process was painfully naive.

"I don't want to be queen!" I blurt immediately. Everyone over the age of thirty smirks. Theo's expression remains carefully blank, while Henry looks intently back and forth between his brother and me.

"Your wishes are irrelevant, because it will never happen," says Graves. "When the King is officially crowned in less than two weeks, this whole mess with your marriage certificate will be forgotten."

"How did the press get ahold of it?" I ask, my accusatory gaze settling on Theo's security guard.

"We're looking into it," Theo says. "A picture of the certificate was sent via phone, and we now suspect our phones have been hacked."

"Is your phone safe, Birdie?" Mom asks. On the American side of the table: me, my stunned parents on a video call, Brooke, Naomi, and Comet snoozing at my feet. There was some dispute about whether they should be present for this (i.e., no one wants them here) but Brooke insisted that if *His Majesty's* people get to be present, mine should too. I know she's not over the surprise wedding reveal, but I'm thankful she has my back, because the vibes in this room are not exactly welcoming.

As in, everyone here fucking hates me.

I thought being lost at sea after a perilous thunderstorm was the coldest and most miserable thing I'd ever experience, but that was before half a dozen furious Brits were testing out the phrase "if looks could kill" on me, slowly freezing the atmosphere in this room with hostile words and frigid glances. The press people especially seem to loathe me, their stares full of bitter accusation. The message is clear: I am a problem to be solved.

"I have canceled all remaining tour appearances," the tour secretary says now.

Any inclination I might have to apologize is stemmed by Brooke, who is pressing her fingernails into my knee under the table. "Don't let them blame you," she whispers.

The communications officer places half a dozen pieces of paper in front of Theo, who has been avoiding eye contact with me since the news of our wedding broke. "We need a story to feed to the press while we deal with this marriage problem. I have prepared a number of statements, and we must decide which one to run."

She wrote the statements, and *they* will decide. I might as well not even be here, for all they care about my opinion. "Do you even need to deal with it?" I ask, dodging the daggers thrown from her eyes. "Not that I *want* to stay married—" Theo's gaze finally lifts to mine, his eyes unreadable. I feel like I'm in free fall. I miss the time when I understood all his expressions. "What I mean is—are we sure we're actually, legally, married?"

"We are not sure of anything, Ms. Wheeler," she says tightly.

"Which is why we need time." She turns to Theo. "I recommend that we run the first statement. It will prevent anyone from questioning your decision-making ability."

"Does everyone in this room think I'm crazy?" Theo asks abruptly.

"*I* wouldn't have done it," Henry mutters.

"Getting married to a stranger on a whim makes you seem *young*, Your Majesty," Graves says.

"It's almost as if a teenager shouldn't be put in charge of an entire country. No, wait! It's almost as if people shouldn't be put on pedestals at all," Theo says, and I'm confused all over again about his feelings toward his new life, his title, and how I fit into any of it. "I suppose you think Wren tricked me into marrying her?" he asks wryly.

The man on the laptop screen speaks up. "We do not know what to think, as you have not provided us with any justification for this senseless decision."

"You will be disappointed to learn that Wren didn't trick me at all. Quite the opposite."

This revelation garners the biggest response yet, but it's something I feel more than witness. The air shifts, the tension heightens. If possible, the glares in my direction intensify. It's strange, to feel so utterly powerless and yet so significant at the same time.

"Even so, statement one is the way to go," the communications officer replies, nudging the paper into Theo's direct line of sight and sweeping the rest into a stack, which she taps curtly against the table. "Total denial."

Theo's brow furrows as he reads. "This makes it sound like Wren forged the certificate because she's obsessed with me or something."

"That's not explicitly stated."

"I don't want to talk about the statement right now. We need to tell Wren the plan for keeping her safe," Theo says. The communications officer sits, while others shift uneasily in their seats.

"I'll be fine," I say quickly. "As long as you don't paint me as some psycho stalker in your statement, I'll be fine. It'll blow over."

"Tell her," he says, looking at Graves. When Graves doesn't speak immediately, Theo's jaw clenches. "Henry?" He turns to his brother for help.

"It'll be bad," Henry confirms.

Theo's face turns pleading. "Wren, the press will stalk you. They'll tap your phone, put trackers on your car, and chase you like they did today. They won't care if it puts your life in danger."

"I don't drive in the city," I say weakly.

"They'll try to camp outside your dorm room. They'll film you while you walk to class. They'll harass your family and friends."

"For what? A glimpse of my mom power walking in the suburbs? I'm sorry, I don't see it."

"Does she know about Dad?" Henry asks quietly.

Graves speaks quickly. "If Wren thinks she can handle it—"

"She can't," Theo snaps. "Mr. and Mrs. Wheeler, can I ask for a favor?" he says, directing his attention to my parents on the video call.

"Of course, Your Majesty," my dad says. My heart tilts at the tremor in his voice. I look at the screen and can't miss the concern in my parents' eyes.

"Show Wren what's already started," Theo says.

The camera leaves my parents' faces and I catch a shaky

glimpse of Wally on the carpet as they carry the phone to a window at the front of the house and direct the camera lens at my front yard. A rock drops in my stomach when I see a handful of reporters camped out on the lawn.

"There's more across the street knocking on the Singhs' door, and Mrs. Beasley is giving an interview in her yard right now," Mom says.

Black spots fill my vision. "What about Naomi's parents?"

"They've closed their curtains and locked the doors like we have," Mom says.

"My DMs are already filled with news outlets asking for an interview." Naomi's voice sounds far away. My life is slipping so far out of my control I can't remember how to breathe.

Theo stands, places his hands flat on the table, and gives everyone in his entourage a hard look before returning his gaze to mine. Those blue eyes always make the rest of the world fall away. I want to believe that we've survived worse than this, but something about the raw fury in his expression makes me doubt myself.

Maybe this is worse.

He takes a deep breath, his eyes never leaving mine. "What's happening now is the tip of the iceberg, and because the Firm refuses to give you security in America . . ." His next words land in my chest like an atom bomb. "You need to come to London."

CHAPTER 9

Brooke, Naomi, and Henry all speak at once, but I can't hear anything except the blood rushing in my ears. "Stop!"

Everyone shuts up.

"For how long?" I ask.

"You owe her security!" Brooke jumps in. "The marriage certificate never would have leaked if you hadn't taken it from her."

"Arranging full-time security takes time that we don't have and money that belongs to the British taxpayer," Graves says coolly.

"Sell one of your castles," Brooke snaps.

"For how long?" I ask again.

"A week should give us enough time to protect you while we deal with the press and the marriage . . . problem. It will also give His Majesty time to appeal for the funds to hire security on your behalf, if he chooses to do so. We do not wish to keep you in London against your wishes, and of course you are free to decline our offer, but the King feels very strongly about keeping you shielded from the media, and I must admit, I do believe the situation will be less than ideal if you return to Chicago on your own."

"A week is cutting it awfully close to the coronation," the man on the laptop warns.

"We need to deal with this story so that it doesn't *overshadow* the coronation," the communications officer points out.

"Heaven forbid." Henry rolls his eyes.

I turn my attention to my parents, both of whom are choking back tears. "What should I do? I don't want to make your lives harder."

"Don't worry about us, Birdie. This is about doing what's best for you," Mom says.

"It sounds like you should go with them," Dad agrees.

"Classes start next week," I protest.

"Nothing happens in the first few days of freshman year. And you're smart. Find the class syllabuses online and get started on your reading," he says.

I'm painfully conscious of Theo's eyes on me. This is all happening so fast; we haven't even had a proper conversation, and now he's asking me to get on a plane. My stubborn side wants to refuse, but something in my gut tells me I'd be stupid to ignore their warnings about the press.

Underneath the table, Theo's foot nudges mine, sparking another painful memory of us together on a train in Italy, his foot bumping into mine while his finger traced idle circles on my knee. Could we have that again? *Do I want that again?* I don't know, but the brief contact still has the power to leave me scatterbrained.

"If she decides to go to London, I'm going with her," Brooke says.

"No," Graves says flatly.

"There's no point arguing with me. I've made my mind up, and I won't let a foreign government take my sister hostage—"

The communications officer stalks out of the room, throwing her pages of carefully worded statements into the air.

"Take it down a couple notches," I tell Brooke. *No need to make them hate us more than they already do.*

"Brooke can come," Theo says. "Naomi too, if she wants—"

"I do!" Naomi says quickly.

I look at her in surprise. "What about school?"

"The press has already figured out that I'm your best friend. I don't want to be stalked either!"

"Not even in the name of higher education?" I raise an eyebrow.

A slow smile spreads across her face. "If you're running away with the royals again, I'm coming with you this time. School can wait a few days."

I swallow thickly and look back at Theo. The last time we decided to run away together I was alone, desperate, and scared. This time, I have my sister, my best friend, and my dog.

What could go wrong?

I knock my foot against Theo's and allow myself a small smile. "Let's go to London."

⚹　　⚹　　⚹

As we're leaving Theo's suite, the Firm "advises" me not to stray farther than the private elevator. (So much for the discreet staff.) Comet needs to go outside, so Brooke offers to take him for a walk around the courtyard, and Naomi and I return to our room.

"What happened to Theo's dad?" I ask once I've closed the

door firmly behind us. I can't forget the apprehension on Henry's face when he asked Theo if I "knew" about their father.

"He passed away a few years ago. He got really sick and was gone within a few weeks, if I remember right," Naomi says.

"Was the press hard on him?"

"They're hard on everyone, even the royals," she says absently, thumbing through a room service menu. "How much room service do you think we can get away with ordering?"

"Order everything. What do you know about Henry?"

"He was the spare, but now he's the heir, and the public *loves* him."

"Why?"

"The curly hair? The dimple? He sticks out in a royal lineup, but people love that he's different. He's also authentic in a way that Theo's not." She winces. "No offense to your husband."

"I thought you were mad at my husband?"

"I am!" She crosses her arms defensively. "But it's harder now that I've met him. I blame the accent." (Fair enough.)

I can only ruminate on the royal family for so long before the conversation quickly turns to the room service menu. Brooke returns with Comet, and we spend the evening eating charcuterie and cheesecake, watching our social media followings go up faster than we can hit refresh, and playing fetch with Comet in the hall.

Shortly after dinner, Victoria's personal stylist stops by the room with a delivery of clothing for each of us, and it quickly becomes obvious that she only knows how to dress rich people.

"We look like Easter eggs," Brooke says critically as we stand together in front of the bathroom mirror, still steamy around the edges from three showers in a row. We're dressed in silk pajama sets in various shades of pastel.

"If Easter eggs wore matching underwear," I say.

"Do you think this is what princesses wear when they sleep?" Brooke muses.

"Ask Wren, she's the queen consort," Naomi quips.

"Not that those stuffy assholes would ever admit it," Brooke grumbles.

"It *is* kind of weird that an American teenager can suddenly become their queen," Naomi says.

"That's because royalty is weird. No offense to Wren's boyfriend, but if you're going to put a nineteen-year-old boy in charge of the country, you can't be surprised when he makes questionable choices because he's horny."

"That's unfair! Marrying Wren is a great choice." Naomi leaps to our defense. I'm starting to feel dizzy.

"The monarchy is unfair," Brooke counters. She begins ticking the problems off on her fingers. "Colonialism, racism, elitism—"

"That's not *Theo's* fault—"

"I need fresh air." I grab the empty ice bucket off the bathroom counter and look at them both in the mirror. "Be done arguing by the time I get back."

I escape to the hallway, bucket in my hand, and lean against our closed door, gulping air until my head stops spinning. I can't believe that twenty-four hours ago Naomi and I were going to our first college party, and now I'm trapped in a Canadian hotel, unable to go outside without having my picture taken. And just in case that's not confusing enough, I don't know how Theo feels about any of this. A small part of me has been hoping he'd come visit my room so we could finish our conversation from earlier, but he hasn't. Apparently, it was too much to call, too much to write, too much to walk three feet from his door to mine.

If I were anyone else, I'd tell me to get a grip.

When my head is no longer swimming and I think I've given Brooke and Naomi enough time to stop squabbling, I wander the hall until I find the ice machine. I'm filling the bucket when I hear a voice behind me.

"I'll never understand Americans' obsession with ice," Theo says.

I jump, and ice goes skittering across the floor. "Shit." I kneel down to sweep it into a pile.

"You all right?" he asks, holding out a hand to help me up. "Sorry for scaring you."

"Hi! Hey! Yeah, I'm fine!" I stand, suddenly conscious of the thin silk of my pajamas. I hold the bucket against my stomach, an icy barrier between how good he looks in sweats and a T-shirt and the way my skin feels like it's overheating.

He nods in the direction of our rooms, and we slowly fall into stride next to each other.

"I'm sorry again, about this," he says, running his hand through his hair. "If there was any other way, I wouldn't have suggested bringing you to London."

Ouch. How does one respond to being told by their maybe-husband that spending a week together is a literal last resort? It's unfair how our time apart has robbed me of my ability to speak to him, while it's only made him hotter.

"I thought you'd dye your hair back" is all I can think to say. I wish he had. His blond hair had no power against me.

"I can say the same to you." He quirks a curious eyebrow.

"Why didn't you?"

"Apparently, you mucked up my natural shade. The palace hairdresser was furious with me."

We reach my door, and I lean against it, unable to smother my grin as I imagine a stuffy British hairdresser yelling at Theo.

"Same question," Theo says, his eyes tracing my vibrant locks.

I shrug, suddenly feeling defiant over my decision to keep the reddish-orange shade. "Just because you don't like it doesn't mean other people don't."

"I never said I don't like it," he argues.

"You implied it."

"Not once. Who are these other people who like it? Blokes?"

"*Me*. I like it. The entire world was so quick to move on after the comet. Sometimes it feels like everyone else has forgotten about it. But I don't want to forget, so I kept the hair." My chest burns with the admission.

He winces, looking down. "Well, if I didn't say it before, I like it," he says. "It suits you." He reaches out and brushes a strand from my face. The smallest sliver of his finger touches my forehead, and I feel like I'm on fire.

"Thanks." We stare at each other a beat too long. I wait for him to say something, to do something, but he doesn't. If I stand here another second, the heat radiating off me will melt everything in this ice bucket. "I should go."

"Okay." He nods.

I open the door and slip into the Gold Suite. The front room is empty, TV sounds floating in from the bedroom. Brooke and Naomi seem to have called a truce.

My hands are shaking as I set the ice bucket on the nearest flat surface, my heart pounding cartoonishly fast. I feel flushed everywhere, like I have a fever. My hand reaches out to the door handle, brushing it once. I drop it.

Don't go there.

I turn, walk all of three feet, then spin around again. I bite my lip in indecision, feeling insane.

I swing open the door and come face-to-face with Theo.

CHAPTER 10

Theo leans toward me, his hands on either side of the door frame, his body filling the open space. He looks at me almost in disbelief, like he's not sure if I'm real. He swallows, forcing the next words out on a rasp. "Do you want to come to my room?"

I'm struck by a swell of memories: images of Theo braced over me, his hands fisted in the sheets. His lips on my neck, my hands in his hair, his weight pressing me down. My breath hitches as my eyes fall to his mouth. "I'm not sure if that's a good idea."

"I didn't mean it like that," he says quickly.

It's the most humbling moment of my life. "Good night, Theo."

He sticks his foot out to stop me from shutting the door in his face. "Please." His voice scrapes my spine like gravel. "We need to talk. There are some things I should have said the moment I saw you in the park."

"Say them here."

He's silent for several seconds before taking a deep breath. "I'm sorry for leaving you in Greece."

The sincere ache in his tone chips away at my defenses, but I'm not ready to let them go. "Is that all?"

A door opens and Henry appears in the hall. "Don't mind me, just going to check on Victoria." He ducks his head and knocks on another door, disappearing the instant it cracks open.

"C'mon. We're not doing this out here," Theo insists. He ushers me down the hall, where he opens the door to his dimly lit suite, and we step inside. He sits on the sofa in front of the fireplace, which is now alight with a crackling fire. I sit on the other side of the sofa, realizing too late how small it is; even sitting on the opposite end puts me almost directly next to him.

He picks up the open beer from the end table, then sits forward with his elbows on his knees. "I'll never forgive myself for leaving you, and I wouldn't blame you if you don't forgive me either, but I need to apologize anyway." Light from the fire flickers on his face, casting half of him in shadows.

I clear the swelling emotion from my throat. "The pilot implied that you asked her to fly me home. Is that true?"

He blinks at me in surprise. "Of course it is. Did you really think—" He shakes his head. "You thought I left you there to die alone?"

I tuck my legs under me because I need the illusion of distance between us. My shoddy defenses are crumbling. "It happened so fast, and you were furious . . ."

He tilts his head to the side and studies me sadly. "I thought you knew me better than that."

"And *I* thought you'd never forgive me for turning you in."

He runs a hand over his face. "I was being a stubborn and shortsighted git. I fooled myself into believing we had a chance outside the bunker because I wanted it to be true so badly, but you were the only one thinking clearly. Listen to me, Wheeler." He leans in, shrinking the distance between us. "There's nothing to forgive."

And just like that, my defenses have collapsed, taking three months of pent-up guilt with them. "It was an impossible situation; there weren't any good choices."

"I should have done more. I should have demanded that you be let in the bunker." He scrubs a hand through his hair. "I'm gutted every time I think of your face as the car drove away."

It's strangely comforting to know that I'm not the only one who spent the summer lost in a supercut of memories. "You did the best you could with the circumstances we had."

"I wish we had different circumstances," he says quietly.

My heart is in my throat. "We do now, don't we?" It somehow feels like the bravest thing I've ever said.

He smiles wryly and tips his head back against the sofa. "Look at what they're saying about us online and tell me it doesn't feel like the end of the world."

"I think your press team would rather deal with a second comet than with me."

He rolls his head to the side to look at me. "You're not wrong, Wheeler. At least the comet was predictable." He sighs. "I'll ask again about the security detail. I know you don't want to come to London." He picks up the beer bottle.

"How can you be so sure?"

He pauses, the bottle halfway to his mouth, and swallows, his throat bobbing. He gently sets the bottle down and turns fully toward me. His face is open with want, and for the first time all day, I'm pretty sure I know what he's thinking. Warmth from the fire feels like it might devour the room whole. My fingers stray to the chain around my neck, his ring still hidden from view. I wonder how he'd feel if he knew I was wearing it.

I wonder how I'd feel if he asked for it back.

"Come here?" he asks.

My heart thumps painfully in response.

A knock pounds on the door.

"You in there?" a voice yells from the other side.

When Theo opens the door, I catch a glimpse of Henry. "Can this wait?" Theo asks in a low voice.

Henry cranes his neck to see over Theo's shoulder and waves to me. "Victoria sent me to get the dog."

"My dog?" I ask incredulously.

Theo looks over his shoulder at me. "Wait here?" he asks. "I'll be back soon." The door to his room swings shut, leaving Henry and me inside.

"Why does she think she can take my dog?"

"She's used to getting what she wants," Henry says.

"She's not getting Comet."

He shrugs on his way to the refrigerator. "I bagsied the fried rice, but there's some egg rolls in the fridge if you want." He grabs a carton of leftover Chinese food and sits next to me.

"Why aren't you ever wearing a shirt?" I ask.

He laughs. (Dimple confirmed.) "Are you excited to come to London?"

"Should I be?"

"I bet Theo has told you all about how horrible our lives are, but it's not so bad. I can show you around if he's too busy brooding to do it." He takes a giant bite of fried rice and pushes a mess of dark curls out of his eyes. "Sorry I was standoffish earlier, by the way, it's just that I thought you might be a nutter."

"You never know. I still could be," I say, which makes him laugh again. It's easy to see now what Naomi was talking about. He seems completely unselfconscious, and I can see why people are drawn to him. What I don't get is why he would be excluded from an outing specifically designed for the public if everyone loves him. "So why were you uninvited from the park this morning?"

He takes another large bite and chews for a long time. "I'm sure you've figured out pretty quickly that the tabloids are ninety-five percent rubbish?"

"Yeah," I say, thinking about how half the internet has already diagnosed me with clinical narcissism based on absolutely nothing.

He tosses the empty carton into the fire. "That means five percent of it is true."

I lean forward. "Like what?"

"Google is free," he says with a smirk. The firelight glints off his eyes, and I realize they're not as dark as I thought; his irises are bronze with a ring of green around the pupils.

I glance at the door. "Will Theo be gone awhile?"

"Depends on how persuasive my sister is."

"She's *not* getting my dog."

Henry chuckles. "So I've heard."

"I guess that means I have time to do some reading," I say. He salutes me cheekily on my way out the door. As I'm leaving, I see Theo and one of the men from the meeting—his communications secretary, Graves—arguing in the hall, their backs to me.

I'm about to slip past them when I hear Theo say, "It's not fair to ask her to do this." I assume they're talking about me (maybe the internet was right to call me a narcissist), and I pull the door almost shut while straining to hear what they're saying over the machine-gun barrage of my own heart.

"We didn't ask, you did," Graves replies.

"And now I'm *asking* the Firm to loan her a security detail so that she doesn't have to disrupt her life."

(I *knew* it was about me.)

"For how long?" Graves asks in a steely voice.

"Just until this mayhem dies down. You can feed the press a more interesting story. Mum used to do that all the time."

"If we provide this random American with her own personal security, it implies that she's important to you and to the monarchy. It will only increase public curiosity. They'll expect her to stick around. *Is* she sticking around, sir?"

I stopped breathing several sentences ago.

"No," Theo says. "She's going back to Chicago."

"Is she important to us?"

Theo's spine straightens, and he looks at Graves dismissively. "Don't be daft. She's just a girl I spent a few days with."

My throat burns with the pain of holding back tears.

"Then don't throw a spanner in the works, let us do our jobs, and she'll be gone in a week," Graves says, before turning on his heel and marching down the hall.

CHAPTER 11

'm on my second private jet in three months, sitting across from a boy I once loved who does not want me here. It's as awkward as it sounds, which is why I spent a good portion of last night brainstorming ways to get out of this.

I'm morally opposed to flying private. (True.)

I'm too sick to fly. (Technically true, since my stomach is churning.)

I'm pregnant. (And it's not Theo's.)

The easiest escape route would have been to tell Brooke and Naomi what I overheard, but it won't help anyone if they murder the king of England.

"Do you think Princess Victoria will be on our flight?" Naomi asked when we were all in the car early this morning, a notepad of hotel paper clutched tightly in her hand.

My stomach churned anxiously. "Probably. Why?"

"I've made a list of conversation topics to help Theo's siblings get to know you. First, I'm going to tell them about the time your pet hamster died, and your parents buried him in the backyard, and you couldn't stop crying so you dug him up and walked around for three days with a dead hamster in a shoebox."

I gaped at her. "Please don't."

"It's charming! Second, I want to know if it's true that she doesn't squeeze her own toothpaste. That one's not about you. Third, I'd love to know her thoughts about *weather*."

"As a general concept?"

"Yes. Exactly." Her eyes scanned the paper. "I guess most of these aren't about you."

When the ride ended, Naomi stepped onto the tarmac, stared up at the dreary, pre-dawn sky, and declared that it would be a great day. She then fired off a dozen emails to her roommate, her RA, her student adviser, and her professors, informing them all that she's on a diplomatic mission and would be back in a week. Brooke, still behind on sleep after spending an entire night driving to Canada, wordlessly slunk to the back of the plane and conked out.

I was surprised to learn that most of Theo's team would be on a second plane leaving later today, and that this morning's flight would just be us, the royal siblings, Comet, and Winston. I overheard snippets of heated conversation about whether the direct heirs to the throne would be allowed on the same plane as Theo, but it sounds like Victoria and Henry wanted on the first plane out of Canada. In the end, Theo overrode royal protocol to allow all three of them on the same flight.

I feel mortified every time I look at the King, flushed with the shame of thinking he wanted to kiss me in his suite last night, that I ever meant anything to him. I'm glad he left when he did, and even more glad that he didn't come around asking for Comet. He would have found me in a bad mood, unwilling to give up my dog, and deep down a rabbit hole of Googling his brother.

I can feel Theo's eyes on me now from across the small plane, and it takes everything I have not to acknowledge him. His presence is so distracting; I can practically *feel* when he blinks. But that doesn't matter. From last night onward, I am indifference personified.

Henry takes the seat next to me and opens a book. Without taking his eyes off the page, he says, "Find anything interesting?"

Given the way our conversation ended last night, I'm pretty sure he's talking about my promise to look him up online.

It's hard to know how to separate fact from fiction when it comes to the royal family, because their fans and haters won't shut up and log off. I could have read all night and still not scratched the surface of royal family lore. One pattern was easy to spot, though, and it's exactly as Naomi said: Henry gets disproportionately positive press. He's consistently named the "hardest-working royal," with more than twice as many royal engagements as Theo and endless puff pieces about his charity work.

Theo, on the other hand, is the face of a monarchy in crisis. I didn't pick up on it when I was just scrutinizing pictures of him and Comet, but apparently public support for him is waning, especially outside the UK. He's suspected of drinking too much and enjoying his job too little. According to some outlets, this (now-scrapped) royal tour was a desperate and doomed effort to gather goodwill for a capricious teenage king in the weeks leading up to his coronation.

I'm not about to discuss any of this with Henry, however. "What are you reading?"

He tilts his book so I can see the cover. *Sceptre, Throne, and Crown*. It looks like a dense nonfiction book about the history of his own family.

I laugh out loud. "Everyone already likes you best! You don't need to do all this."

He uses his finger as a bookmark as he closes the book. "You *did* research me."

"Is that why you weren't at the park yesterday? Because you've been getting too much good press?"

He raises a cryptic brow before flipping the book back open and returning his eyes to the page. I'm dying to lean forward and look at Theo, but I heroically resist the urge.

The smell of nail polish fills the cabin. Eager for a distraction, I push myself up onto my knees and turn around, resting my chin on the back of my seat. Naomi is painting her nails a kelly green while Victoria frowns at her. I realize with a stab of jealousy that Comet is lounging on the seat next to the princess.

"Hey, Theo. Can you change Mum's rule about colored nail polish?" Victoria asks, running her hand over Comet's head.

"You wear colored nail polish all the time. You're wearing it now," Theo points out.

"Barely." Victoria rolls her eyes at her pale pink nails. "And the press still won't put a sock in it. I want to wear black. Or neon purple with silver sparkles. I want my nails to be two inches long with charms hanging off."

He cocks his head. "You do?"

"I want the option."

"Do it. You know *I* don't care."

"Also, I'm done with tights. They make me feel like a grandma."

"I'll write a statement," Theo deadpans.

"Never complain, never explain," Henry says ominously.

"What is that?" I ask.

"Our family motto," he says proudly, and I remember Theo telling me how the Queen forbade him from talking about his depression. I can't help but wonder if she saw it as complaining, and my impression of her plummets even further.

I glance at Theo, and my heart surges. "That doesn't seem fair," I say to Henry.

He shrugs. "No one wants to hear rich white people complain about clothes or nails when there are families struggling to put food on the table. It makes us seem out of touch."

"We *are* out of touch," Victoria and Theo say at the same time.

I slide back down in my seat. "Even so, I'd rather live naked at the North Pole than get my brother's approval on my *nail art*."

"You should know that if you stick around, you'll be expected to follow the same guidelines," Victoria says.

"She's only staying for a few days," Henry answers for me. "Right?" For clarification he turns to his brother, who is watching our conversation with interest. "Once the wedding fuss is cleared up, she's going back to Chicago?"

"You two aren't together?" Victoria butts her way into the conversation now, but my gaze is still locked on Theo's. My face heats as I think about the conversation that I overheard last night.

"No," I answer, before Theo beats me to the punch. "No, we're not together. Yes, I'm leaving London as soon as possible."

Theo stands and crosses the aisle. "Switch with me," he says to his brother.

"Is that an order, Your Majesty?" Henry jokes.

At least I think it's a joke until I see Theo's jaw clench.

Henry raises his eyebrows at me. "That's the trouble with my brother. If it were me—"

"Sod off," Theo says gruffly.

"Attaboy! Way to take charge!" Henry bows and sweeps his arms out to the side, dramatically giving his seat to his brother.

Theo sits and buckles himself in and motions to his brother. "In case you doubted that he was better for the job . . ."

He's too close. I stand up. "I have to go to the bathroom."

"Safety hazard," Theo says. "The pilot never cleared us to take off our seat belts."

"I'll risk it." I step toward the aisle, but his arm reaches out, blocking my path.

"I have it on good authority that you've been known to hide in the loo. You wouldn't be planning on doing that again, would you?"

I close my eyes against the memory of him and me in a public bathroom on the Eurostar: I counted the number of times his legs touched mine by the giddy spikes in my pulse. When the world was on the brink of disaster, everything else was simple. There were no consequences to worry about or futures to plan. It was just him and me, bumping knees and hiding smiles.

Fate had to play out exactly right for us to have ended up on that train together, in a situation we couldn't run from, but I sure as hell am running now. I wrap my fingers around Theo's wrist (a grave error in judgment), momentarily frozen, when the pilot makes an announcement.

"We're expecting rough turbulence ahead. Please stay seated with your seat belts fastened."

One side of Theo's mouth hitches up in a wry smile. I can't tell if he's being flirty, or if he's just happy to be right. I drop into my seat and buckle my seat belt, my eyes firmly on the window.

"I think I'm missing something," Theo says to the back of my head.

I want to ignore him (well, I want to *want to* ignore him), but doing so would be the opposite of unbothered. "I don't think so," I say coolly, turning to look at him.

"I'm sorry I left last night."

"I'm not upset about that."

"But you *are* upset?" he prompts.

Great. Two seconds into my unbothered act and I'm already failing. "Nope!" I turn my gaze back to the rain-speckled window.

"Why won't you talk to me?"

"What do you want me to say?"

"The truth."

I whirl on him. "I can't!"

His jaw clenches in frustration.

I lean back with a sigh as the plane hits turbulence and jostles me against him. I quickly lean away, removing all points of contact between us, only to be thrown back into his side. My hand lands in his lap. "I didn't mean to!" I quickly withdraw my hand.

"You're *not* responsible for the turbulence?" he asks in mock surprise.

The plane hits another huge bump, and he grabs my hand and squeezes hard. I look at our intertwined fingers in surprise before glancing up at him. "I didn't mean to," he says sarcastically.

My head slams into the window as Theo's shoulder collides with mine. "Ow!" I yelp in pain.

"Switch seats with me," he says immediately, but I wave him off. I don't need special treatment, and I'm too scared to unbuckle now anyway. This storm is rougher than anything I've ever felt. Books, water bottles, and phones crash through the cabin; Theo and I duck to avoid being hit as we strain against our seat belts.

Silence settles over us as the turbulence intensifies, until Naomi yells "Sorry about the nail polish on the leather" from the back of the cabin.

"Where's Comet?" I ask.

"Buckled in his safety harness," Victoria confirms from somewhere behind me.

"Buddy system?" Naomi jokes. "In case we crash or whatever."

"We're not going to crash," Brooke says. "Flying is safer than driving."

"Even so, you probably shouldn't have let all three of us on the flight, Your Majesty." Henry's voice is strained, and Theo's jaw clenches in response.

I close my eyes and try to slow my breathing, but I can feel my panic bubbling to the top. "Remember we're in Jell-O," I say loudly.

"Care to explain that?" Henry calls, his fingers gripped tightly around his history book.

"The plane is a shaken-up cup of Jell-O and we're the peas safely inside. It's physics," I say, fairly certain that I could explain it better if I wasn't worried about our plane falling out of the sky, cracking the Jell-O cup, and crashing our little pea bodies into the ocean.

"Do Americans eat peas in their jelly?" Victoria asks, managing to sound haughty even in dire circumstances.

"Who said anything about jelly?" My fingers are starting to ache, but then Theo relaxes his white-knuckle grip, and I realize the turbulence is lessening with every second. I open my eyes and look around. The cabin is a disaster, and rain still lashes at our dark windows, but the worst of it appears to be over. The chaos churning inside me settles.

Winston appears from the front of the plane and physically checks to ensure that Theo's seat belt is fastened. I use the moment to quickly swipe tears off my cheeks.

I pull my hand from Theo's loose grip and shake off the remaining terror. My heart hasn't caught up with my brain, and it's brutalizing my rib cage. "Do you think it's over?"

"I reckon, yes," he says.

A voice comes through the speakers. "Ladies and gentlemen, this is your pilot speaking again. Storm conditions have shifted rapidly. If the cabin loses pressure, oxygen masks will deploy."

"Just a precaution," Theo says quickly.

"We're going to be fine." I smile tightly.

"We're Jell-O." Somehow his hand has found its way back around mine.

"We're *in* Jell-O," I correct. "But if something goes wrong, no worries, Your Majesty. Everyone will help you put your mask on first."

"You would take the piss out of me even on the brink of death," he whispers back, a glint in his eye.

"So dramatic." I try to swallow my fear, but my throat is burning with it, my eyes brimming with unshed tears. For about a week this summer, I thought I was going to die, but I never came to terms with it; I wasn't ready then, and I'm even less ready now.

He squeezes my hand, and I squeeze back, all my flimsy

resolve about keeping my distance vanished in an instant. Our knees are pressed together, and I've made a liar of myself. It's just a little turbulence, but we're conditioned to reach for each other as if the world is ending.

"Do you remember when we jumped off a ferry because we thought it was capsizing?" I ask as fear prickles along my spine.

"Is now a good time to be reminiscing, Wheeler?"

"This is just like that. It feels like the plane is crashing, but it's not. I'm sure we'll be laughing about this in a—"

The lights go out, and the plane plummets. Oxygen masks fall. A strong tug behind my belly button nearly yanks me out of my seat. For a heartbeat or two, our luggage hovers in midair.

All I hear is screaming, pierced through by Comet's scared whimper. I picture him hiding under his paws, and I might throw up. Theo's fingers are bruising on the back of my hand. I close my eyes and brace for an impact that doesn't come.

Disaster is slower than I thought.

The plane evens out, and I'm stunned. Theo and I stare at each other in pure disbelief. His eyelashes are wet with tears and my entire body is shaking.

"Are we dead?" I'm only half joking.

The speaker turns on. "Ladies and gentlemen, we've lost both engines."

We look out the window and see flames. I can't breathe. I bend in half and place my head between my knees. My vision goes fuzzy. Theo yanks my shoulders back and clamps an oxygen mask over my face. I turn to see him putting on his own.

"Life preservers are under the seats. Brace for impact," the pilot shouts. "MAYDAY MAYDAY MAYDAY."

Winston throws a life preserver at Theo. My hands shake

violently as I find mine and loop it over my neck. Someone in the back of the cabin is sobbing hysterically.

On second thought, that might be me.

I move the oxygen mask. "I love you, Brooke. I love you, Naomi," I scream.

"I love you, too," Brooke yells back. Naomi doesn't respond.

Theo's face is deathly white. "I can't remember the last time I said that to anyone, even my siblings."

"Now might be a good time." My fists are clenched, my nails digging crescent moons into my skin.

"We don't do that. It . . . it's not natural for me. But I should have said it." He screws his eyes shut tight and forces the next words through gritted teeth. "When we were in Greece, I should have told you that I loved you."

Loved. Past tense.

It's absurd that my brain picks *this* to focus on, but I take comfort in knowing nothing would have changed if he'd said it.

I close my eyes and concentrate on breathing in and out as the plane spirals through the air. I'm covered in tears and snot, shaking so badly it's painful.

"Time to face the facts, Theo." I shout to be heard over the sound of our personal apocalypse.

"What's that, Wheeler?"

"Every time we're together, the universe tries to kill us. It was never going to work."

PART II

CHAPTER 12

The plane hits the ocean with a life-altering crash.

For the space of a heartbeat, there is only shouting, fire, and water.

I frantically scrabble at my seat belt, my hands fumbling against metal. It won't unlatch. I'm stuck. I forget everything I know about anything and tug vainly on the strap until Theo reaches across my lap and unlatches the seat belt with a flick of his wrist.

The frigid water is up to our shins. The side of the plane is on fire. Where the wing used to be, there's nothing.

"*Theo, now!*" Winston snaps from behind us. "This could explode at any moment." He throws an arm around Theo's torso, but Theo jerks free from his guard's grasp.

"I'm with her," he growls. And then to me, "Do *not* let go of my hand."

My teeth chatter violently as I nod.

Theo pulls me to my feet and drags me toward what used to be the back of the plane. It's torn open, and everyone is gone. My stomach pitches violently, thinking of Brooke and Naomi getting sucked out of the cabin. There are jagged shards of twisted metal everywhere, and water is rushing in. It's up to my chest now.

"Brooke—" I scream.

"This is the buddy system," Theo yells. "Trust me." He yanks the rip cord on my life preserver, then his, and pulls me close to his side as we fight against the current streaming into the wreckage. The water is at my chin. "Deep breath!" he says.

I tip my head back, and in the last seconds before the water closes over my mouth, I fill my lungs with air. Theo places his feet against the plane and shoves hard, propelling us out of the cabin and into the water. He swims toward sunlight, but something heavy pulls at me, dragging me away from him. I kick frantically, only to be tugged back. A strap is wrapped around my ankle and pulling me down like an anchor. I try to untangle myself with my free hand but can't, not with Theo tugging me in the opposite direction.

The water pushes and pulls, disorienting me. All I know is Theo's hand in mine and his words.

Do not let go. Trust me.

If I hold his hand for another second, we'll both drown.

I wrench my hand from Theo's and reach down to feel for the strap around my ankle. It's my backpack, and it's tangled in a chunk of metal. A *literal* anchor. My lungs burn as I'm dragged toward the seafloor. I finally shake free and kick up, almost sure that I won't make it. My lungs don't have anything left in them. It feels like swimming through cement, but I keep kicking, rejecting the instinct to inhale a mouthful of seawater.

It's over, my brain lies to me. I kick harder, my fingers clawing at nothing, until I finally break the surface and gulp for air.

I push my hair out of my eyes, trying to get my bearings,

when a churning piece of metal drags against my arm. The pain is instant and blinding. I bite my lip and grab the wound; it grows slippery with blood under my fingers. I'm dizzy. I float onto my back and hope I don't black out.

"Wren!" Brooke's voice cuts through the din. *She's alive.* I snap into focus and swim through the metal, luggage, and burning debris littering the water.

When I reach the rest of the group, I see that Winston is half submerged on a floating piece of wreckage. His leg is lying at an unnatural angle that makes me sick to my stomach. Brooke, Naomi, Henry, Victoria, Comet, and the pilot are floating around the injured bodyguard.

I turn back to the direction I came from, searching for Theo. *How did I get here first?* "Theo!" I yell. It's hard to see anything with all the debris. "Theo!"

"Wren," Naomi says softly. She shakes her head, and I must have lost too much oxygen underwater, because I don't understand what's going on.

"What?" I ask. No one will make eye contact. An abandoned life vest crosses my vision, floating away from the wreckage, and my brain struggles to keep up with what the rest of me already knows.

White-hot dread seeps into my veins.

"Where is he?" I snap.

"Looking for you," Victoria says flatly.

"Why isn't he wearing his life jacket?"

"He took it off to dive for you," Naomi says quietly.

Victoria narrows her eyes. "If he dies, it's your fault."

"Oh, shut up!" Brooke says.

But Victoria's right, I realize numbly; I abandoned the buddy system, and he put himself at risk just to save me.

There's noise behind me, and Theo breaks the surface of the water with a huge gasp. I'm too weak with relief to speak.

Victoria doesn't have that problem. "Don't you dare do that again, you bloody, gormless *wanker*!"

And she's not the only one who's mad.

"Bloody hell, Wren!" Theo pushes hair and water out of his face with an unsteady hand. A range of emotions flits across his brow before settling on fury. "Why'd you let go?"

"There was a backpack . . . it was an anchor . . . pulling me . . ." I trail off as the adrenaline drains from my system. He waits for me to explain myself, but I'm too exhausted from the emotional and physical whiplash of almost dying, not dying, almost dying again, then thinking Theo had died, to do it properly. Especially not when all I can focus on is the water dripping over the bridge of his nose and landing on his lips.

I miss the days when the end of the world had a countdown clock.

"I had to save myself," I say weakly.

He blinks away the anger until he looks simply shattered. "I thought I lost you," he says.

"And I thought I was being promoted," Henry jokes.

"Sorry to disappoint you and the rest of the world." Theo rolls his eyes.

"You literally can't die, because I will burn Buckingham to the ground if Henry becomes king. We all know he wants it too much, and that's bad for business," Victoria says to Theo.

"I do not!" Henry protests. Even I can tell he's lying.

The currents have pushed Theo and me farther from the group, and we doggy-paddle back to the others while Henry and Victoria squabble. I lift my arms out of the water and rest my cheek on a floating piece of junk.

Theo scowls at me. Whatever affection he felt for me during the crash has eroded in the salt water.

"Why are you looking at me like that?" I ask.

"You're bleeding." He lifts my arm to inspect my injury. The silk blouse provided by the royal stylist has torn from shoulder to elbow, and I have a long, jagged gash running the length of my upper arm.

Naomi gasps. "Are you okay?"

"It looks worse than it is. It's already numb," I tell her.

"That's because you're in shock," the pilot says. "Same with Winston and his broken leg." He claps the bodyguard on the shoulder. Winston whimpers. "Once the shock wears off, the pain will set in." He leans closer to my wound and pinches the edges together with his fingers. "We'll figure that out when we get to shore. You'll be all right until then."

"If she doesn't kill us by attracting sharks," Victoria mutters, *just* loud enough for everyone to hear. She smiles in a way that makes me think she'd summon a great white if she could.

"I'll live." I pull my arm from Theo's hand. "And if I don't, it'll be because we drowned at sea, not because of a scrape."

"We're not going to drown," Theo says.

"Cocky, are we?"

"I've got eyes, Wheeler." He points over my shoulder. "We've made it to land." I follow the line of his finger to a rocky shore in the distance and wilt with happiness.

We're going to be rescued, and everything will be fine.

"Brilliant!" Henry claps his hands together. "We'll be home in time for Theo's coronation."

"On second thought—" Theo makes a show of swimming toward the horizon.

"We'll be home in time for dinner if you lot listen to me,"

the pilot says. "By my count, every passenger is here. Is that correct?"

Theo nods.

"Good. I'm Reggie, and if you listen to me, we *will* make it out of this alive, I promise." Reggie has a strong British accent, short gray hair, and a handlebar mustache. He makes eye contact with each of us individually, and I think I love him. In *this* life-or-death crisis, I don't have to plan anything. No one is counting on me to rescue them. I don't even have to count on myself. The relief is staggering.

Reggie continues. "Winston will need help getting to shore, obviously, and her arm is in bad shape." He points to me. "Does anyone else have injuries that will prevent them from swimming to land?"

Theo and the others shake their heads.

Reggie barrels on. "The shore is farther than it looks, but the tides are in our favor and we're not in a rush."

"*I'm* kind of in a rush, mate." Winston speaks for the first time, his eyes screwed shut against the pain of his broken leg.

"Me too," Naomi says through chattering teeth. Her lips are turning blue.

He points to Naomi. "You, Victoria, and Henry are responsible for getting Winston to shore. Take turns towing him, don't let yourself get too tired, and stick together."

"I'm in charge of Comet," Victoria says quickly.

"No, I'll take him," I correct her.

Theo groans. "Not the time."

"The dog will go with the first group, but he's not a priority," Reggie says.

Indignation burns in my chest. "What did you say?"

"Are you bloody joking?" Victoria has a fire in her eyes; it's the first likable thing she's said so far.

Reggie rolls his eyes. "Don't risk Winston's life for the sake of a *dog*."

"No one was saying that, mate," Henry says gently. "Between the three of us, we can manage them both."

"Then go," Reggie orders. "The noninjured American and I will gather luggage."

"If anyone sees my black Prada bag, please save it," Victoria says over her shoulder. I roll my eyes at the back of her head.

"Why do we need luggage?" Brooke asks.

"In case rescue takes more than a few hours to get here and we need supplies," Reggie explains.

"I guess that makes me the injured American?" I ask. *What a legacy.*

"*You* just focus on getting to shore. Flip on your back and kick if you get tired. You're losing blood and you look paler than a polar bear," Reggie says.

"What about me?" Theo asks.

"Swim to shore."

Theo exhales in frustration.

"Welcome to the club; I'm too weak and you're too important," I say.

"You're not weak, you're injured. When you get to shore, find Winston," Theo says, then turns to Reggie. "I can help. I want to help."

"Your Majesty." Reggie nods his head in a quick bow. "Are you willing to take orders from me?"

"Tell me what to do and I'll do it. Don't treat me differently than anyone else."

"Help us with luggage and keep an eye on this one." He nods in my direction, which is annoying. *I'm fine! I don't need Theo to babysit me!* To prove myself, I swim toward a scrap of metal floating about ten yards away and untangle the black purse hanging off it. I wrinkle my nose when I see the Prada logo. Of course it would be Victoria's bag.

I loop it across my body and start to swim, but the leather strap across my chest and the small drag as I swim make me anxious. I kick and kick and kick, but the purse feels like an anvil; every pull makes it harder to breathe. My head is spinning, and a panicky feeling is mounting in my veins. Tears burn my eyes. I unloop the bag from my chest and hold it in my hand instead.

Without the weight of the bag across my chest, my anxiety ebbs. I flip to my back and gently kick myself to shore, the swell of each wave propelling me forward.

A reusable water bottle floats by my head. To avoid being *completely* useless, I grab on to it and keep my eyes on the sky until I hear voices.

"How do we climb it?" Victoria asks.

I roll onto my stomach and crane my neck up.

We've made it to shore. Unfortunately, this shore is not like the one where Theo and I once said our vows. Instead of soft moonlit Grecian sand, we've washed up to a craggy cliffside straight out of *Wuthering Heights*.

I make eye contact with Victoria.

"No sharks?" she asks in a disappointed voice before flicking her gaze back to the rocks.

I unclench my fist and let her Prada bag sink.

"This route looks like our best bet." Henry's finger traces the outline of a rocky set of steps naturally carved into the cliff. "I'll carry Winston up first."

We form a line, and by the time I'm climbing the craggy bluff, Theo, Brooke, and Reggie have caught up and are tossing luggage onto a rocky outcropping at the base of the cliff.

My stomach feels violently empty, every limb in my body shaking with exhaustion as I crawl over the ledge onto the spongy green moss. My throat is screaming with thirst. I untwist the metal bottle still clutched in my hand and tip it over my mouth.

One drop hits my tongue. Just enough to make me ten times thirstier than I was before.

I collapse onto the ground and stare up at the gray sky until it goes black around the edges.

CHAPTER 13

I sit up quickly and blink away the black spots in my vision. Lying down was a bad idea; if I do it again, I'm afraid I won't get back up. A warm rush of blood trails down my arm. I lift my hand and my head spins when I see blood dripping off my fingertips.

I push myself into a standing position and sway on my feet. The world glitches, a slow-motion catastrophe. I shake my head and time trips over itself to catch up. Henry is in front of me, peeling off his soaking-wet shirt and pressing it to my arm. I blink and he's gone. Comet is running frenzied circles around me until Victoria pulls him away. I open my mouth to yell at her but I can't hear anything except waves crashing against rocks. My head aches, my throat burns, and my soaking-wet clothes are plastered to my freezing body.

The shirt does nothing to stem the flow of blood. I drop it.

Instead, I tear a clump of crimson-stained moss from the ground and hold it against my wound.

I step forward on wobbly legs and almost trip over a rock. The rugged shoreline stretches for miles in either direction. Inland, however, the moss becomes tall grass and eventually a dense forest that slopes upward into a mountain.

I don't see a single sign of human life.

(Devastating. I was hoping we'd washed up on the shores of Majorca.)

I pull the moss away from my cut and nearly faint. We need to get out of here immediately.

Reggie is on his knees trying to start a fire with damp moss and a cigarette lighter. I stumble over to him. "When are we getting rescued?" I ask.

"I'm working on it," he says.

"Will it be soon?"

"We're with His Majesty and the two people next in line for the throne. What do you think?" he snaps.

I think the sky is empty, the island is deserted, and that moss is never going to ignite.

"I think I'm in trouble." Since we're not on the verge of being rescued, I need to figure this out myself. Theo told me to find Winston, so I trudge to where he's lying near the edge of the cliff. His eyes are screwed shut and his teeth are clamped hard on a stick.

Victoria is transporting handfuls of clothing up the cliff from the rescued luggage down below, and Naomi and Henry are using wet pants to tightly wrap Winston's broken leg. A first aid kit lies on the ground next to him.

"No one was going to tell me about this?" I motion to the kit with my injured arm. A wave of nausea rolls through me.

Naomi looks up from the bodyguard and gasps. "Oh my gosh, Wren. Sit down! Your cut didn't look this bad in the water." Her eyes fly to Henry's. "Where's Brooke?"

"Reggie sent her to look for firewood."

Naomi swears. "This is bad. She looks awful."

"Funny, because I've never felt better." My lips and finger-tips tingle numbly. I breathe slowly through my mouth to avoid blacking out. I don't know if it's dehydration or a panic attack or blood loss or all of the above.

"Stop joking. It takes too much energy."

"My sarcasm fuels me." The spongy moss reminds me of a bed. I allow myself to lie down with the help of Naomi's insis-tent hands. I feel a tongue on my ankle.

"Actually, you lose a liter of blood every time you say some-thing snarky," Naomi says.

"She'd already be dead." Theo's voice cuts through the din. His face hovers above mine. Icy water drips from his hair into my eyes, but I can't look away. He looks *pissed*. (American ver-sion.) "Why hasn't she been stitched up yet?"

"We're working on it," Henry says. I glance at him. He's attempting to thread a needle with an unsteady hand, and my stomach churns. I close my eyes.

"Work faster," Theo orders. "You all right, Wheeler?"

"Mm-hmm."

"I'm going to need more than an 'mm-hmm' to know you're okay," he says, his voice at point-blank range. I open my eyes and find myself staring directly into his. I could kiss him, if the thought of moving didn't make me want to die.

My eyelids feel heavy.

He places his hand on my cheek. "Don't check out on me now."

I inhale something sharp and painful. (I didn't realize pain could be a smell.) My eyes water as they fly open, and my brain catches up with reality.

Theo is crouched next to me, a pinch between his brows. "Tell me you're okay." It's a command if I've ever heard one.

"Did you lick my ankle?"

"That was me," Henry says gravely.

Theo's eyes widen in alarm until he looks down and sees Comet at my feet. His gaze returns to mine, and I use the very last ounce of energy in my body to wink. He pushes up to his feet, but not before giving his brother a hard shove. "She's fine."

A ringing endorsement. I'm too tired to say it.

"How's Winston?" he asks.

Winston's eyes are still closed. He gives the King an unenthusiastic thumbs-up. Naomi and Victoria are hovering by his side.

"We gave him some painkillers from the first aid kit and did our best to stabilize his leg, He's going to be okay. We're all going to be okay," Naomi says.

"Let me know if you need anything. I have to go." Theo turns to his brother. "Henry," he says in a steely voice.

"I'll try not to make it worse," Henry says.

A beat passes. "If anything happens to her—"

"No dead Yanks on my watch. I've got it," Henry says.

"I'm serious," Theo says, and then he gazes down at me. "Go easy on him." He stalks away, leaving all of my focus to land on the needle in Henry's hand.

"You might want to turn your head," Henry says as he takes Theo's place by my side. He pinches my cut between two fingers and Naomi and Victoria both inhale sharply. Naomi covers her eyes with her hands.

"Naomi, can you go find Wren's sister?"

"I'll be right back," she says.

"Take your time," he mutters as she runs toward the forest. He lifts the needle again, but even I can see Victoria flinch in my periphery. "You've got to go, Tor."

She stands with a huff and whistles for Comet to follow her.

When we're alone, Henry takes a steadying breath. "You ready, darling?"

I'm so thrown by the word "darling" that I forget to anticipate the pain, and before I know it, he's made the first stitch. The tug of needle and thread is sickening.

"Victoria wants to push me over the cliff."

"Hmmm?"

"I bet the Firm would be *chuffed* if you let her do it."

"*Ah.*"

"She'd take your crown as the most beloved royal, for sure. They'd be grateful for the person who solves this problem for them." I'm rambling, but I can either talk, or pass out from pain.

"A bit of a stupid thing to say to the person who has a needle in your arm, innit?"

"I liked it better when you called me 'darling.'"

"Bite this and stop talking." He places a stick between my teeth.

Time crawls like molasses, until I feel one final tug, followed by a pinch. "Done."

I spit out the stick. "Thank you."

He cleans up his supplies and closes the first aid kit. "With any luck, someone who knows what they're doing will fix it soon."

"I think our luck ran out the moment the plane went down," I say.

His gaze travels to the bodyguard a few paces away from us. "Winston's asleep."

I watch the bodyguard's chest move up and down. "I hope he's not in pain." Sleep sounds ideal. I want to sleep until we're rescued.

We lapse into a long stretch of silence. Henry sits with his arms on his knees, staring out at the ocean while I lie on my back and look at the empty skies. I feel strangely untethered, like if no one is watching, I might dissolve entirely.

Every time Henry shifts, I expect him to leave, and I'm newly shocked each time he doesn't. "You don't have to wait with me."

"I'm afraid I do," he says.

"You don't even know me."

"Doesn't matter."

I want to know a lot more about that, but when I push myself into a sitting position, I'm distracted by my view of Theo, who's aggressively sorting through the salvaged luggage down on the beach below. When he doesn't find what he's looking for, he pushes his hands through his hair. A wave crashes into the rocks, covering him with ocean spray.

Muscles ripple across his shoulders as he lifts his arms above his head and dives into the water. "He's not—" I cut myself off, because *he is*. I watch in horror as he swims toward the flaming wreckage. "What is he doing?"

"Looking for something."

"It's dangerous! It's reckless, and—"

Henry places his hand on my arm. "He'll be safe."

"I'm going to get him. He's being stupid." I stand up and my vision goes temporarily black.

Henry catches me when I stumble sideways. "You're not getting in the water."

I pull myself out of his arms and sit back down. I hate that he's right. "I've only been around the royals for a day and I'm already sick of being told what to do."

In the distance, Theo drags himself out of the water and

stops to catch his breath. He shakes out his arms and dives back in. Even now, his gravitational pull is so strong that I'm tempted to jump in after him.

"Theo's trying to do what's best for you," Henry says.

"What's best for me is getting off this island," I grumble, trying to ignore my burning thirst.

"Once we're rescued and back in London, you should let him."

My pride bristles, and I can't help but roll my eyes. "Of course he knows best, because he's a *man,* and I'm just a silly eighteen-year-old girl."

Henry picks up a rock and chucks it off the cliff. "I'm not saying that. I'm saying that you might consider the possibility that the person who was born for the throne knows more about the dangers of proximity to the royal family than you do."

"I get that it sucks to be written about in tabloids—"

"You don't," Henry cuts me off. "And that's not your fault, because there's no way you could understand."

My stomach squirms. "What happened to 'it's not so bad'?" I use air quotes to remind him of what he said about royal life back in the hotel room.

He picks up another rock and tosses it between his hands, as if weighing his reply. "My brother and I both understand the drawbacks of our life, but I believe in the monarchy as an institution in a way he never has. At least not since—" He abruptly cuts himself off.

"Since what?" I press. It's annoying to realize there's still so much about Theo I don't know.

He sighs. "That's a story he should tell you himself."

"Cop-out!" I shout.

"It bloody well is, I won't deny it!" He laughs. "The point

I'm trying to make is that being a royal is complicated, but most of the time, I like it. I don't know if you've noticed, but the world is kind of shite right now—"

I bark a laugh; it feels like the understatement of the century.

"—but my family is a unifying force for our nation," Henry continues, ramping up his passion as he goes. "The monarchy connects us to our past. It's good for the economy, good for tourism, good for charity work, *and* more politically stable than other forms of government."

I roll my eyes. "What's so complicated about that?"

"The point is, we have the power to do a lot of good. Right now, my brother is trying to use the power of the monarchy to protect you from the dangers of it."

"You make it sound like you're radioactive."

"*We are,*" he says, with a conviction that feels like a premonition.

I wrap my arms around my knees and watch Theo's head bobbing in the water. "If Theo's trying to do what's best for me, who's trying to do what's best for him?"

"Everyone is doing what they think is best for the Crown."

"I'm talking about *Theo*."

Henry chucks the rock into the water. "I think you know the answer to that."

CHAPTER 14

Naomi and Brooke return from the forest, and in the commotion of them seeing my stitches for the first time, Winston wakes up. Henry helps the guard move farther inland.

Brooke shudders. "I had no idea your cut was that bad."

Naomi puts on a bright smile. "It actually looks better than I expected!"

"Don't lie. I know it's awful," I say with a glance at my puckered skin. I'm so emotionally numb that I can't muster a single feeling about it.

"They'll fix the stitches when we're rescued," Naomi insists. "You won't even be able to tell it happened."

"Speaking of rescue . . ." I let my unspoken question hang in the air.

"I'm not worried yet," Naomi says.

Brooke's pensive gaze tracks from the gray sky to the empty horizon, where the last pieces of plane wreckage have disappeared in the distance. "They won't ever find us if Reggie doesn't get a signal fire started. I'll bring him the kindling and show him how to do it. At this rate, he's going to run out of lighter fluid before doing anything useful." She walks away, cradling an armful of sticks, and part of me stings with jealousy that she has something to do.

My gut screams at me to *Do something! Fix this, find a way out, make a plan.* But for the first time in my life, I'm utterly paralyzed. There's nothing to be done but sit and wait to be rescued.

"Am I in a nightmare?" I ask. The pain feels real, but it's the only thing that does.

"Not unless I dreamed it too," Naomi says.

"Our plane fell out of the sky, and we hit the water." *Nope.* Saying it out loud doesn't sound any more believable.

"Our *private* plane filled with royals."

"Maybe we're dead."

She groans. "Before I got to go to college? The ultimate tragedy. Can you imagine?"

I don't want to, but now that she's sent my mind down this path, I can't help it. "What if no one finds us?"

She sighs heavily. "Do you want a real answer, or do you want me to make you laugh?" Her eyes light up hopefully, and it's obvious she'd rather not talk about the worst-case scenario.

"*Please* make me laugh," I beg.

She immediately brightens. "If we don't get rescued, then you'll have plenty of time to get in good with Victoria."

"Why would I care about that?"

"Because if she likes you, and Theo likes you, maybe the Firm won't give you such a hard time when we get to London."

"Victoria does not like me."

"Not *yet.*"

"If we don't get rescued, my relationship with Theo is a nonissue."

She raises her eyebrows. "If we don't get rescued, we'll need to start a new civilization, and your relationship with Theo will be one of the *only* things that matters." She wiggles her eyebrows suggestively. "Almost everyone else here is related; repopulation will be your responsibility."

Pain shoots through every muscle in my body as I laugh.

"Imagine if they rescue us in ten years after you've made a bunch of royal babies who all call you 'Mum.' The Firm would *have* to accept you after that."

I laugh harder, too deliriously tired for this conversation. "I am not going to baby-trap the king of England!"

"Say that again when we've been here for a year without condoms or birth control," she says before devolving into a fit of giggles.

"Stop! Laughing hurts too much!" I gasp. "It doesn't matter whether Victoria likes me, because nothing is ever going to happen between Theo and me."

"He *married* you, Wren, and then he strong-armed the Firm into bringing you to London. He obviously plans to Stockholm-syndrome you into being his queen."

"He really doesn't." There's a difference between being in love with me (present tense) and not wanting me to drown. Maybe he *did* love me (past tense), but in the light of day, when the world isn't falling apart around him, I'm barely a blip on his royal radar. His intentions were made crystal clear in the hotel hallway last night. In his mind, I *am* just a girl, and after this small detour in my life is over, I *will* be going back to Chicago.

"Speak of the devil," Naomi says as Theo approaches us. His lips are blue and he's shaking violently, but he's never looked happier.

I scramble to my feet in anticipation of good news. "What'd you find?"

He grins slowly, and I swear he's drawing out the moment just to torture me.

"Tell me."

"Or what?"

"I'll push you off the cliff, Your Highness."

He has the audacity to laugh. "I found a phone."

My jaw falls open. "With service?"

"One bar."

"What are we waiting for?"

"The battery is low. We might only get one chance at this. Do you want to be there when we try?"

Naomi shrieks and throws her arms around Theo before running toward the group. Theo sticks his hands in his pockets and rocks on his feet. "You ready to be rescued, Wheeler?"

I'm overwhelmed with a rush of hope. It's *euphoric*. My body hums with a surge of adrenaline, and unlike Naomi, I have no way to channel it. I can't casually hug him like she did. Nothing between us has ever been casual—not since the very first day.

I fall into stride next to him. "You're lucky I'm too excited to give you an ego check." I nudge him with my uninjured shoulder.

He nudges me back, and for a second, it feels just like three months ago, before the weight of the future smothered whatever we had. Back then our circumstances were even more impossible, but at least we both wanted to try. Now, I force myself to remember what I overheard in the hotel, and step away from Theo, allowing the distance between us to grow.

⚹   ⚹   ⚹

The phone rests flat in Victoria's palm; all six of us gather around her and stare at it like it's the Holy Grail. Naomi's nails dig into my skin as she squeezes my hand in excitement.

"That's mine." Henry pretends to shrug modestly. "You may direct your thanks toward me. I'm accepting cash, compliments, phone numbers . . ."

Theo's expression turns stormy. "It might be your phone, but I found it," he grumbles. "It was on the rocks underneath the luggage. If you weren't such a wanker, you'd have remembered to check your trouser pockets before climbing the cliff."

"How much battery is left?" Winston asks from his spot on the ground. We were all relieved to see him aware and talking after his short nap.

"Twelve percent," Victoria says.

"Is it in airplane mode?" Brooke asks.

"Was it supposed to be?" Henry asks sheepishly.

Naomi's eyes widen. "Phones can interfere with airplane signals!"

All eyes snap to Henry. He shakes his curls out of his eyes like a guilty puppy.

"Bloody hell." Theo lifts his gaze to the sky.

Reggie frowns. "It wasn't the phone, it was the storm."

"Whatever it was, we should conserve the battery while we decide who to ring," Theo says.

I grimace. "I hate to be the one to point this out, but now there's no service."

Reggie grabs the phone and starts pushing buttons. He holds the phone up to his ear, shaking his head when the call doesn't go through.

"Don't drain the battery!" Theo reaches for the phone.

Reggie jerks away from him and pushes a few more buttons before dropping the phone back into Victoria's outstretched hand. "Now it's on airplane mode," the pilot says.

"And ten percent battery. Well done." Victoria takes the words right out of my mouth.

"Why would you try to make a call with no service?" I ask, and I'm not even being sarcastic. Genuinely, *why* would he do that?

"To prove that this is a waste of time," Reggie says defensively. "We're better off working on a fire so the planes know exactly where to find us."

"We're better off not wasting our battery on calls that won't go through," I mutter under my breath.

"We'd have a fire by now if you'd listened to me," Brooke tells Reggie, and suddenly everyone is arguing, and the phone is being yanked from hand to hand.

"You're not going to find a signal—"

"We wouldn't be here if—"

"Stop yelling—"

"Help is coming—"

"What if it doesn't—"

"Stop!" I scream. Shockingly, the group falls silent. My need to do *something* is stronger than ever. "We need to find a signal." I pluck the phone out of Theo's grasp. The sudden motion of skin tugging against stitches hurts like hell. I breathe slowly through my nose. "Where were you when the phone had service?"

Theo points to the coastline. "I'll go with you," he says in a rush.

My eyes fly to his and quickly away. It's probably best for me if I'm not alone with him right now. "Anyone else want to come?"

"Theo and I can go alone," Victoria says, then freezes. Her eyes dart back and forth, a confused expression crossing her brow. "Did you feel that?"

"Feel what?" Henry asks.

She shakes her head. "Never mind."

Theo and Henry exchange concerned glances. "You need to stay here and rest," Theo says. "Wren and I will look for the signal on our own. When we find one, we'll make the call."

"Everyone else should be looking for firewood and a freshwater source. Don't go far and be back here before sundown," Reggie says.

"Are we going to have to sleep here?" Naomi asks. Tension is heavy in the air as we glance uneasily at each other.

"Let's hope not," Reggie says.

I miss his confidence from earlier.

"Shall we?" Theo asks me. My stomach flips with foreboding.

I quickly survey the group. On the ground, Winston's face is screwed up in pain. Naomi is putting on a brave face, but I know she's terrified. And every ten seconds, Theo glances at Victoria as if she's made of glass. I don't know how long we've been here, but the "what if" voice in my head is growing louder as the pain in my arm grows worse.

My heart kicks into high gear as I tightly grip our dying lifeline. If we can't find a phone signal, I don't want to think about how much trouble we'll be in.

"Lead the way," I tell Theo.

CHAPTER 15

I've lost all sense of time since the plane crashed. It feels like it happened in another lifetime, but we can't have been here for more than three or four hours. Unless I'm totally wrong, which is possible. You could tell me it's been ten hours, or ten minutes, or maybe ten days, and I'd probably believe you, especially if you distracted me with something to drink.

Time is meaningless, except that it's not. We have three days from the time of the crash to find water, or nothing else matters.

(When Reggie said rescue would come soon, he must have meant sooner than three days, *right*?)

At this point, water is kind of all I can think about. I'm 3:00 A.M. thirsty, the kind that wakes me up with a dry throat only to realize I forgot to bring water to bed. And because I'd rather die than get out of bed when I'm cozy and comfy and warm, I become the thirstiest person who has ever existed on the planet.

There's something about wanting what I can't have that drives me to the brink.

"We can survive three weeks without food, three days without water, three minutes without air," I tell Theo as we walk along the coast, the phone still clutched tightly in my sweaty hand.

He smiles to himself. "I remember when you told me that at the corner shop in London. I didn't think it'd be relevant."

"We didn't think the world would exist long enough to worry about drowning or starving or dehydration."

"Lucky us, to have made it this long," he says.

"An honor and a privilege," I agree. The line between sincerity and cynicism has never been thinner, and even I'm not sure which side I'm on.

Every day since the comet didn't hit has been a bonus, and I'd started to foolishly believe that I had an entire life of bonus days ahead of me.

"Have you been brushing up on that bucket list?" he asks.

"Skinny-dipping was the only thing that ever mattered," I tease.

He shakes his head with a smile, his eyes downcast, and it stirs something in my chest that I'd thought died in Greece.

I don't *want* to want him again. Not like this. Not when my future is so fragile and unclear.

I'd convinced myself my feelings for Theo weren't real because they were so tangled up in the fear and chaos and hope of Comet Week, but maybe I was wrong. What if the fact that I can't separate Theo from all my biggest emotions is a feature, not a bug? The thought of brushing my knuckles against his makes me so sick with vulnerability that I could pitch myself off this cliff, and that has to mean something.

What if what we had was the only thing that meant anything, and he doesn't want it anymore?

"You're thinking about skinny-dipping, aren't you?" he asks.

I smile to myself. I wasn't, but he definitely was. "What's the plan here?" I hold up the phone.

"We should stay along the coast and away from the trees and the mountain for our best chance of picking up a signal."

"If you say so." I'm starting to wonder whether Theo imagined seeing a signal on the phone. The ocean stretches forever in front of us, an empty horizon from here to the end of the world. I'm not sure where he thinks the cell towers are hiding.

"You don't agree?" he asks, his brow raised in that cocky way of his.

The opportunity to banter with him materializes effortlessly, a bright, shimmering invitation. I want to engage, but I'm worried it'll only make me feel worse. We bantered nonstop on our trip from London to Greece, and that ended with a wedding on the beach and a honeymoon night that I can't forget, no matter how many times I've tried.

I sidestep the bait. "I'll take the phone off airplane mode when we get to the spot where it had service."

"Here," he says after another minute of walking. "This was the spot."

I switch the phone out of airplane mode and watch the battery immediately drop to nine percent. My stomach tightens. "Are you sure?"

Theo glances around, doubt creeping over his features. "Maybe not. Let's keep walking." After a long stretch of silence, he speaks again. "How's your arm feeling?"

"It's fine."

"Did Henry do all right?"

"I'm no longer on the verge of bleeding out." I walk faster.

"Did it hurt?"

I stop walking and whirl around. He crashes into me. "Yeah, Theo. *It hurt!*"

If I'm "just a girl" to him, I don't want him to pretend that he cares about me. A flare of annoyance burns in my chest. I seize that feeling and wrap myself in it. If I direct all my attention at being *Mad. At. Him,* I don't have to feel scared or heartbroken or anything else.

Theo looks pained. "I knew he'd take care of you."

"Well, he did," I say flatly.

Dueling hurt and defensiveness flash in Theo's eyes. He crosses his arms with a scowl. "I was looking for something important."

"And lucky for us, you found it! A completely useless brick!" I wave the phone in the air.

It vibrates with an incoming text.

I fumble the phone. It slips out of my hand and lands on a sharp rock. The screen splinters. Theo and I both lunge for it, but our competing hands send it right over the edge of the cliff.

It lands ten feet below us on a flat rock, just inches from the water. The screen is shattered, but the phone lights up and vibrates as dozens of messages flood in, one after the other. The phone dances closer to the edge of the rock with each vibration.

Theo and I are sprawled on our stomachs, our heads hanging over the edge of the cliff. We look at each other with wide eyes.

"It has a signal," he says.

"And almost no battery left," I reply.

"We need to get down there."

"There's not room for both of us on that rock." There's barely room for *one* of us. Unlike the cliff that we scaled to get onto the island, this one doesn't have handholds and footholds to follow. The ten-foot drop is sheer, and the rock holding the phone can't be wider than seven or eight inches.

I hold my breath as a wave crests precariously close to the top of the rock.

"I'm going," Theo says.

"How will you get back up?"

"One problem at a time, Wheeler." He takes off his shoes and pulls his shirt over his head, and it's not lost on me that my stomach fills with butterflies. I shake away visions of skinny-dipping in the Mediterranean and fix my eyes back on the phone. Another wave nearly sweeps it away.

"Don't jump too close," I warn. Theo springs away from the mossy cliff and dives into the slate-colored water. He waits for his own waves to settle before doubling back to pick up the phone.

"Four percent battery," he yells before chucking it up to me. "My hands are too wet."

I catch it with a scream. "Who do I call?" I yell.

"Penny, or my sister Louise." He pulls himself out of the water and balances on the rock. He leans his forearms against the cliffside, craning his neck up to see me.

I scroll Henry's contact list with shaking hands and find "Penny," the woman who has been the royal nanny since Theo was a baby. He once described her as his second mother. I bite my lip and hope she's waiting for a phone call.

I press her name.

The sound of the phone ringing catapults my heart straight into my throat. "It's ringing!"

The call drops before the second ring. My hope collapses in

on itself like a building marked for demolition. Turned into a pile of smoke and ash in three seconds flat.

Battery life: three percent.

"The signal's gone."

"Find it again!"

I keep my eyes glued to the phone screen as I jog along the edge of the cliff. My heart pounds so hard I might collapse. When the world's weakest signal bar flickers to life, I click on the contact "Lulu."

The phone rings once before sending me to voicemail. "My name is Wren Wheeler I was on a plane with your siblings. We crashed near an island but we're all alive—"

The phone dies in my hand. It's not perfect, but at least someone will know we're alive. If they look along our flight's route, they'll find us.

I turn and sprint back to where Theo is still waiting. I drop to my hands and knees at the edge of the cliff and gulp giant breaths of air, fighting a new wave of dizziness. "The phone's dead now, but I found another signal. I left a voicemail."

"For Penny?"

My left arm is trembling. I transfer all of my weight to my right elbow. "Your sister."

A full smile breaks across Theo's face, and it feels like seeing sunshine for the first time in days. "Louise?"

"Yeah. Lulu."

His expression clouds over. "Lulu? You called *Lulu*?"

"You told me to!"

"Lulu isn't my sister."

"Then who is she?"

He drags a hand over his face and nearly topples back into the water. "Henry's ex-girlfriend!"

"Okay. *Well*." I cross my arms defensively and try not to wince from the pain. I was too jittery to question it when I saw a "Lulu" in Henry's contact list; I assumed it was a nickname. "It doesn't matter. She'll get the voicemail."

"No, she won't."

A knot cinches in my stomach. "Why not?"

"She blocked Henry's number when they broke up."

"But the phone rang."

He looks skeptical. "How many times?"

"Once."

Theo sighs heavily. "That's what happens when you call a phone number that's blocked you. It rings once and then sends you to a separate voicemail box that doesn't send notifications."

The knot in my stomach doubles in size. "It might have rung twice." My voice wavers. I'd flop hard in Las Vegas.

Theo lets his head drop forward until it rests against the side of the cliff. "Do you know what this means?" His tone is resigned. He's not blaming me, but he doesn't need to; I'll blame myself enough for the both of us. I'm the "you had one job" meme personified.

Of course I know what this means.

Screwing up that phone call means I wasted our one chance to call for help. It means we're probably not getting rescued tonight, and maybe not tomorrow. It means I have to live with bloody stitches, and "three days without water" suddenly feels a lot more relevant.

I gaze over the cliff into Theo's eyes. "It means Victoria will finally have a legitimate reason to hate me."

CHAPTER 16

"Are you sure you don't want to yell at me?" I ask several minutes later. I think I'd feel better if he did, because then I could defend myself. Instead, he's been unbearably quiet since I doomed us to reenact *Lost*.

Theo is trapped on the small rock. His many attempts to climb back up have failed, so he's crouching with his back against the sheer cliff, staring at the horizon and most likely thinking about how badly I've screwed up. ("Lulu" and "Louise" aren't interchangeable, when you think about it.)

"I'm not going to yell at you," he says wearily.

"It might make you feel better."

"I can't emphasize enough how much it won't." He tips his head back to look at me, and his eyes remind me of smoke from a fire that's been doused in water. It scares me more than everything else combined. "You could bodge up everything, and I don't think I'd care."

I'm hit with another memory: Theo and me lying together in a bed in France, him whispering that he was afraid he'd give up on himself. His apathy feels just like that, and now I can't breathe.

"Do you want to try grabbing my hands again?" I ask. Last time he'd tried, my stitches had started to tear. As soon as he saw the trail of blood leak down my arm, he'd let go and resigned himself to life on the rock.

"Go back to the group without me and get some help," he says. "Don't bring Henry. He'll just gloat."

"And admit that I fucked up our rescue call?" I can't think of anything I'd rather do less. It's not just that, though. Theo is withering before me, and the thought of leaving him out here alone, perched precariously on an eight-by-eight-inch rock, makes my stomach riot with anxiety. I can't leave until he has some fight in his eyes.

"What did you wish for at the sunken gardens?" Theo asks suddenly. His dehydration-induced rasp makes me nervous.

"It's embarrassing," I warn.

"The best wishes usually are."

I clear my throat and prepare to humiliate myself. "I wished that meeting up with you in High Park wouldn't ruin my memories from our trip."

He's quiet for a painfully long time. Embarrassment threatens to burn me alive. I'm suddenly glad he's stuck on the rock.

"Feel free to pretend I didn't say that."

"Can I ask some follow-up questions?"

I close my eyes and prepare for the worst. "If you must."

"Why did you think that seeing me would ruin our memories?"

My breath hitches at the word "our." These days it doesn't feel like we share anything except for bad karma.

"When we were in Europe, I never thought of you as 'the prince.'"

He laughs sharply. "I remember."

"All I have from that time is one Polaroid and a week's worth of memories." My hand goes instinctively to the ring hanging under my shirt. "I was worried that meeting 'the king of England' on a *royal tour* full of pomp and circumstance would make those memories feel less real, somehow. I didn't want to lose the guy I thought I knew."

"No need for the air quotes. I *am* the king, unfortunately."

I shrug. "I'll believe it when I see the crown."

He laughs again, his blue eyes flickering to life. I take my first easy breath in at least three minutes.

"What's the verdict, Wheeler? Am I the guy you thought I was?"

He is *now,* but this isn't real life. "The jury's still out."

He nods slowly, his eyes locked on mine. "I wasn't searching for a phone."

Tears well in my eyes. A secret for a secret. We've played this game before. "What were you hoping to find?" I ask.

"Victoria's insulin. She never travels without it, and if she goes more than a couple of days between doses, she'll be in serious danger." His mouth twists with suppressed emotion, but his eyes scream for help.

My chest tightens. "I had no idea."

"She'll never admit when she's not feeling well, and I'm scared shitless for her."

"It's only been a few hours," I tell him, and hope it's true.

His throat bobs. "It's hard not to worry."

I push myself to my feet and pick up his shoes. "I'll find her and make sure she's okay, and I'll bring someone back to help you up."

"No," Theo says quickly. "I don't want to stay here alone."

I look around, confused about what he's suggesting. "I can try to pull you up again."

"No. You walk along the shore, and I'll swim next to you."

"It's too far," I argue. "You'll be safer here."

"Nah. I'll drive myself crazy if I'm stuck alone with my thoughts that long. I'm swimming."

"What if you get tired?" I call after him as he dives into the water. He backstrokes a few paces until I'm jogging to keep up with him.

"I guess you'll have to jump in and save me," he yells back. And it might be a trick of the sunlight, but I swear he winks.

⚜   ⚜   ⚜

It doesn't take long before Theo's request is put to the test.

"I'm tired!" he pants.

"You're doing a great chicken-star-rocket!" I yell back. The water looks cold, and I don't want to be cold.

A wave crashes over his face while he's in chicken position. "A what now?" he sputters when he can breathe again.

"Chicken, star, rocket." I mime the positions for him.

"Is that an American thing or a Wren thing?"

"It's what my swim coach called it when I was five."

"It sounds mental, but I like it," he muses. "I can picture a five-year-old Wren shouting 'chicken star rocket' from the pool."

"Stop talking so much or you'll drown," I call back.

"What's taking so long?" he moans, and I wish I had an answer. The coast was to our left on our way out, and it's to my right on the way back. There's no way we could have gotten lost, but it feels like we should have reached our makeshift camp by now. I'm about to say this to Theo when I see smoke in the distance.

"Fire!" I shout. A new shot of adrenaline courses through me.

"I'll meet you there," he says.

I run while Theo swims, but I outpace him and reach the small, smoky campfire first. The group is gathered around it while Brooke tends to the flames. "I can't believe you made fire! Scratch that. I can't believe you convinced Reggie to let you make fire," I tell her. A lungful of smoke triggers a coughing fit, but I can't contain my smile. This is the first thing that's gone right all day.

I instinctively check the sky for rescue helicopters and am only a little bit devastated that it's still empty.

"We found water too!" Naomi hands me a bottle. "There's a stream that runs through the forest." I close my eyes and tip the water over my tongue. It's the best thing I've ever tasted—no contest. I drink until my empty stomach protests the sudden rush of liquid. I twist the cap on the bottle and hand it to Naomi. She's leaning back-to-back with Victoria, whose head is tipped against her shoulder. Victoria's face is pale. Like everyone else, she looks filthy and exhausted.

I kneel next to her. "Do you feel okay?"

She slowly lifts her head and looks at me blankly. "Why wouldn't I?"

I wither. She has a special way of making me feel like an idiot for asking a simple question. "Theo said . . ."

Her gaze hardens.

I trail off as I realize she doesn't want to talk about this. With me. In front of everyone. Maybe at all.

The rest of the group stares at me expectantly.

Henry leans forward. "Well?"

I move closer to the fire. The smoke burns my eyes, but the muscles in my shoulder unclench for the first time in hours. It feels unbelievable. "Theo's on his way. He should be here any second," I tell them.

Reggie sighs impatiently. "Did the phone work or not?"

I pretend to choke on another lungful of smoke to buy myself a few more miserable seconds before I have to drop the news. I got so distracted by the fire and the water that I momentarily forgot about the phone.

When I open my watery eyes, everyone is staring at me. I stare directly into the flames. I can't bear to look at any of them.

"That's a no," Victoria says flatly.

"You couldn't find a signal at all?" Naomi chews her lip anxiously.

"We did," Theo says as he joins the group. Water drips off him onto my shoulders. I scoot over to make room for him in front of the fire. He sits next to me and leans into the heat. "We found a signal. I tried to ring Louise, but my hands were shaking so badly they slipped, and I ended up calling Lulu instead."

Henry's jaw drops. Mine does too. "You don't have to—"

"Yeah I do," he says evenly. "I have to tell them what happened. I left Lulu a message, but I think she still has Henry's number blocked, so she probably won't get it. Then the phone died."

"That's not funny," Henry says.

I open my mouth to confess, but Theo cuts me off by putting his hand on my leg, narrowing the universe down to that single touch.

I stare at the fire as my eyes well with tears. Hopefully everyone will assume it's from the smoke.

The first day I met Theo, it was raining, and I had just sprained my ankle. He wanted to call me a cab to take me to the airport, but I'd refused to let myself be saved by Prince Charming. If I had let him, I probably would have made my flight in time.

Maybe I don't need to be saved, but it sure does feel nice.

"Tell me this is a bloody awful joke," Henry demands, and his sharp tone takes me by surprise.

Theo squares his shoulders.

"Can you do one fucking thing right?" Henry shouts. Theo's eye twitches, but otherwise he's frozen. The pressure of his hand on my knee increases, and as unreadable as he's felt these last couple of days, I recognize his plea immediately. This is some deep-rooted brother shit, and he wants me to stay out of it.

I don't. "You don't know what you're talking about," I tell Henry.

"Wren," Theo says sharply.

"He doesn't! We wouldn't have even found that phone if it wasn't for you. It's not your fault that his battery life was decimated because he didn't put his phone on airplane mode."

Henry scoffs.

"You should have some water," Naomi says quietly as she holds out the bottle to Theo.

"Make him get his own." Henry snatches the bottle from Naomi's hand. "We found water *and* made the fire, while Theo hasn't done a bloody thing to help. He says he doesn't want special treatment just because he was born first. Time to stop giving it to him." He unscrews the top and drains the bottle in one long gulp.

"You've always been an arse when you're drunk," Victoria says.

"How could he be drunk?" I ask.

"He found booze with the salvaged luggage," Victoria says.

Winston groans from his position flat on his back on the rocky ground. "Got any of that left?"

"Is there food down there?" Brooke asks Henry.

"Ask my brother, he's the one hoarding stuff."

"Am not," Theo protests, but Henry's accusation is a fuse that quickly burns through everyone's short temper. Soon nearly everyone is yelling over each other, slinging accusations in all directions.

I draw my knees into my chest and rest my cheek on them. I turn to Theo, who is slumped over with his head in his hands. Smoke curls in the distance between us. I nudge him. He looks at me warily.

Thank you. I mouth the words.

You too, he mouths back.

Naomi leans forward to be heard over the fighting. "Do you want to get out of here?"

"And go where?"

She grins. "I've got an idea."

CHAPTER 17

aomi pulls me to my feet while the others argue and Brooke
slips Winston the last of the airplane booze.

"Where are you going?" Reggie demands, looking up from
the campfire.

"Be back soon!" Naomi calls over her shoulder. She leads me
down the coast in the opposite direction Theo and I came from.
We're both barefoot, stumbling wearily across the mossy rocks
in the dying light, with Comet hot on our heels. "The royals are
intense. Do you think Theo really hid the alcohol?"

"I—"

"Henry was being a total jerk. I don't blame him for being
upset, obviously, but he shouldn't have yelled at Theo like that.
Major ick."

"Actually—"

"We're all hungry, tired, and scared, but that's no reason to
be rude." Naomi stops to peer over the edge of the cliff. "This is
the spot! We're climbing down."

"Nay." I clutch her forearm. "I need a minute." My hand is
shaking.

She wraps her arms around me in a tight hug and lets me sob on her shoulder until we're both covered in salt water and snot. "I'm so scared," I say when I can finally choke the words out.

"Don't tell anyone else, but me too." She laughs at herself as she wipes tears off her cheeks. "I'm trying to stay optimistic, but . . . you know."

"I know," I say. I reach down to stroke Comet's head. He immediately twists himself between my legs and nudges me with the stick he must have stolen from the firewood pile. I cock my arm back and give it a ride. He tears off in a frenzy.

Naomi and I both turn our eyes to the water. The cloud cover has finally broken and the sun sits on the edge of the horizon; the ocean is stained a vibrant orange that ripples gently in the breeze. It looks like a scene from a movie, a romantic one, where there's not a plane crash and no one needs emergency medical attention. Once upon a time, I would have wanted to take a picture of Naomi with the wind in her hair. Now, I wish I could close my eyes and forget this ever happened.

"I made the call to Henry's ex-girlfriend," I confess as Comet drops his stick at my feet and waits for praise. I scratch him behind the ear and throw it again. "It wasn't Theo. It was me, and if anyone dies before rescue arrives, it's my fault." I picture Winston gritting his teeth against the pain of his broken leg and Victoria's pale face as she insists she's fine. I'll never forgive myself if anything happens to either of them.

"A plane will see our fire tonight. I think we're going to be rescued," Naomi says, and I'm grateful for the lie. She takes a deep breath. "This was my plan. Cliff jumping in the sunset." She gestures (with jazz hands!) to a slope of climbable rocks leading to a large flat one that juts out over the water's edge. "Also, I have to pee."

We quickly shed our pants and Naomi helps me undo the buttons on my ripped blouse because my arm is too sore to do it myself. She clasps my hand and then my best friend and I scream "Cannonball!" on three and jump into the salt water under a twilight sky. Comet leaps down the rocky path to the shore, splashing in behind us. Naomi and I are both shaking and shivering and laughing when we come up for air, and I feel alive again. I'd almost forgotten what that was like.

I float on my back while Comet paddles circles around me and we wait for Naomi to do her business. Soon my teeth are chattering, and Comet has pulled himself out of the water. It's fully dark now and the breeze has picked up. "Hurry up!"

"I'm coming back."

I climb onto the flat rock in my bra and underwear, and I'm reaching my hand out to help her up when she screams.

My heart spasms. "What's wrong?"

"Something stung me!" she gasps.

I grasp her with my right hand and haul her onto the rocks. Blue tentacles are wrapped around her foot, and she's writhing in pain. Without thinking, I reach out to pull the creature off her, but she grabs my hand to stop me.

"Don't! It will sting you too!"

I pick up a rock. Naomi and I both scream as I try to nudge the squishy creature off her leg.

"Why are you screaming?" she yells.

"Because it's gross!" My body shudders involuntarily.

She presses her forehead into the rock. "Get it off me!"

I use the rock to scrape it off her. We both scurry away as it lands with a squelch.

Theo crashes quickly over the edge of the cliff, nearly colliding into me. "What's happening? I heard screams."

"Careful!" I grab his biceps and pull him out of the way before he steps on the blob. "That thing stung her."

"Is it a jellyfish?" she gasps, eyes screwed tightly shut against the pain.

Theo bends to inspect the creature in the dark and swears loudly. "It's a man o' war. The 'floating terror.'"

"Is it deadly?" Naomi cries.

"No," I insist, before throwing a questioning look at Theo.

He shakes his head. "Rarely."

My stomach drops. Rarely isn't never. I needed the answer to be never.

He continues. "The stings are excruciatingly painful, though. One of my mates at school said it was the worst pain he'd ever experienced."

"I could've told you that," Naomi says through clenched teeth.

"How do we help her?"

"I don't know."

"Someone just pee on me already!" Naomi shouts.

Theo and I stare at each other in horror, and that's the moment I register that I'm soaking wet and barely dressed. His eyes fall to my breasts before he immediately catches himself, wrenching his gaze all the way up to the sky.

"Not it," he says quickly.

"Baruch HaShem," Naomi says. "No offense, Your Majesty, I'm a big fan of yours, I don't think I've told you that yet. I defended you when Wren called you spoiled and outdated and—"

"Keep it moving, Nay," I tell her.

"Right. Anyway, you seem great, but I'll never live it down if you, you know—"

Theo looks at me with wide, panicked eyes. "I'll get help."

He climbs back up the rocks and out of sight. I send Comet with him.

"I don't know if the pee thing is true," I say to Naomi.

She presses the heels of her hands against her eyes. "I'm willing to risk it."

"But—"

"If you're my best friend, you will pull down your silk princess underwear and pee on my damn foot!"

"Fine! But we're never talking about this again, understand?"

Brooke's head appears over the cliffside. "Keep your princess underwear on, Wren. Don't pee on her."

"Why not?" Naomi demands.

"It's a myth and it won't help. Bring her up here. Winston says we need hot water and we're heating some over the fire now. C'mon, give me your hand, Naomi."

We quickly get dressed, and then I walk behind Naomi as she crawls up the rocks. At the top, Brooke and I each take one of her arms and sling it over our shoulders so we can support her weight between us. Henry meets us on our way back to camp and takes over, giving my throbbing arm some relief.

The group moves to make room for Naomi as he sets her next to the glowing fire. Theo looks stressed. "I could have done that."

"Well, you didn't," Henry barks in response.

Naomi presses her face to my shoulder with a whimper. Winston twists his torso to inspect the sole of Naomi's foot. "Nasty one, innit?"

"It feels like . . ." She pauses to pant for breath. "Like bolts of electricity . . . are shooting into my body. It won't stop."

"Is she going to be okay?" I ask.

"Why were you in the ocean after dark?" Reggie demands. The veins in his neck are bulging.

"Where's the hot water?" Winston asks.

Theo uses a stick to knock the bottle away from the fire and rolls it to Winston, who covers his hand with a spare piece of clothing before twisting the bottle open. "Don't want it to burn ya, but it should be as hot as you can handle, understand?"

"Will she be okay?" I ask again, Theo's *rarely* still echoing in my brain.

Winston tests the temperature of the water on the inside of his wrist before gently pouring it over the long, stringy red welts on Naomi's skin.

Naomi sucks in a breath through her teeth. "It still hurts . . . but it's helping."

"I need something hard and flat, like a credit card, to scrape the nematocysts out of her skin," Winston continues.

"On it," Theo says. He runs off before Henry can offer to do it.

"The nema— What?" Naomi's voice is frenzied. She quickly pushes herself up and tries to look at her foot.

"The stingers. Those little buggers hurt like a bitch. We need to remove them."

Theo returns, handing a rock to Winston. "Try this."

"Brilliant. A rock," Henry deadpans.

"It's flat and sharp. It'll work," Theo snaps.

"I need a distraction," Naomi hisses as Winston gently scrapes the rock across her skin.

"If you weren't out there in the dark, this wouldn't have happened," Reggie says. Between this and the "don't prioritize the dog" comment, I'm starting to hate him.

Brooke kneels next to Naomi. "During my freshman year at Northwestern, I was in this biology class—"

"What? No! Biology is boring. Next?" Naomi waves Brooke away with her free hand before draping it over her eyes. The pain must be *bad* bad if not even school is enough to distract her.

I rack my brain to think of something that will. "The weather—"

"No! Next?"

"Oh! Henry, come here!" I say, avoiding eye contact with Theo. I know he's still annoyed with his brother, but Theo won't give Naomi the royal tea she needs to take her mind off the pain. "Tell her about the book you were reading on the plane."

"*Sceptre, Throne, and Crown?*"

"Yes!" Naomi cries. "Tell me every sordid historical detail. Don't leave out a single illegitimate baby."

Henry jerks his head back and I can't help but laugh. For all of Naomi's practicality, she's always had stars in her eyes where the royals are concerned.

"Stingers are out," Winston announces. "Next up, antibiotic ointment, I'll wrap your foot in a bandage, and Bob's your uncle!"

Once the guard finishes wrapping Naomi's foot, she pushes herself into a sitting position and moves closer to the fire.

I sit next to her. "How are you feeling?"

"Relieved that you didn't pee on me, and jealous that I've never had a scepter."

I exhale in relief. "So, you're okay?"

"I think so." She nods. "It still hurts, but my brain doesn't feel like it's being shoved in an outlet."

"We'll take another look at it in the morning," Winston

says. "You might have some welts that will make it difficult to walk."

"I'll fill the water bottles. The rest of you stay here. I'm responsible for you, and from now on, you don't move without my permission," Reggie says. He looks each of us in the eye before stalking toward the dark tree line.

"Calm down, my guy," Victoria mutters under her breath, without much bite. It's the first thing she's said in ages, and even though she doesn't want me to, I can't help but worry about her.

Henry arches his brows at Theo. "You shouldn't let him speak to you like that."

I scoff. "You're one to talk."

Theo's lips twitch as his eyes sweep over my face. Firelight throws shadows across his bare chest and stormy eyes, but then he blinks, and his expression is so carefully blank that I can't read anything in it.

Tension grows and stretches between the two brothers, and quiet settles over the group until the only sounds are the pounding surf and the popping of damp sticks in the fire.

The adrenaline that has been driving me drains away, leaving only a smoldering ember in my gut. I feel restless and antsy, so I tell the others that I'll help Reggie get water and jog toward him. Theo catches up to my side in seconds.

Reggie looks over his shoulder with a scowl. "I told you not to move. That was a close call with your friend back there."

"How many more close calls can we survive?"

"There won't be another one if you kids would just *stay put* until we're rescued," Reggie says.

"For how long?" Theo asks.

"Until. We're. Rescued." Reggie enunciates each word insultingly slowly.

"And what if that doesn't happen tonight, or tomorrow, or the next day? We can't just sit and wait," Theo argues.

Reggie shakes his head. "That's exactly what we'll do. We're safest right here."

Theo's jaw tics, and I can feel the frustration radiating off him. Despite his earlier protests to the contrary, he wants to be making the decisions right now. I don't blame him, even if the prospect sounds ridiculously, exhaustingly overwhelming. (Even worse than choosing a major and a future and a whole life path, which is saying something.)

"Do you have any idea where we are?" I ask Reggie.

"We're on an island off the coast of Portugal."

"Which one?" Theo asks. "Madeira? São Miguel? Flores?"

"Yes," Reggie says tightly.

"That's not an answer," I point out.

"Flores."

Theo blinks in surprise. "People live on Flores."

"There's a settlement on the east side." Reggie drops this bomb like it's nothing, and I can't help but wonder why we're not doing anything more to find help. Not that I want to be in charge again, because I don't. But still, it wouldn't hurt to do *something* to give fate a nudge in the right direction.

Theo squints into the dark, appraising the mountain at the center of the island. "How long would it take us to get there?"

"We're not leaving the west side," Reggie snaps.

Theo draws himself to his full height. "Why not?"

"Because this is where the plane went down, and staying out of the trees gives us our best shot at being spotted from the air."

"But that could take days," I say, although I'm starting to worry it'll take even longer than that.

"Victoria doesn't have that kind of time. She needs food and insulin immediately." Theo sounds more stressed than ever.

Reggie doesn't flinch. "We have no supplies. We have no food. It is not wise to use our energy stores traipsing all over this bloody island where anything could happen to you."

Theo grabs the pilot's shoulder and stops him in his tracks. "I don't care about me. Victoria needs our help."

Reggie ducks his head. "I am in service to the Crown. Keeping you safe is my number one priority."

Theo blinks at Reggie in shock. "Don't you care that she could die?"

"I do. But respectfully, sir, you are the monarch. Your life is worth more than hers."

My hands fly to my mouth. I've never heard anything so callous.

Theo stares the pilot down, silent fury radiating off him in waves. "Respectfully, Reggie, you can fuck off." He stalks into the trees.

I snatch the water bottles out of Reggie's hands. "Don't come after us," I warn, before following Theo into the dark.

CHAPTER 18

My chest burns with righteous vindication as I storm away from Reggie (*I knew I didn't like him!*), right up until I realize that I can't see anything under the canopy of trees. The farther I press into the forest, the less moonlight filters through the leaves, and Theo's long legs are moving quicker than I can keep up with. The only reason I know I'm going in the right direction is because he makes no effort to be quiet.

My side cramps, each breath more painful than the last. The ground slopes up and my legs join the long list of body parts that are in pain. (At this point, it's everything except three fingers on my right hand.) I'm starting to worry how far Theo's anger is taking him away from camp when the sound of his footsteps is drowned out by flowing water.

I duck through a thicket of trees and step into a clearing. Squinting, I see the outline of Theo standing on the bank of a small stream, barely there moonlight reflecting off his rigid shoulders.

I take a tentative step forward.

"It's not a good time to be with me, Wren," Theo says. There's an unfamiliar note of warning in his voice.

I exhale a long, slow breath. "Okay."

He stuffs his fists into his pockets, but not before I realize that he's shaking. It creates a schism in me, dividing my life into two parts: there is before I saw Theo silently falling apart while trying to keep himself together, and there is after.

"Why are you still here?" he asks after a long stretch of silence. The words scrape painfully against his throat and my heart.

"You don't have to be alone right now."

"What if I want to be?" he asks sharply. Impossibly, his gravitational pull only gets stronger. Not even a rescue helicopter could pull me out of here, because I recognize a defense mechanism better than anyone.

"If you want me to go, look me in the eye and tell me to go."

He turns, and my breath catches. Even in the dark, his eyes simmer with rage and heartbreak. He tips his chin up and holds my gaze.

I'm sure he's used to people backing down, but I won't. I pull my shoulders back in the way I've seen him do a hundred times. "Tell me to leave, Theo."

His eyes shutter when I say his name. He turns his head and swallows heavily. "I can't." His hoarse voice cracks on the last word, snapping off a piece of my heart in the process.

I cross the distance between us and wrap my arms around him. I press my cheek against his chest and listen to his heartbeat while his body shakes. I hold him tighter, not to keep him from splintering apart, but to let him know I'll gather the pieces when he does.

"It's okay," I whisper.

"It's not." His voice is thick with restrained emotion.

Hot tears spill over my cheeks and run down his chest. I hate his family for teaching him that a stiff upper lip is more important than anything else. "It's okay to not be okay when you're with me."

I feel his intake of breath, and then the whole weight of his body at once as his shoulders crumple. He presses his face to the hollow in my neck and shakes. I don't realize he's crying until his tears slide over my skin. I cry harder.

The almost-apocalypse robbed me of the fantasy that life will be fair. I'll never expect that again. But I still don't understand how a nineteen-year-old with no political aspirations can end up with the weight of a country on his shoulders. Or why I fell in love with someone who only fits into my life when our world is ending. Or how a boy with no parents is supposed to accept that his sister might die, and the people around him won't let him do anything to help.

I know the world isn't fair, but I wish it weren't this emotionally devastating.

I cry with him until my knees buckle and we both end up on the ground, tangled together on damp soil. I rack my brain for the right thing to say, but he speaks first.

"What am I going to do?" he asks at last, repositioning us so that we're sitting side by side.

I begin turning over possible solutions, sorting through our short list of drastic options. I lean forward and dip my hand in the cold water before unscrewing the lid of one of our bottles and filling it to the brim. I hand it to him.

"Start with a drink" is the only thing I can think to say.

Theo's fingers brush mine as he accepts the bottle, and the

last inches of me that didn't hurt, those three fingers on my right hand, ache with painful wanting.

He takes a long sip, then looks at me with a cocked head and a grim smile. "Problem solved," he says solemnly, and I can't believe I ever thought I didn't love him. It was pure denial—like swimming in the ocean and claiming I wasn't wet.

"We'll figure something out," I tell him, because I'd say just about anything to smooth the crease between his eyes. "We'll make a bigger fire and write a message in the sand and search for food for Victoria. It hasn't even been a day since the crash. We still have time."

His gaze sweeps up to the looming mountain. "We need to go over it."

My stomach pitches uncomfortably. "Maybe Reggie will change his mind."

"Did Henry tell you about our dad?" he asks abruptly.

I sit back in surprise. "No. Why?"

"Do you hear that?" He cocks his head to the side. I hold my breath, but all I hear is rushing water. Theo stands and sticks out his hand to help me up.

I'm too tired to move. "Tell me about your dad, Theo," I say softly.

He rolls his shoulders and shakes out his hands, suddenly skittish. "I need to work up to that."

I let him pull me to my feet. "Then start with Henry. Why are you two always competing?"

He glowers into the distance, his hands on his hips. "It's a boring story," he warns.

"Try me."

He sighs and runs a hand through his hair. "It's just jealousy. It drives me mad that he wasn't the heir when he should have been. You don't see *him* out here throwing a wobbly in the forest."

I recognize his self-deprecating tone and give him a light shove. "Cut yourself some slack. He's never been under the pressure you have."

"He would have handled it better." His voice is strangled with emotion. "If he got the chance to be the monarch, he'd make Mum proud in the way I never could."

"And what about your dad?" I prompt.

He cuts me a sideways glance. "While we're walking," he says, and that's when I realize this is a conversation that he needs to distract himself from. He won't be able to talk about it unless we're also doing something else. If this is what it takes, we'll walk all night.

We follow the stream to higher ground. The air is wet with mist, drops of it gathering on thick moss and glossy leaves. The trees here are denser than ever, and as we scramble over a fallen trunk, I can't help but think this forest feels prehistoric; it's astounding that the natural environment is still so lush and untouched, even on an inhabited island.

We walk for long enough that I wonder if Theo is ever going to tell me his story. "Rock here, be careful," he says, pointing to a loose rock a step ahead of us. His voice is scratchy with emotion or thirst or disuse, but he continues. "Royal marriages are historically fucked up."

A sharp laugh escapes me, and I clap my hand over my mouth. "Whatever happened to 'Once upon a time'?"

"Not that kind of story," he says. "Rock." He grabs my hand and helps me over the obstacle.

"Sorry. It's just—you weren't this cynical about love when we—" I bite my lip as my cheeks heat. I almost said "when we got married." In our wedding vows, he said we were fate. He made me want to believe in it too. "When we first met," I finish.

"Who's talking about love?" he says wryly. "And anyway, I didn't know then what I know now."

"Which is what?"

"I'm getting there. Duck." He holds a tree branch up so I can duck underneath it. "First, you must understand that royal marriages are usually balls-up, and Mum and Dad's was no exception. When you add political pressures and media scrutiny on top of regular old relationship rubbish, it's a disaster waiting to happen."

"Is that what happened to your parents?"

"My dad came from a wealthy family that everyone approved of, and he and my mum loved each other in the beginning. That's what they told us, anyway. But my mum was the heir, and there was so much attention and pressure on them to have a bunch of babies and make it work. Add that on top of my dad's depression and the constant cheating rumors, and it was never going to have a happy ending."

I slip on a muddy rock. Theo reaches for my waist, his hands spanning my hips. I swallow as his gaze sweeps across my face. "I thought he got sick."

"He did. But not in the way people assume." There's something achingly stoic in his tone that tells me this story is going to break my heart.

"They decided to separate. The news was leaked to the press, and the media scrutiny was relentless: paparazzi stalking Dad, articles about what he did wrong, what she did wrong, which kids would stay with which parent, body-language experts dissecting every public appearance they'd ever made. The press hounded him relentlessly and dragged fifteen years' worth of speculation onto the front page of the tabloids. It was utterly unsurvivable." He clears the emotion from his throat. "He died by suicide a few weeks later, though the Firm covered it up and blamed his death on other health problems."

My stomach plummets. I reach for Theo's hand. "I'm so sorry," I whisper.

"Just wait!" Theo says, like he's building to the best part in a campfire story. "There's more trauma coming." He places his lower hand on my back to steady me. "When my mum died, I got access to a bunch of her stuff: documents and emails and everything. I was combing through it all, looking for information from that time, and would you believe that everything came from her? The divorce story, the hit pieces on my dad, all of it."

My mouth falls open as a chill seeps into my bones. Yesterday I was lying on a speeding car floor, being chased by cameras. I can still feel the way my heart stopped. I'd never felt less human. "Why would she do that?"

"*Redacted,*" he says sourly.

"What does that mean?"

"My best guess is that the press had a different story that she didn't want to go public. Her marriage with my dad was falling apart anyway, so she offered him on a silver platter instead."

We follow a bend in the stream that takes us to the mouth of a large waterfall. The trees have opened up, letting moonlight glimmer off the pounding water. It's jaw-dropping, but after Theo's revelation, I don't feel a thing except heartache.

He turns to me. "You said that maybe Reggie will change his mind about letting Victoria get sick. This is how I know he won't. These people will do anything in the name of protecting the Crown." His voice is hollow, and the truth is awful, and there's nothing else for either of us to say.

He threads his fingers through mine and I lean my head on his shoulder until we're soaked with the spray of the waterfall. I feel almost sick with nostalgia, wishing we could go back to the Eiffel Tower or the beach in Amorgos. I mentally add "enchanted misty forest" to the list of locations where I've loved Theo, and I can't help but wonder how few places I have left.

"You ready to go back?" he asks.

I'm not, but I nod wordlessly anyway.

CHAPTER 19

I wake up at dawn and am not lucky enough to have even a second of groggy confusion. I know exactly where I am, because even in my sleep, it was impossible to forget the scratchy moss under my cheek or the stitches tugging at my itchy skin.

I've never been this filthy or sore or exhausted in my life, so of course it's the perfect time for a sharp cramp attack. I curl into a ball while I wait for the pain to pass. Mercifully, it's just from hunger. (But also, I didn't know it was possible to be *this* hungry.)

Comet nudges my side with his snout. "Hey, boy." He nudges me again and whines.

Victoria, Winston, Henry, and Naomi are asleep around the dying fire. My eyes sweep over Victoria, who looks okay, as far as I can tell, though I'm not sure what symptoms I should be looking for.

Brooke is lying on her back with her eyes open, a look of intense concentration on her face.

"Help me get Comet a drink," I whisper. She pours water

into my cupped hands and Comet quickly laps it up. "What were you thinking about?" I ask as we repeat the process.

"I was retaking the LSAT in my head. I think I could have gotten a higher score than 178."

I shudder, remembering the stressful month when Brooke locked herself in her bedroom while she studied for the law school entrance exam and cried a lot. "That's normal."

She puts her hand on her hip. "Don't sound so judgy. I have to think about *something* to keep myself from going crazy."

"No judgment!" I say seriously. "But everyone knows you're supposed to be a lawyer. Unless you're suddenly dying to be as directionless as I am."

She rolls her eyes. "Yes. Obviously, I'm thrilled to be back at square one, exactly like an undeclared college freshman." She takes the now-empty water bottles and leaves with a huff. Comet follows her, a stick in his mouth.

"Do you really feel directionless?" Naomi asks as she rubs the sleep out of her eyes.

"Compared to you and everyone else who knows what they want to do with their lives, *yes*. How's the foot?" I'm in desperate need of a subject change.

"Really bad! The worst," she says brightly. "I'd show you the blisters, but Winston told me to keep them covered so it doesn't get infected."

"We'll be off this island before that can happen. I predict that help will be here in five, four, three, two . . . one."

We stare at the empty sky.

"I could have sworn that was going to work," I say.

She bites her lip. "Do you think anyone is looking for us?"

"*Yes*. They know the route our flight was taking. The British government is definitely looking for us. Well, they're looking for the royals, but I assume they'll let us hitch a ride home too."

She sighs dramatically. "I bet everyone at home thinks we're dead. Oh my gosh, Levi thinks I'm *dead*."

I wince at the thought of my parents watching news stories about our plane. The stomach cramps are back with a vengeance. "He'll know you're alive soon."

"I bet he posted something sad about me and a bunch of grief vampires are in his DMs, trying to hook up with him."

"Levi would never."

"Tom Hanks's wife did, in that movie with the volleyball," Naomi argues.

"Tom Hanks was on that island for years. Theo's too important to be left presumed dead. They *will* find us."

She rubs her eyes with her hands. "At least your boyfriend knows you're alive. Really, I love that for you."

I roll my eyes. "Theo's not my boyfriend." I watch him pacing with Reggie at the edge of the cliff. Unlike yesterday, when his temper matched the weather, the gloomy clouds have been chased away by sparkling sunlight, which is glinting off the crystalline water that might as well stretch from here to the end of the world. A gentle breeze ruffles the trees behind us.

Naomi gasps and sits up tall, grabbing my forearm. "Forget about the boys. What if I'm dropped from my classes and Northwestern makes me enroll in Psych 101 or Intro to Acting?" She looks like she's going to pass out. "I need a distraction."

"Turn around. I'll fix your hair. That way you'll look hot in the rescue pictures."

I extract two elastics from what are left of her bedraggled and lopsided space buns and finger-comb her hair into two Dutch braids while Naomi ponders what kinds of memorabilia will be left outside the dorms in her memory, and whether it would be tacky to keep them when we get back to Chicago.

"We survived a plane crash. If you want to keep the teddy bears, you're allowed to keep the teddy bears."

"People left hundreds of teddy bears in front of the palace after my mum passed," Victoria says, finally waking up and joining our conversation. "As if Mum was the teddy bear type."

My eyes sweep over her face. *Does she look clammier than yesterday?* I squint and lean closer. *Or am I imagining things?*

She wrinkles her nose. "Why are you looking at me like that?"

"Sorry." I straighten.

Naomi's stomach growls loudly. "What's the first thing you're going to eat when we're rescued?" she asks. "I want peanut butter."

"Are we talking about food?" Henry asks, shaking the curls out of his eyes as he joins our little group. We spend the next several minutes daydreaming about all the food we're going to eat when this is over. Henry wants shepherd's pie, Naomi wants chocolate and peanut butter babka, I want deep-dish pizza, and Victoria wants us to shut up because we're making her hunger worse.

"What was that?" the princess suddenly asks. She presses her hands to the ground on either side of her.

"What?"

"You didn't feel that?"

I glance at Naomi, who shrugs. "Feel what? A raindrop?" I ask.

"With cirrus clouds in the sky? Be serious," Naomi says, motioning to the wispy cotton candy strands.

"Brilliant. I'm losing my bloody mind out here," Victoria mutters.

Reggie struts back toward our makeshift campsite and glances at us, clearly unimpressed. "When you're done with your makeovers, we need more firewood."

"Already taken care of," Brooke says, dropping two handfuls of wood next to her fire, waking Winston up in the process. "I also refilled our water supplies." She drops a full bottle next to the wood. "Do you think rescue will find us today?"

"These things take time," Reggie says.

"That's not what you said yesterday," Winston points out.

Brooke crosses her arms. "It's been what—eighteen, twenty hours? Shouldn't they know where our plane went down?"

All eyes turn to Reggie. He doubles down. "The most important thing to remember is that we must stay together—"

"Where are they?" Brooke demands.

Reggie's eyes dart around the group, sensing an impending mutiny. "Our radio went out before the storm forced me to reroute. I was attempting to make an emergency landing in Portugal, but unfortunately, no one on the ground knows that."

My lungs feel like they're collapsing. "What does that mean?"

Reggie wets his lips, his expression uneasy. "There is a chance that they're looking for us in the wrong place."

Naomi's hands fly to her mouth, Henry drops his head into his hands, Victoria swears loudly, and Brooke and I exchange a wary glance. *This is so much worse than we thought.*

"Why didn't you say that yesterday?" Brooke asks.

"We're not far off course. Help *will* come."

"I'm leaving." Theo appears, shouldering a backpack that must have been salvaged from the rest of the luggage. "I'm going to look for help on the east side of the island."

My stomach sinks, but I'm not surprised. After last night, I knew Theo would never agree to sit here and wait.

"No," Reggie says.

"I don't need your permission," Theo says sharply.

"Your Majesty, I can't climb that mountain." Winston gestures to his broken leg.

"Technically it's a volcano," Brooke notes.

Reggie continues. "Winston can't move, and we need to stay near the scene of the crash where we're safe."

"*Victoria's* not bloody safe!" Theo cries. "Every minute that we sit here and do nothing is wasting time she doesn't have."

"And what if I don't want to go?" Victoria asks. A line of sweat beads on her upper lip, and she's as pale as Naomi's cirrus clouds.

Theo's face falls. "I'm trying to help you."

She crosses her arms. "I want to stay with the group."

"I'm with Wren!" Naomi blurts out. She elbows me in the side and everyone's attention swivels to me.

I elbow her back. "This isn't about me." I *want* to support Theo's decision, but I can't ignore the foreboding feeling I get when I think about trekking over the mountain.

Henry holds up his hands. "Let's not do anything drastic, Theo."

"Our *situation* is drastic!"

"We can wait a little bit longer and think this through," Henry says.

"No, I can't. Winston—mind if I ransack the first aid kit?" Theo asks.

"Take whatever you need. If one of you lot dies on my watch, I'll be sacked for sure."

Henry grabs Theo's shoulders. "You don't always look at things rationally."

Theo shoves his brother away from him. "Sod off. I'll go alone."

"Sir—" Reggie tries again.

"I can't just sit here and wait for help!" Theo turns to Victoria, his voice thick with emotion. "I don't want to wait until it's too late. We've lost too much. I can't go home and look Louise, Charlotte, and Andrew in the eye if something happens to you. I won't survive it." He turns to me, pleading for someone to take his side, to trust him. "I *have* to do this."

Out of the corner of my eye, I see Victoria's hand tremble as she takes a drink of water. My stress level rises by a factor of ten.

Winston holds his hands up. "Sir. If I may, sometimes your mind lies to you—"

"Don't tell me about my own mind!" Theo shouts. His eyes travel over everyone in the group, landing on me last. "Wheeler."

My name is a sigh and a plea that cracks my heart open all over again, and I can't help but wonder how many times it will break for him.

Theo and I may be doomed to live in terror for the rest of our lives, but at least we've always been in this together.

I can't justify it, can't put words to the part of me that is willing to put my destiny in his hands. I fell in love with him and gave fate a hostage.

"Let's go."

CHAPTER 20

'm the first domino; once I fall, the others quickly follow. In a matter of minutes, Naomi, Brooke, and Henry agree to trek across the island with Theo and me in search of help. When Victoria sees that her options are to come with us or stay behind with Reggie and Winston, she grudgingly relents.

Theo's shoulders relax for the first time since the crash. He makes eye contact with me across the group. *Thank you,* he mouths, and my chest feels tight. Like deciding to leave Heathrow on the eve of the apocalypse and meeting Theo in a pub, it feels like nothing else was ever an option.

I turn to Naomi. "Will you be able to hike with your injury?"

"I'm not worried; it's just a few blisters." She stands for the first time all morning and instantly doubles over in pain. With a hand braced on her knee, she looks up at me with a wince that she pretends is a smile. "The blisters heard me, and they laughed. I can't come."

"No! Are you sure?"

"I can't even put weight on my foot. I'll never make it."

"But I don't want to go without you."

"Ironic, because I won't let you stay. I'm trusting you to get us rescued." She hugs me tightly and we promise to see each other soon.

Before I have a chance to catch my breath, my sister, three royals, my rescue dog, and I walk into the foggy forest with the ocean at our backs and a mountain that is "technically a volcano" in front of us.

A recipe for success.

"We'll take the direct path, straight through the middle of the island," Theo explains as we move through the dense trees. Vegetation swallows us and blocks out the rest of the world; the ocean waves are soon muted and sunlight filters weakly through the leaves. I swat a mosquito off my elbow.

"It'd be easier to walk along the coast. Less chance of getting lost," Henry says.

"This is faster. We have no idea how long the coast is," Theo argues.

Henry puts his hand out to stop Theo. "You want to climb over a volcano? *Really?*"

We form a small circle, and I can see Theo is getting frustrated again. The tension between the brothers has been thick since last night, and I have a feeling Henry is trying to get a rise out of him. Theo's right. If we're taking the risk to make this journey, we may as well do it the quickest way possible.

Theo points toward the north shore. "The crater is off center. We're going up and over the base. It's the fastest way."

Henry crosses his arms. "I disagree."

Theo's jaw tics.

"C'mon, Your Majesty, pull rank on me. You know you want to," Henry says.

"Get over yourselves and stop fighting," Victoria snaps. "Let's vote on it."

"The democratic way!" Brooke smiles sarcastically at the royals.

"Brilliant," Theo says dryly. "All in favor of traveling as the crow flies?"

Theo, Brooke, Victoria, and I raise our hands. Comet barks in agreement.

"Well, that's hardly fair." Henry gestures to me. "Wren was going to agree with you regardless."

"I'm agreeing with him because he's right about the distance, and because this path gives us easy access to fresh water."

"You lost even without the wife vote. Deal with it," Victoria tells Henry. She looks between the brothers. "No more whinging from you two, understand?"

They both look chagrined as they nod.

I raise my hand. "Just to clarify, I'm not actually his wife."

"Probably for the best. Given that we wouldn't have been on that plane if it weren't for you, the press will blame you for all of this," Victoria says.

"Enough. I tricked her into marrying me. It's my fault. Now let's go," Theo says, the mention of our *marriage* sending little electric prickles down my spine. It's taken a heroic effort on my part not to broach this particular subject, but I'm not going to miss the opportunity now that I have it.

I let the others take the lead and fall into place next to Theo. "Speaking of our wedding . . ." He visibly flinches, and I pivot to the least awkward question I can think of. "Do you have any idea who mailed me our marriage certificate?"

"Eleni?" he suggests. Eleni was the daughter of the Greek

family we stayed with, and one of only three people in attendance at our midnight wedding.

"I think so, too. Do you think she knew you were the prince the whole time we were in Greece?"

Theo holds back the branch of a fern to let me walk around without getting smacked in the face. "I hope not. It's bloody embarrassing to think that I was running around pretending to be Blaze Danger if everyone knew who I was."

"Maybe she had no idea until she saw the marriage certificate with your name on it."

"That must have been a proper shock."

I stop him with my hand on his chest and block his path. He has a dusting of facial hair on his cheeks, highlighting how hollow they've gotten in the past few months. Now that I've had a couple of days to desensitize myself to his face, I also notice purple shadows under his eyes. "You think it was a shock *for her*?"

He winces. "That was a stupid thing to say."

I look ahead and realize we've widened the gap between ourselves and the rest of the group. The distance makes me feel bold. "Were you ever planning to tell me that you signed your real name, or were you going to pretend it never happened?"

He blows out a breath. "It was the first thing I thought about when the comet was destroyed. I felt like the biggest arsehole on the planet. And then my mum died, and I was gutted. Couldn't think about anything else. Didn't get out of bed for a long time." His voice strains, and it makes my heart ache.

"Penny did her best to be there for me, but she's busy with the little ones, especially since Mum passed. She's literally all they have now. Eventually Graves kicked me in the arse and told me that I had to start making public appearances, do my first royal tour, and prove that the monarchy is still strong despite being led by a depressed teenager who doesn't want the job." He half laughs and half groans as he drags his hands over his face. "As much as I hated him, forcing me into action did help. I had no choice but to do the job."

I feel a small sting of jealousy; Theo and I both spent the summer spiraling in an existential crisis, and I can't help but be envious that he didn't have to sort through a mile-long course catalogue and more than 116 different undergraduate degree programs to find his way out. I know he feels stifled by the lack of options, but I feel overwhelmed by the sheer volume of them. It'd be kind of nice for fate to step in, block off all other paths, and point me in the direction of destiny.

Or at least tell me whether or not I'll ever actually need that 8:00 A.M. psych class.

"You really did look happy in Canada," I tell him.

He barks out a laugh. "That's 'cause I was drunk. I've been at least a little bit drunk in every appearance since her death."

"*That's* why you looked so happy in all those pictures?"

He arches an eyebrow. "You were looking at my pictures?"

I scowl at him. "I was looking at *Comet*."

His lip twitches. "You're a bloody awful liar, Wheeler."

I put a hand on my hip. "And you never looked me up online?"

"What is it you Americans say? 'I plead the fifth'? Although . . ." His eyes fill with mischief. "I *have* always wanted to spend an American Fourth of July on the beach, eating hamburgers and waving sparklers, the full monty."

I squint at him. "Are you drunk *now*?"

He laughs. "No. But I was self-medicating for most of the summer. It was the only way I could deal with what I did to Mum. I couldn't face any of my choices. Couldn't even call you."

I blink, confused. "Theo, your mom had a heart defect. Her death had nothing to do with you."

He sighs heavily. "And my dad died of 'natural causes.'"

"You don't believe the story about your mom?"

"Yes. No. I don't know. I think it's awfully convenient that her heart attack happened days after I ran away."

"Sometimes terrible things just happen, and there's no reason for it."

"I'd like to believe that, but my disappearance put so much stress on her."

My heart tugs me toward him. I press my hands on his shoulders until he's sitting on a mossy log. We're shrouded in a swirl of dense mist that blocks out the sounds of the forest. "There were a lot of stressful things happening. I don't know if you remember, but there was this whole thing with a comet." I wave my hands like it's no big deal. My joke earns me half of a reluctant smile. I'll take it. "I know you have a healthy ego, but in the case of *Missing Prince v. World-Ending Asteroid*, I think you're coming in second place, Theo."

"Ouch." He covers his heart like I've shot him.

"I'm serious. She didn't have a heart attack because you ran away. She had a heart attack because she had an untreated medical issue, and *maybe* because the world was about to end." After she died, I spent many a sleepless night reading about her sudden death and hoping that Theo was okay.

He mulls this over. "What you're saying is . . . I always came in second place."

"No!" I have a mini internal panic attack.

He laughs. "Yes, you are. And you're *right*. Mum's allegiance to the country always came before me."

"That's not what I meant!" I try to backtrack, but Theo's not having any of it.

He stands and paces the forest floor, the thick moss deadening the sounds of his footsteps, his face locked in concentration like he's fitting the puzzle pieces of his life together. Finally, his expression clears. "Shite, Wheeler. I never thought I'd be so relieved by the knowledge that my mother loved the country more than she loved me, but I am. Thank you."

I narrow my eyes, suspicious of how well he's taking this. "I don't know if I feel terrible for you or happy for you."

"Please don't feel sorry for the sad rich king." He sticks out a hand and pulls me to my feet. "I think I just needed to hear someone say it wasn't my fault."

"Look at me," I say, even though our eyes are already locked together. He tugs me into him, and I bump against his chest.

The air is wet with fog, and it's suddenly hard to breathe as Theo's eyes burn into mine. "I'm looking," he says, his gaze dipping to my lips, and then lower.

"It's not your fault, and I'm sorry no one else told you that."

His fingers brush against my sternum and pause there, feeling the outline of his ring under my shirt. I hold my breath, on the precipice between wanting him to ask and hoping he doesn't. "And I'm sorry I didn't tell you we were married."

My response sticks in my throat. "You should be apologizing for secretly marrying me in the first place."

"I only give apologies I mean," he says with a wink that leaves me utterly speechless. I blink at him in shock—and that's when it hits.

A picture I posted after the Fourth of July. Me on the beach in Chicago, a hamburger in one hand, a sparkler in the other. Posted to my stories, only available for twenty-four short hours.

My jaw drops as I stare at Theo. I'm trying to process this revelation, but I don't know how to reconcile it with what I overheard him telling his press secretary.

All I know for sure is that I wasn't the only one who spent my summer looking at pictures on the internet.

"I can't hear them anymore," he says suddenly. His eyes sweep the forest as we strain to hear footsteps or Comet's barking or Brooke and Henry's chatter.

Nothing.

"We should go." He turns away, but I grab his hand and hold him in place.

"Not yet."

A wicked grin spreads across his face as his eyes dance in the mist. "Something else on your mind, Wheeler?" His eyes fall once again to my lips, and I'm close enough that my mouth tingles in response.

"I heard you tell the press secretary that he doesn't need to worry about me because I'm not important," I say in a breathless rush.

"Shite." His eyes widen in understanding. "So that's why you were mad at me on the plane."

"Can you blame me? I drove all the way to Canada to talk to you, and you told Graves that I'm 'just a girl.'"

He shakes his head. "Wren, no. Just, *no*. I'm so sorry you heard that, because it's not even close to being true."

"Then why would you say it?"

He blows out a heavy breath. "The last thing I want is for the Firm to know how important you are to me."

A jolt of hope hits me straight in the chest. "Why?"

"If they get wind of the fact that I . . . that I'm . . ." He seems unable to find the words he needs. He swallows heavily and closes his eyes. "If they know that I care about you, they'll ruin everything."

I narrow my eyes, unsure what to do with this information. He cares about me. Well, okay. I care about my grandma, and pet adoption, and whether or not I'm having a good hair day. Or he *cares* about me, and that's why I could have sworn we were just about to kiss.

"So, what does that mean for us? I have to spend the rest of my life pretending not to know you?"

Theo's face falls, and before he can answer, a shriek pierces the muffled silence.

CHAPTER 21

Theo and I sprint in the direction of the scream. As we run, I effortlessly imagine a hundred terrible things that could have gone wrong, most of them involving Victoria. I have no idea how much time we have before she gets seriously sick, but judging by the tense expression on Theo's face, I think the answer is: *not a lot.*

Comet's bark echoes through the trees, leading us in the right direction. When we finally stumble upon the group, they're gathered on the banks of a trickling stream. Henry is drenched all the way to the ends of his curls, laughing and hollering as Comet splashes circles around him. Something in my brain clicks, and I recognize the screech from before as a happy one. My pulse slows.

Victoria is gulping water straight out of her cupped hands, and Brooke is sitting with her arms around her legs watching Comet and Henry splash around.

"Welcome back," Victoria says when she sees us.

I lean against a tree to catch my breath. "I thought you were dead."

"That's dramatic."

"What were you two doing?" Henry's insinuation is not subtle.

"None of your business," Theo responds. "Is everyone okay? We shouldn't split up again."

"*We* didn't split up. *You and Wren* disappeared," Brooke says. "We stopped here to give you a chance to catch up. It's not our fault you two can't stop making doe eyes at each other long enough to—"

"Are those berries?" Theo cuts her off. He points vaguely in the distance and leapfrogs over a fallen tree to get the hell out of this conversation. At the thought of food, my mouth fills with saliva and my hunger pangs triple. If he's lying to avoid Brooke, I don't blame him, but I will kill him for giving me false hope.

"Verdict?" I call after a minute. My legs are about to fall off. No food, no moving.

Theo returns to the group and displays a rough, purplish fruit in his hand. "This time you may direct your gratitude to me," he says, grinning smugly at his brother.

"What is it?" Victoria asks.

"We're about to find out." Theo lifts the fruit to his mouth.

"Wait!" Henry slaps the fruit out of his brother's hand and catches it with his free one. He holds it up for inspection. "Let me have the first honors. Wouldn't want this to kill you, Your Majesty." He winks, and I genuinely can't tell if he's joking or not.

Brooke surveys this exchange with a critical eye. I've been on the receiving end of that expression too many times in my life to not be terrified of it. Henry's about to find himself in the middle of a Brooke Wheeler cross-examination. "Why would you eat it first?"

"We don't know what this is. It looks safe, but it might not be," Henry says.

"Okay. And?"

"If I don't get sick, Theo can eat it."

Brooke narrows her eyes, zeroing in on her target. "So, you're doing this to protect Theo, *specifically*."

Theo winces, but Henry just smiles. "Have you heard of the phrase 'the heir and the spare'?"

"If we're being technical, you're now the heir, and I'm the spare," Victoria says. "I should eat it first."

"So, because he was born first, you're going to taste all of his food in case of poisoning? That can't be a real thing."

"No. At home, we pay someone to be the poison tester," Victoria says with a dramatic eye roll.

"I'll eat it," Theo protests.

"No, I will," Henry says.

"And if you *die*?" Brooke asks.

Henry tips his head to Brooke. "It's in the name of protecting the Crown."

Theo groans loudly.

"I have loads of food allergies, so that's how you know I'm willing to risk it all for you, brother." Henry winks.

"Oh, bollocks; pineapple gives you an itchy tongue. You're not risking anything," Victoria says.

"Explain to me why his life is more important than yours," Brooke says to Henry.

"Brooke, come on," I say. If she'd seen Theo's expression last night when this exact topic came up with Reggie, she'd realize how unnecessary this little lecture is. "That thing's not going to kill anyone. It's probably just a passion fruit."

"That's not the point!"

I snatch the fruit from Henry's hand and bite it open. A tangy, sour flavor floods my senses. I suck out the yellow, pulpy insides and I don't drop dead or get violently ill. Crisis averted.

I open my mouth and stick out my tongue. "Passion fruit."

"How egalitarian of you," Theo deadpans.

"You know what I always say, everyone deserves equal rights to die by poisonous tropical fruit."

Henry salutes me. "Thank you for saving me from a potentially itchy tongue."

I roll my eyes. "I only did it so my sister wouldn't murder you."

"Stop flirting with my sister and get us more fruit," Brooke says. Theo and Henry look at her, and then me, and then each other. Theo stalks into the trees, his brother hot on his heels.

A few minutes later Theo drops a large handful of passion fruit into my lap before settling next to Comet and me, and I make a silent wish that Reggie, Winston, and Naomi have also been able to find something to eat. Henry moves to sit with us but Theo glares at his brother until he joins Victoria several paces away.

"I'm sorry about Brooke. She can be intense," I whisper to Theo.

He shrugs. "I don't disagree with her on principle."

"She doesn't, like, *want* you to be poisoned. You know that, right?"

One half of his mouth hitches up. "I understand. She wants me to have an equal chance of being poisoned when we're playing Mystery Fruit Russian roulette."

"Exactly."

We grin stupidly at each other, and for a few perfect seconds I forget about all our problems. "Do you think your brother is flirting with me?" I tease.

Theo takes a bite of passion fruit. "Yes."

"Does that bother you?"

He slants me an exasperated look. "Yes."

I smother a smile and for a fraction of a second I can picture it: Theo and me doing this every day. The banter, the flirting, the being-on-the-same-continent. *In the same palace.* I close my eyes and let myself sink into the fantasy, and for the first time in months, my future shimmers with exciting possibility. I look down and am startled to discover that in my daydream, I'm wearing a gown.

I shake my head and snap back to the present.

Across from us, Victoria rolls an uneaten passion fruit between her hands before dropping it on the untouched pile at her feet. I watch her out of the corner of my eye for a while and am surprised that she's not eating. Instead, she continually dips her hands to the stream to gulp more water from them. She drinks so much that it's no shock when she grabs her stomach like she's in pain. My eyebrows pinch in worry, but she glares at me and stalks off by herself into the woods. I glance at Theo, wondering what he'd make of this.

"Will the fruit help your sister?"

"Maybe? I don't know. She needs to eat, but not too much sugar . . ." He exhales heavily. "What she really needs is her insulin. If she doesn't get it, she could become hyperglycemic, which could lead to diabetic ketoacidosis."

"What would that look like?"

His eyes stray to the spot in the trees where she disappeared. "She'll get tired. Blurred vision. Increased thirst. Nausea. Her breath might smell weirdly fruity. And then . . ." He trails off again, the worst-case scenario left hanging in the air like a fog.

I try to swallow my terror, but Theo's not done talking.

"I really hoped I'd be able to find her purse in the water. There was so much other stuff floating around, I thought there was a chance."

My head snaps up. "Her purse?"

"Yeah. It had her insulin in it. That's why she asked us to look for it."

Passion fruit churns in my stomach as I replay the crash in my head.

The backpack strap around my ankle, pulling me under. Victoria asking for her black Prada bag. Thinking she was just being spoiled. Kicking toward shore. Looping Victoria's purse around my body. Letting it sink anyway because she was rude to me.

The truth covers me like a wave, until I'm drowning in it.

This is my fault. Victoria's in danger because of me.

⁂

We finish eating and continue toward the center of the island. The evergreen trees start to thin, the ground sloping upward at the base of the volcano. I stay at the back of the group, my eyes fixed on Victoria like a hawk, my thoughts bouncing between her and Naomi back at camp, wishing I could push us faster, worrying whether Victoria will be able to keep up, and stressing over whether I should tell Theo about Victoria's symptoms. Every time he tries to talk to me, I feel worse. I can't even look at him without thinking about Victoria gulping that water like she couldn't get enough.

I spend the next hour alternating between fantasies of being rescued and making myself sick with worry that we'll never be found. I count the steps we take up the slope of this Portuguese volcano, wondering what fate has waiting for us on the other side.

When I can't stand the sound of my own thoughts for one more exhausted step, I sidle next to Victoria and Comet. I hold her back until the rest of the group has passed us, although Theo raises his scarred eyebrow and swivels his head to watch us. I wait until he's out of earshot.

"We need to talk." My pockets are filled with passion fruit, my fingers sticky with juice and dirt. My arm throbs where it was sewn back together, and the wound has started to swell. I've never felt so hideous in my life, but somehow Princess Victoria is rocking the shipwrecked look in a pencil skirt that she's ripped to her thigh.

"Pass," she says, before bringing her hands to her mouth like she's going to be sick all over the forest floor. Her complexion is a worrying shade of gray.

"How are you feeling?"

"Do us both a favor and stop asking me that."

I try again. "Theo told me that increased thirst and nausea might be symptoms of—" She cuts me a warning glare, and the rest of my sentence gets caught in my throat.

"And?" she demands, a hand on her hip. "What's there to do about it?"

"Let us know if you feel nauseous or tired or you need a break—"

"I can take care of myself." She throws me a sidelong glance. "I don't even know you. You're just some random girl—"

I've been trying to be nice, but my temper flares. "That your brother married."

Her eye roll is epic. "You're not staying married. The Firm would never allow it."

"Well, until they rescue us, grant your brother and me a quickie divorce, and kick my ass back to America, you're stuck with me. Don't want to cooperate? Fine. I'm not letting you out of my sight, *Your Highness.*" I dip into a shallow curtsy, just to get under her skin.

"That's going to be awkward, because I have to wee." She ducks out of sight to do her business, and when she's done, she rolls her eyes to discover that I'm still waiting for her. "I told you, I am more than capable of looking after myself. You can piss off." She flips her hair and picks up her pace, patting her thigh so Comet follows her as she catches back up to the group.

I sigh. *That went about as well as expected.*

I whistle, calling Comet back to my side. "Comet! Come here, boy!"

"Keep him back there," Brooke calls over her shoulder. "He stinks."

"Don't listen to her." I bend to pick up the stick Comet has dropped at my feet and am almost knocked backward by the smell of rotten eggs. I cover my nose with my hand. "Okay, wow. I don't love you any less, but you need a bath."

He cocks his head, begging for me to play with him, and despite the gag-inducing smell, I can't help but smile.

"Don't forget who your human is, okay?" I scratch him behind the ears. He picks up the stick and presses it into my leg. I laugh. "Fine, fine!" I pull back my good arm and let the stick fly. It lands out of sight and Comet takes off, leaping over a ridge to retrieve it. His bark carries easily through the quiet air, and I'm starting to wonder what's taking him so long when he lopes back over the ridge.

"No stick?" I ask.

He nudges my hand with his dripping-wet snout.

I laugh. "Are you the smartest boy ever? Did you already take that bath?" It's just his muzzle that's wet, though.

He barks again for my attention, and I jog with him over the ridge. The land gently slopes down to a small crater filled with a deep pool of water in the center, and the rotten egg smell intensifies. Comet's stick is floating near the shore.

"You found water!" I rub his head affectionately and reach my hand into the water to retrieve the stick.

Then I pull my hand out in shock. "Did you feel this?" I slowly dip my fingers into the warm water again, closing my eyes as a soft sigh escapes my lips.

When Theo and I were on the run and facing the end of our lives, even the smallest luxuries felt like heaven: a bed, a shower, clean clothes. But I was wrong.

Heaven is a Portuguese hot spring.

CHAPTER 22

The tranquil blue-green water is the temperature of a steaming shower at the end of a long day. Hot enough to turn my skin scarlet, on just the right side of scalding. It feels so amazing that I sink my uninjured arm in up to my shoulder, and my sore muscles turn to goo. *Bliss*.

"Wren?" Brooke's voice floats through the trees.

"Get over here!" I call.

Henry reaches me first and sees me soaking my arm in the water. "What's that smell?"

"Forget about the smell and feel this water."

"One does not simply forget about the smell of swamp arse."

I laugh. "You will when you feel it."

Victoria dips her hand into the spring and her eyes widen in surprise. "What is it?"

"A hydrothermal spring," Brooke says as she joins us. "The groundwater is geothermically heated by shallow bodies of magma."

"How do you know that?" Victoria asks.

Brooke shrugs. "Everybody knows that."

"I can assure you they don't," Theo says. He pulls his shirt off in one fluid motion and catches me watching.

I quickly pull my gaze away and glance at the sky. The setting sun has already dipped below the treetops, and it'll be dark before long. Comet's already resting under a tree, we're all exhausted, and as much as she's trying to hide it, Victoria looks like she needs a break.

"We should stay here for the night," I say.

"Smashing. I'm getting in." Henry toes off his shoes and flips into the water. When he springs back up, he flings his hair out of his eyes, showering me with water drops. "What's everyone waiting for? Get in! It feels amazing."

Brooke, Victoria, and Theo waste no time stripping down and sinking into the warm water, but I drag my feet, avoiding the inevitable.

After a moment of soaking in the hot spring, Theo turns and rests his chin on the back of his hands. His eyes glint in the golden light. "Forget how to swim?" he teases, a sharp contrast to his wistful expression.

The memory of us skinny-dipping under a midnight Grecian sky is dizzying. I swallow a painful lump in my throat and spin my finger in a circle.

"I already know you're wearing princess knickers; I heard Naomi yelling about it after she was stung," he says. My mouth falls open as he laughs and turns around.

"No one will be seeing my knickers!" I unbutton my shirt and hang it on a tree branch, keeping my pants on, and make my way over to the hot spring.

"You shouldn't get in," Brooke says.

"Why not?"

"This water is probably teeming with bacteria. Your cut could get infected."

I glance at my arm and am startled to see that the skin around my sutures is growing redder and puffier by the hour. "It's not that bad!" I protest.

"It looks a bit minging," Henry agrees.

"You're the one who did the stitching," I point out, before my eyes stray longingly to the water.

"I wouldn't risk it," Theo says regretfully.

My heart sinks. The idea of not getting in makes me want to cry.

I glance at Victoria for a fourth opinion. "What do you think?"

She shrugs. "It's your life."

I sigh heavily. If *she* thinks I should do it, it's probably a bad idea.

I blink back tears, embarrassed to be getting so emotional over a hot spring. "Fine. I'll keep the stitches dry, even though I'm pretty sure rich people would pay thousands of dollars at a wellness spa for this kind of shit and call it a healing soak," I grumble.

I sink in until the water hits my waist, but the bottom is steep and slick, and gravity drags me deeper. I grit my teeth and hold my arm nearly straight in the air. Only a few seconds later, the muscles are burning, then shaking, then screaming in pain.

I've never been a quitter, but not even my pride can keep my arm in the air for another painful second. I drop it with a frustrated whimper.

"Come here. I'll do it for you," Henry says.

"You'll hold my arm in the air?" I ask doubtfully.

"Sure. Or you can put it around my shoulders. I'd be honored."

"No thanks." I pull myself out of the hot spring and into the chilly air, my wet pants plastered to my legs. Goose bumps travel across my skin. "Enjoy your bacteria bath," I say dryly as I pull my blouse over my wet skin.

"You can start a fire if you're cold," Brooke offers.

"Reggie let us take the lighter?" Henry asks in surprise.

"*Winston* and *Naomi* let us take the lighter. I was going to steal it if they didn't," Victoria says with a satisfied smirk.

"Do you think they'll be okay without it?"

"The fire was pretty big by the time we left. Reggie would be an idiot if he let it die," she says.

I personally think Reggie's an idiot even if he doesn't let the fire die, but that's beside the point. I find the lighter in Theo's backpack and scan the ground for kindling. Brooke shouts instructions from the hot spring, but by the time the sky is painted tangerine, I still haven't managed to light anything for longer than a few seconds. I press my cheek to the ground and blow gently on the kindling under the log-cabin structure. It catches, but the dried leaves burn up in a bright flame and turn to ash and smoke before igniting the wood. I refuse to look at the water, but I can feel Theo watching me.

I push my knotted hair behind my ears and try again. My fingers fumble over the lighter as a strong breeze whistles through the trees, stirring up ripples in the water and extinguishing my flame.

I let out a frustrated groan. "Why is this so hard?" I throw the lighter. It lands unceremoniously in the grass, and I don't feel any better for having hurled it out of my hands. I have wood, and I have a lighter, but I don't have fire. At this point, not even the laws of physics are on my side. "The universe hates me. It is conspiring against me."

"To what end?" Theo's gravelly voice floats over on the breeze.

"To annoy me." I spit the words, refusing to look at him. I feel wretched. I look wretched. My stitches burn and my cheeks sting with the first sign of sunburn. I'm hungry, I'm tired, I'm dirty, and with every passing hour in which we don't see a rescue plane or boat, it feels more and more like we might never get off this island.

I hear footsteps approach. Theo retrieves the lighter and then crouches next to me. "Can I help?"

"No," I say flatly. My throat burns with the effort of holding back tears. I clench my jaw and wait for him to stop staring at me. The only thing that will increase my humiliation is if I start bawling because I can't start a fucking campfire.

"Need my help?" Henry calls from the water. "I'm better at it than him!"

Theo ignores his brother. "Talk to me, Wheeler," he prods, his infuriating gentleness making me want to scream.

"Stop being nice to me," I whisper-hiss so the others don't hear us.

"Why?"

Because if anything happens to your sister, it will be my fault, and neither of us will be able to untangle our relationship from yet another tragedy.

The guilt is suffocating.

I finally turn to look at Theo and am startled to find him so close. His eyes bore into mine.

"Because it's painful," I tell him.

"Any luck with the fire?" Victoria calls in a mocking voice from the water, and whatever is left of my sanity crumbles.

"Why does your sister hate me?" I snap at Theo.

"She's a teenager whose mum just died; she hates everyone."

"She doesn't hate Naomi."

"That's because she's not threatened by her."

I'm dumbstruck. "Why on earth does she feel threatened by *me*?"

His face is pained. "Because her entire world has been turned upside down, *twice*—and then you come along, bringing all the media attention in the world with you. I'm sure it reminds her of our parents."

"And that's my fault?"

"No!" He pushes his hands through his hair, looking desperate. "I'm not explaining this right. But life was just settling down. The royal tour in Canada was supposed to prove that we're okay, that our family is strong and capable of leading the monarchy. It was the last chance before the coronation to get the public on my side . . . but then I looked up at the sunken gardens in High Park, and there you were . . ." He trails off, looking lost in his own thoughts, and it's not hard to imagine that he's thinking about paparazzi ambushes and car chases and emergency meetings with the Firm.

"And life was chaos again?" I ask, hoping he'll deny it.

He exhales. "Yeah."

My chest collapses, but I refuse to cry. "That's what she thinks? Or that's what *you* think?"

He winces. "It's not your fault—"

"I get it." I cut him off before I have to hear him let me down gently. I don't want to hear again that he cares about me, because now I know that it's not enough.

Fate was never going to put me in a royal ball gown.

"Maybe we'd both be better off if we'd never met," I say.

Theo winces. "I don't know how to do this."

"Neither do I." For the first time since Italy, I feel like I could use a drink. I walk away, and with a glance back at Theo, I open his backpack and rummage through the first aid supplies and spare clothes until I find a small bottle of booze like the one that Brooke slipped to Winston.

"Wren!" Henry swims to the bank of the hot spring, wet curls plastered across his grinning face. "Come settle a debate between Brooke and me. And bring the whisky with you."

Chapter 23

"Where'd you find that?"

Brooke motions to the small whisky bottle in my hand as I sit on the bank and dip my feet into the steaming pool.

I spin the bottle between my fingers. "In the backpack Theo was carrying."

"I didn't know it was there," he says, slipping into the water and swimming to the other side of the circle.

"Never have I ever lied about hiding booze from my fellow castaways." I arch a brow.

"Neither have I," Theo says.

"Over here." Henry motions for me to throw him the bottle. "I nicked it and didn't tell anyone. A lie of omission." He grins, flashing his dimple in the dusky light.

I toss him the bottle and he looks very pleased with himself as he untwists the cap and takes a small sip.

"What were you and Brooke debating?" I ask.

"Whether the monarchy has a place in modern society, but I won. She can't argue with the fact that countries with monarchies are more politically stable *and* have more money than countries without."

"To be fair, I'm not sure that's justification enough in the twenty-first century," Victoria says.

"Traitors, both of you." Henry motions between Victoria and Theo.

Victoria rolls her eyes. "Everyone our age hates the monarchy, and we need to change to keep up with the times."

"You haven't heard my strongest argument," Henry says.

Victoria quirks an eyebrow and motions for him to continue.

Henry holds up his hands and waits for silence. "It's really fucking wicked to live in a palace! Debate that, Brooke!" He takes another drink.

Brooke rolls her eyes. "I don't debate eighteen-year-olds."

"Told you I won." Henry smirks proudly. "What about you, darling?" He turns his attention to me. "Ever given it any thought?"

"Given what any thought?"

"Living in a palace."

I do not let myself look at Theo as my face turns scarlet. "Not really."

"Too bad. We could have fun togeth—"

"Cut the shit," Theo snaps.

"What?" Henry shrugs innocently. "I'm not stepping in the middle of something, am I?" He throws Theo a loaded glance that makes my insides squirm.

"Never have I ever been jealous of my brother and pretended I wasn't," I say pointedly.

"Nice try," Henry says. "I've never pretended I don't want what Theo has."

I feel like the ground has shifted under me, and I need to

get this conversation back on track. "It must be easy to defend the monarchy when you get all of the privilege but none of the drawbacks."

Henry chuckles and tips the bottle toward me. "Never have I ever wished I was born into a different family." Without looking at Theo, he hands the bottle off to his brother. Theo tosses back a small sip. Henry's face clouds, the mask on his vulnerability slipping for a fraction of a second. I can't help but think how much of his constant cockiness and flirting is just to cover how much he wants Theo's life.

Theo holds the bottle up to his sister. "You should probably drink too, but that seems like a bad idea. How are you feeling?"

Victoria wipes sweat off her brow. "I'm all right. I'm—"

A tremor travels across the surface of the water, scattering ripples across the hot spring. "What was that? Who did that?" My gaze travels over to Comet, but he's still sleeping undisturbed under a tree.

"You didn't feel it?" Victoria asks.

"Feel what?" Brooke says.

"The ground has been shaking on and off since we landed. I've felt it at least a dozen times."

"What, like bloody earthquakes?" Theo asks. Our eyes meet, the way they always seem to. He raises an eyebrow like, *Can you believe this shit?*

We're cursed, I mouth back.

Victoria shrugs. "I don't know what else it would be. It only ever lasts a couple of seconds, and no one else has noticed but me. I thought I was going a bit mental."

"A dozen of them?" Henry is skeptical.

"Earthquake swarms are common in volcanic regions," Brooke says.

"Is that dangerous?" I ask.

We fall quiet as we scan our surroundings. We're on a beautiful tropical island, but we're also climbing the side of a freaking volcano. Everything about the island that once felt peaceful takes on a menacing air, from the shadows in the trees to the inky-black depths of the hot spring.

"I wouldn't worry about it," Brooke decides, but a telltale crease forms between her brows. "Pass me the bottle?" She holds her hand out to Theo.

"Uh-uh. You've got to play the game," Henry says.

"I need the bottle to play the game."

"One drink left," Theo says as he passes the booze to my sister.

"Sorry, Wren, this is going to be a short game and you're not legal yet." She takes a deep breath. "Never have I ever dropped out of law school and secretly regretted it every day since." She downs the rest of the whisky and wipes her mouth with the back of her hand.

"I knew it!" I cry. "How long have you known?"

"Since about three days after I had my quarter-life crisis and made a huge point of telling everyone that I was taking time off to 'find myself'?"

"And you're positive this time?" I lean forward, wondering how she can be so certain.

She nods.

"All the jobs in the world and you want to be a bloody barrister? Interesting," Henry muses.

"What did *you* decide about law school, Wheeler?" Theo asks. His tone is cool, but he looks at me like my answer is the only thing he cares about.

"I agree with Henry."

"Do you now?" Henry throws his brother a cocky grin.

I sigh and scrub my hands through my tangled hair, regretting bringing this up in front of everyone. "It's a lot of pressure to choose the right path, that's all." I feel a burn at the back of my throat and look down at my lap. "I almost died—*twice*—and when we're rescued, I don't want to screw up my second chance at life."

"*If* we're rescued," Victoria says ominously, and an awkward silence settles over all of us.

"New game!" Henry claps his hands together. "Truth or dare?"

"No."

"Are you kidding?"

"Pass."

"Absolutely not."

I sigh. "Let's play something less likely to get us in trouble." Truth or dare always results in the wrong people kissing, or someone getting naked, or someone doing something irredeemably stupid. Plus, there's a couple of truths I'm currently planning to take to my grave. "Have you ever played two truths and a lie?"

Henry's face brightens. "What's the reward for guessing right? Or the punishment for guessing wrong?"

"The punishment is being stuck on this godforsaken island," Victoria mutters.

"I have a better idea," Brooke says. "Would You Rather. It's simple and we don't need rewards or punishments." When no one protests, she continues. "Victoria can start, and we'll go in a circle."

Victoria closes her eyes and grimaces. "My question is for Wren. Would you rather move to London where you can see

Comet all the time, or stay in Chicago and never hang out with him?"

"I don't understand the question."

"Which part?" Her face is impassive.

"The part that assumes that Comet is going to live anywhere other than with me. He's *my* dog."

"It's hypothetical," she says evenly, but I recognize the trap. She's trying to get me to admit that I don't need Comet because she wants to keep him.

"I—I don't—that's not—"

"You have to pick one," Brooke says.

"While I reject the premise of the question, Chicago is *literally* where I live and where I'm going to school and it's where all my family and friends are, so I guess I'd rather stay in my own country."

"Without your dog?" she prompts.

"If that's the question," I say through gritted teeth.

She frowns like she's disappointed by my answer, which I don't understand at all. I thought she wanted me as far away from her family as possible.

"Your turn," she says. She moves to the bank of the hot spring and leans against it.

I sigh, wishing I could slip fully into the water and float away. "Henry. Would you rather be able to fly or see the future?" I'm already regretting letting Brooke overrule my idea to play two truths and a lie. At least in that game I would have had control of the information I shared with this group.

"That's an easy one, innit? Considering our circumstances, I'd fly," Henry answers. "My turn?"

"That question is boring!" Victoria whines. "The game's not fun if you don't ask something hard."

"Too late. She only gets one," Henry says. "My question is for my brother."

"Of course," Theo drawls.

"Would you rather give up the throne—"

"That one," Theo says.

Henry smiles. "I'm not finished."

"I don't need more information."

"You might." Henry's grin turns wicked, and dread prickles the skin at the back of my neck. "Would you rather give up the throne, or give up your marriage?"

Theo's expression is hard to read in the dying light. "What?"

"It's just a hypothetical. Wren, or the throne?"

Theo's eyes dart to me, and I feel like I'm sinking, like I might never breathe again.

I wrench my eyes away. "What if he doesn't want either?" I quip. My attempt to relieve the awkward tension only makes things worse. Brooke's expression fills with a sympathy that makes me want to catapult myself off the island.

"You're a prick. I'm not answering that," Theo says.

Henry smirks in delight. "Are you pulling rank, Your Majesty?"

"Yes." Theo looks at me. "My question's for Wheeler. Would you rather—"

"Get rescued right now or stop playing this game? It's a toss-up."

"Game over." Brooke lifts her hands.

"No, it's okay. I'm not too scared to answer," I say. The truth is, I'm dying to know what question he'll ask.

"Would you rather go back in time three months, or jump three months into the future?"

"That's too easy!" Henry protests. "In three months, we'll be rescued—"

"Or dead," Victoria adds helpfully. She tucks a piece of her hair behind her ear with trembling fingers.

"But if she goes back in time, she can get on her plane in London and avoid meeting me completely, which means she never would have been on the plane that crashed in the first place," Theo says, never taking his eyes off mine.

The stakes are spelled out for everyone. He's calling my bluff. He wants to know if I really regret meeting him, and everything that came after. The wedding. The heartbreak. The three months of feeling like I've been caught in a current, unable to do anything but gasp for breath and wait for the ocean to spit me onto shore, tired and bruised and too scared to try again.

My chest burns as I meet his unflinching gaze. I'm tempted to fall back into old habits: to avoid my feelings and bury them under ten layers of sarcasm. It never worked on him before, but there's so much strange, distant tension between us that it might this time. We're under the same sky, but I'm starting to wonder if we're the same people we used to be.

Steam curls over the water, and maybe it's the heat going to my head, or the way the starlight glints off Theo's bare shoulders, but if the comet taught me anything, it's that I can't pretend away my feelings. Hiding them never got me anywhere I wanted to go.

"I'd go back in time."

He doesn't flinch.

"I don't feel good," Victoria says suddenly. She vomits on the shore and then slumps against the side of the hot spring.

"Get out of the water," Theo commands, already swimming toward her.

I reach her first and help her boost herself out on trembling arms.

"My head . . . I'm dizzy." She sounds like she's out of breath. She shakes me off and stands on her own, but then she stumbles forward.

"Wait. Let me help you." Theo scrambles out of the water, his feet and hands slipping against the muddy ground. He lunges for his sister, but he's too late.

We all watch in horror as Victoria's knees buckle.

CHAPTER 24

Time slows down, and I feel frozen in shock as Victoria collapses.

"No!" a voice screams (maybe mine), and time speeds back up.

I sink my nails into the soft, muddy grass and pull my feet out of the hot spring. I dive toward the princess, but Brooke's arms close around me. She pulls me away from Victoria's unconscious body as Henry and Theo kneel over their sister.

"Tor! Tor! Can you hear me? Victoria!" Theo screams, shaking her shoulders. Wet hair is tangled across her face.

My stomach lurches. I turn and press my face into Brooke's shoulder. The air is freezing, and our knees knock together.

"She's already weak, and the heat must have gone to her head. I should have said something," Brooke whispers. I pull back and look up at her. Her face is stricken, but if anyone's at fault for this, it's not her. The guilt makes me nauseous.

"She's not responding," Henry says.

I squeeze my eyes shut as a chorus of denial echoes through my bones. *Not now. Not yet. Not now. Not yet. Not now. Not yet.*

"She needs water and food," Theo roars, snapping me back to reality.

This *is* happening now, and we can still save her.

"You get water," I tell Henry. "We'll find fruit."

I grab the backpack and turn it upside down. First aid supplies, Winston's handcuffs, and spare clothes scatter across the ground, but our passion fruit supply is gone, and our water supply is drained.

We sprint into the dark trees, and I'm immediately disoriented. Brooke veers to the left, and I hear Henry to my right, but the pitch black keeps me from seeing anything. I stick my hands out and move slowly, but soon I'm tangled in damp leaves and muddy moss.

"Find anything?" I yell.

"Not yet!" Brooke calls, barely audible over the sound of my jagged breaths.

"Hurry!" Theo screams. The terror in his voice makes my blood run cold. This is taking too long.

My eyes slowly adjust to the dark and I finally run into a passion fruit vine. "I found some!" I call into the black as I untangle myself and load my arms with as many as I can hold. I drop half of what I'm carrying, stumbling over my own feet in panic, but still have a handful of fruit when I reach Theo's side. I drop to my knees and bite open a passion fruit. Theo holds Victoria's mouth open, and I squeeze the juice onto her tongue.

"Do it again," he tells me. "Come on, Tor. Wake up," he pleads, tears slipping down his cheeks.

"We've got more," Henry calls, running out of the forest behind Brooke with loaded arms. They drop piles of passion fruit and a filled water bottle to the ground. Henry tips the liquid into her mouth until she's swallowed several gulps, and then

Brooke and I take turns breaking the fruit apart and dripping pulpy juice into Victoria's mouth.

I'm desperate and frenzied, covered in sticky juice and goose bumps, tears pooling in my eyes and a pain welling in my chest, when Victoria finally coughs and opens her eyes.

"Oh thank god," a voice says. (Maybe me.) I crumple, and Theo catches me, his arms wrapping around my shoulders. The pain in my stitches flares.

"Eat this," Henry says, pushing a passion fruit into Victoria's hand.

Victoria slowly eats, then drains the entire bottle of water. After a long, tense moment, she sits up and sucks the juice off her fingers. "Why all the panicked faces?" She bats her eyelashes innocently.

Henry laughs weakly, but Theo sits back wordlessly, his eyes wide with shock.

"How are you feeling?" I ask.

"Fine." I don't comment on the way her eyes seem to slide out of focus when she looks at me. Then, more quietly, she says, "Thank you for the fruit." She picks up another piece and bites it open.

"You shouldn't get back in the hot spring," Brooke says, handing Victoria one of the extra shirts that we brought with us.

"Obviously." Victoria's eyelashes bob in the moonlight as she avoids making eye contact with any of us. She pulls the shirt on and wraps her arms around her knees, looking more scared than I've ever seen her.

"You should sleep by Comet tonight," I blurt.

"Okay," she whispers. I want to do more, but I feel utterly helpless.

The mood of our little campout has turned quiet and anxious.

Brooke starts the fire in silence, and Victoria is asleep with her head on Comet's stomach by the time the flames are big enough to produce heat. Henry takes the spot next to his sister, his breathing turning slow and even within minutes. Brooke checks in on me to make sure I'm okay (a word that has lost all meaning), and then she dozes off too.

When everyone else is asleep, Theo finally moves from the edge of the hot spring to the last open spot around the fire. He lies a few feet away from me and stares at the inky sky in a silence that neither one of us knows how to break.

"I miss Greece," he finally says.

I take a deep breath, trying to block out the pain in my arm. "I miss when life didn't feel like a curse."

Theo turns his head to the side, his eyes at half-mast. "You were never the curse," he murmurs. His eyes shutter closed and I watch him for a long moment, starlight glinting off his lips and lashes.

I shift onto my side, trying to get comfortable on the cold ground, but pain radiates through my arm, making it impossible to think about anything else. After what feels like hours of tossing and turning, I give up on sleep and tiptoe to the hot spring.

I prod my scarlet, swollen stitches with my finger and hiss in pain.

This might be a mistake, but here goes nothing.

I slip my shirt off and step out of my pants. I leave them carefully folded by the edge of the spring and step into the hot water. I sink down until the scalding, soothing water reaches my neck and tip my head back with a sigh as the throbbing in my arm subsides.

Now that it's gone, I realize the pain was like being in a room with the TV on, the volume inching up little by little. It was background noise until suddenly it was the loudest noise of all, drowning out everything else.

Blissfully, it's finally quiet. My head clears for the first time since the crash, and an old familiar daydream flickers to life in its absence.

Theo and me in Chicago, taking the train like he's not one of the most famous people in the world. I invent a hundred reasons why we'd be out together (taking Comet and Wally for a walk, coming home from a Cubs game, running through an entire roll of film on my Polaroid camera), in a hundred different conditions (the first snow of the season, drowning in humidity, crunching leaves under our feet). We take our time, because the world isn't ending, and no one is dying, and we get to make our own future. The picture is fuzzy around the edges, slipping out of my fingers like a dream the moment you wake up, but I pretend it's the life we'd have if we were different people in different circumstances.

When I get frustrated with the impossibility of it all, I imagine myself in a crown in Buckingham Palace. Weirdly, this future is easier to see, because it's not impossible. Theo can never join my world, but I could join his, and we'd follow a path laid out for generations. I tip my head back to gaze at the stars and lie to myself about destiny.

"What about your stitches?"

Theo's voice startles me. I twist around to see him standing shirtless on the edge of the spring, his toes inches from the water.

I cross my arms over my chest on instinct, though the water's too dark and murky for him to see anything scandalous. "I'm risking it."

He nods distractedly and rakes a hand through his hair. "Okay."

The silence between us stretches paper thin. "You couldn't sleep either?"

"No. I, um—" He clears his throat and paces the side of the hot spring. "I need to say something."

My heart beats double-time.

He stops abruptly and spins to face me. His jaw clenches. "You aren't the reason my life is a mess. I am lucky to know you, Wren Wheeler, and it was criminal for me to imply otherwise. I'm sorry." He looks like the words were tortured out of him.

"Thank you," I wheeze. I stopped breathing somewhere around the word "lucky." "I'm sorry for what I said too. About how I'd be better off if we'd never met." I knew I was a liar the moment I answered Theo's Would You Rather question.

His gaze hits the ground as he rubs the back of his neck. I've never seen him so unsure.

"Is there something else you wanted to say?"

"Yes, but—" He cuts himself off and looks at the sky. At anywhere but me, it feels like. "Do you want to play another game?" he asks suddenly.

Talk about emotional whiplash. "The last one didn't go very well."

His teeth scrape over his bottom lip. "I'm a bit desperate here, and this is the only thing I can think of."

"What kind of game?"

"We're each allowed to ask each other three questions, and we can't lie."

"That's not a game, that's a conversation."

"Something we're notoriously good at," he deadpans.

"Hey! I've gotten better."

"Well then, Wheeler, let's have a conversation." Now that

he's made eye contact, we're locked. I couldn't look away to save my life.

My stomach lurches. I'm getting braver, but sincerity is still the scariest thing. "Three questions."

He nods to the water. "Do you mind if I get in?"

Yes. No. My heart thrums painfully. "I won't stop you."

He cocks his head to the side, annoyed. "See, you're being evasive already."

"Me?" I gasp in faux surprise. "I'm not the one who refused to answer my Would You Rather question."

"It won't happen again," he promises. He unbuttons his jeans. "Fair warning, I'm going to take off my pants now." Maybe it's the heat, but I'm suddenly lightheaded. I don't remember what we were talking about. A soft sigh escapes his lips as he sinks into the hot water.

My throat dries up.

He advances toward me but stops just shy of arm's length, which is probably for the best, because I'm internally freaking out.

"All right, Wheeler, question one. Are you ready?"

My stomach is fluttery, and I feel pinned in place by his eyes. "Do your worst." (My false bravado is out of control.)

"During Would You Rather, you said you'd go back in time. Is that to avoid meeting me . . . or something else?" he asks. Direct and to the point.

I swallow my nerves. "I'd do it again without changing a thing." Even if we'll never get autumn walks past the brownstones in Lincoln Park, I can't bring myself to regret a single minute of knowing King Theodore Geoffrey Edward George.

He edges closer and his eyes flutter closed for a split second.

His shoulders relax a fraction. He's moving in inches, as if worried about scaring me away. He should be. There's a part of me that wants to run, but as always, there's something about Theo and me that feels inevitable. We can fight it all we want, but the universe will run our airplane into the ground before it allows us to outrun each other.

"What's your second question?" I ask.

He looks at me like he knows something I don't. "Turns out I only needed one."

"Are you serious?"

"All right, all right. Er. Oh, I've got one! Is it true that Americans eat peanut butter *and* jelly on the same sandwich?"

I bark out a laugh. "What kind of question is that? Yes, we eat PB and J sandwiches, and yes, they're delicious."

He grins. "Fascinating. Three—"

"You already asked three questions."

"No, I didn't."

"Your first one was when you asked if you could get in the water."

He slants me a frustrated look. "That's against the spirit of the game, Wheeler, and I have a real question this time."

"Why do you call me 'Wheeler'?" I blurt it without thinking and regret it immediately. I hadn't planned on wasting one of my questions on this.

He narrows his eyes and slides an inch closer. "It just happened. It probably started as a doomed attempt to put some casual distance between us, but then I saw the way your eyes sparked when I said it. You looked half annoyed and half in love with me, and I guess I got addicted to that expression."

"No one with an accent like yours should be allowed to be so charming. It's not fair." I never stood a chance.

His expression softens into one of amused delight. "I'll take that under advisement. Question two?"

"Why did you write your real name on our marriage certificate?"

He exhales in relief. "I would have let you have as many questions as it took until you asked me that."

I'm flustered, both dying for his answer and nervous about what he might say. "If it meant nothing, that's fine. I'm not expecting—"

"Wheeler." He moves closer. "I didn't plan it, and I don't have a good explanation, but when we stood on that beach and said our vows, I realized all of mine were true. It's that simple. I did it because I meant it."

He reaches up and brushes a wild strand of hair off my forehead, his fingers trailing fire everywhere he touches. In the water, his foot nudges mine.

"I know that piece of paper has made everything infinitely more complicated, but I thought I was dying, and I loved you, and in that moment, I wanted to marry you as me, not as Blaze Danger. I wanted it to be a decision I made for myself." He wears an expression that I've memorized down to my bones: it's the same look he gave me when I took his picture with a Polaroid camera in Greece, and for the first time, I realize it wasn't the angle or the early-morning magic light or even my mind playing tricks on me.

"I meant it too," I whisper, closing the final distance between us until my body is flush against his. He hooks a finger onto the chain around my neck, his pupils expanding in the dark. He lifts the necklace out of the water and stares at his ring for a long time, before gently letting it slip from his fingers and tucking a finger in the waistband of my underwear.

I'm buzzing everywhere.

"I think that might be a bad idea," I whisper, my lips brushing against his.

"I'm certain of it," he answers, and I squash the flash of guilt that hits me.

There's a warning on the edge of my consciousness telling me there's something I'm forgetting, one more question I have to ask. But when Theo tilts his lips to mine and whispers, "Third question?," the words that come out of my mouth are "Why haven't you kissed me yet?"

His hands rest on my waist, and even in the heat of the spring, his touch is searing. The kiss starts as a question—hesitant and soft. Everything fades away, and we're not in a hurry. I feel rooted to the muddy earth as we melt into each other, the burn in my chest answering the only question that really matters. His tongue presses against mine and the pace of the kiss changes. From question to answer to desperate resolve. He clasps my waist and presses his body to mine, opening an ache in me that I've done my best to ignore. We fit as easily together as we did in Greece, and the months of waiting finally catch up to us. I worry that if I keep kissing him, I won't know how to stop.

I rake one of my hands through his hair and he swears softly in my ear. He pushes us backward until we hit the edge of the spring, where he flips us around and presses my back against the muddy banks. He sinks his teeth into my bottom lip, and I hiss in pleasure. His hands are everywhere: in my hair, tracing my collarbone, pressing an indent of his ring against my sternum, feathering lightly across my stomach. His mouth breaks free from mine and trails down my neck, and then reality hits.

"Theo." My chest heaves with the effort of not kissing him. "I have one more question."

"You already had three," he growls, kissing me behind the ear.

"I know. But it's important."

"Only one more," he whispers, sending shivers across my damp shoulders. "And then I get to kiss you again."

"What are we going to do when we get off this island?"

He draws back, his brows scrunched in confusion. "What do you mean?"

"How are we going to make this work? The public needs a story, and obviously the Firm is going to want to be involved in figuring all this out."

The heat drains from Theo's eyes as his hands fall away from me. "I'm not telling the Firm."

"We can't exactly sneak around without them finding out. You travel with an entourage everywhere you go."

"Right."

Now I'm the one confused. "So we *are* going to tell them?"

"*No.* They'll want to control every aspect of your life. How you dress and where you go and who you spend your time with. You'll become another piece on their chessboard, something to be maneuvered to their advantage, and that's *if* they decide that you're allowed to stick around. If not, Graves will plant horrible stories about you in the press and ruin your life. There is no scenario in which you win."

I finally understand, and I feel like an idiot for not getting it sooner. He won't tell the Firm, because after we're rescued, there'll be nothing to tell. I swallow the emotion in my throat and force out the next words. "What if I don't want to win anything but you?"

"I'm sorry, but I love you too much to ever let you date me," he says simply, like those three little words won't change my entire world.

"You're in love with me—present tense?"

He laughs softly as he lifts our intertwined hands out of the water and kisses each of my knuckles in turn. "Did I not make that obvious? I'm in love with you, past, present, and future, which is why there is no world in which I would ever subject you to the life that killed my father."

I think of my palace-and-ball-gown daydreams. *Theo and Me. King and Queen. Fate. The whole shebang.*

But when I look at him now, my heart sinks. Because I've seen that conviction in his eyes—the one that says he believes in his cause and he won't change his mind. As long as he thinks he's protecting me, love was never going to be enough to keep us together.

"I love you too," I whisper into the dark. The harsh reality of our situation settles firmly around us: Theo and I have not been brought together by fate. The plane crash was just shit bad luck. "Can we pretend?" I don't want the heartbreak yet.

"Anything for you." He kisses me again. I hum softly against his lips as warmth spreads out from my chest, chasing away the shadows in my heart.

"Can we stay up and talk all night, for old times' sake?"

"Mm-hmm," he murmurs, his lips against my ear.

It's decided. Until we're rescued, Theo and I aren't doomed. He's not the king, and I'm not a potential pawn for the Firm to control. We can be two idiots in love, kissing in a hot spring under the stars, pretending nothing in the world could ever change that.

Theo lifts me and brings me in front of him. I wrap my legs around his torso and press my fingers into the soft ground behind his shoulders. As we kiss, the earth trembles under my hands.

CHAPTER 25

DAYS ON THE ISLAND: THREE

He's going to be insufferable when he wakes up."

A voice floats on the periphery of my consciousness. I snuggle deeper into my warm cocoon.

"Only if you keep purposely trying to get his knickers in a twist," says a second voice.

"I'm going to wake them up," says a third, more familiar voice.

If I pretend not to hear them, maybe they'll go away.

"Not yet; they're knackered."

"Knackered" is such a perfect word. I feel completely knackered, and I refuse to wake up.

A sprinkle of water falls across my cheeks.

When I open my eyes to find Brooke staring down at me, the watery early sunlight framing her body, I'm certain I only fell asleep seconds ago. "Not yet," I mumble. Theo and I are tangled together, his legs and arms like weights over mine. I couldn't move if I wanted to. (I don't want to.)

"Victoria's vision is blurring. We don't have time to waste."

I quickly sit up as I feel renewed guilt for dropping Victoria's purse in the water. I watch as Victoria douses the hot embers left over from last night's fire. Beads of sweat roll down her sallow skin. "You shouldn't be working if your vision is blurry," I tell her.

"I'm fine. I just wanted you two to get up."

I have no idea if I should believe her or not. "Are you really?"

She smirks. "Guess you'll never know."

Brooke continues. "I'm hoping to go around the side of the volcano and back down again by tonight. You and your boyfriend—sorry, *husband*—need to wake up." She nudges our feet apart with hers, and Theo finally stirs.

"Is it time to go?" His early morning rasp scratches an itch in my brain. If we'd been alone last night, our hot spring make-out session would have been much steamier than it was, but because we both had family members sleeping nearby, we just talked and kissed. Now, though, seeing his sleep-mussed hair and soft lips, my body aches with want. Where Theo is concerned, I never stop wanting. Even if we had forever, I don't think I'd ever get enough of him.

He presses a sleepy kiss against my shoulder, and I cover my wince so he doesn't realize how tender my arm is. While everyone (including an overjoyed Comet) eats blueberries for breakfast (poison-tested by Brooke), I sneak into the trees to inspect my stitches. Streaks of red radiate out and away from the wound. I sway a little on my feet and arrange my shirt so no one else will see them.

Once our pockets are packed with fresh fruit and our bottles refilled from the stream, we continue our trek, my calves and hamstrings burning as the rocky ground gets steeper. Theo and

I hang at the back of the group, Comet practically glued to my side, and Victoria glances over her shoulder at us every few minutes with a scowl on her face.

"Didn't you once tell me that royals are supposed to keep a stiff upper lip? Because your siblings have the opposite of that," I tell Theo as he trails his fingers along the hem of my shirt, grazing the skin of my lower back; it completely scrambles my brain.

"We're also not supposed to engage in PDA. We're all screwing up the job since we crashed." He tips my chin up until my mouth meets his and kisses me. The morning passes in a haze of brief touches and stolen kisses. Since our days together are numbered, we're going to make them count.

After a couple of hours, we stop for a rest. I double over with my hands on my knees, wheezing as I inhale a jagged breath and choke on a cloud of mosquitoes. Brooke, Henry, and I compare bite counts (Brooke wins with thirty-seven) while Theo checks on an uncharacteristically quiet Victoria.

When he rejoins us, he chucks his backpack to the ground as he sits next to me and leans back against a banana tree whose fruit is depressingly out of reach. The mist from yesterday has lingered, and everything is slightly damp.

Judging by his stormy expression, "checking on Victoria" didn't go well. "How is she?" I ask.

"Heads-up!" Henry shouts as he throws a rock up into the tree to knock loose the bananas. He misses by a mile and the rock falls to the ground with a thump.

Theo shakes his head, scrubbing his hands through his hair with a frustrated groan. "I don't know, that's the problem. She won't answer me."

"She doesn't want you to worry."

He picks up a stick and stabs it into the wet dirt. "Too late for that. I've been worried about her since the moment the plane crashed." He tosses the stick into the brush. "If I'd just found her purse—" He cuts himself off with a groan.

Guilt on guilt on guilt.

As if sensing my distress, Comet places his head in my lap. I run my fingers over the soft edges of his floppy ears. "I wish I could help."

"Maybe she needs to talk to someone other than her protective older brother. Will you try?" he asks.

"She hates me! And I'm scared of her!"

"She's harmless," he says.

My eyebrows skyrocket.

"Mostly harmless."

I cross my arms.

"She means well." He helps me up and then puts his hand on the small of my back and pushes me toward his sister. "Good luck," he whispers, giving me a quick kiss on the cheek. He picks up a rock and chucks it into the tree that Henry is trying to shake with his bare hands. "Ten quid says I can get one down first."

"Uh, hey!" I say as I approach the princess. She's lying flat on her back in the soft dirt, and it worries me how pale she is.

"I'm fine," she replies automatically in a flat voice.

"Tell that to your face."

She scowls at me. "That was rude."

"Yeah, well, so are you." I blow out a breath. "I know you don't like me, and I'm sorry that my coming to Canada caused us to get on that plane, but your brother is really worried about you, and he would feel a lot better if you'd be honest about any symptoms you're having. Tell him when you need to slow down, or take a break, or eat."

She rolls her eyes. "Why do you care if I don't like you? Just because you're hooking up with my brother again doesn't mean we have to be bezzies who braid each other's hair."

Why *do* I care? If there's really no future for Theo and me, it shouldn't matter.

I press the issue anyway. "I think there's a world where we could have been friends."

"There's not."

"Only because you're determined to hate me. You never gave me a chance." It feels like she decided to hate me before we even met, and definitely before the story of the wedding blew up on the internet.

A horrible thought dawns on me, and my brain screeches to a halt.

"Did you leak the story of our wedding?" I ask.

Hurt flashes in her eyes, and I realize immediately that I've made a really stupid mistake. She stands up, smoothing her torn skirt.

"Wait! Come back!" I follow her as she turns on her heel and stalks away from me.

She stumbles, grabbing on to a tree for support. Theo reaches out to her, but she shrugs off his touch. "Keep your girlfriend away from me." She takes off again, surprising me with how quickly she scales over mossy logs and slippery rocks.

"Bollocks." Theo sighs heavily and follows his sister into the mist.

"What happened?" Brooke asks.

"It's my fault," I say miserably. "How far do you think she'll get?"

"She's fast," Henry says.

Awesome. It feels like every decision I've made since the

crash is the wrong one, but this is something I can still fix. "I need Winston's supplies from Theo's backpack."

"Is she hurt?" Brooke asks.

"Not yet, but she will be if she runs herself sick." I unzip the kit, grab what I'm looking for, and chase after Theo.

I catch up to them on a steep, rocky stretch of ground. Victoria is on her hands and knees, her entire body shaking.

"You can't do that again," Theo says, lying next to her on his back, breathing like his lungs have collapsed. He throws a passion fruit at her. It bounces off her forehead and rolls away.

"Watch me." Victoria pushes herself up on shaky legs and manages a single step before tripping and falling, scraping up her palms and shins. She swears loudly.

I kneel next to her and slap one of Winston's handcuffs around her wrist, locking the other cuff around my own. "Howdy, Princess."

"What the bloody hell are you doing?" She tugs her arm away from me. Mine follows.

"The key is in my pocket, and I'll uncuff you as soon as you promise you're not going to run away again."

She looks me dead in the eye. "I promise."

I raise an eyebrow at Theo. "Do you believe her?"

"Give me a couple of minutes to catch my breath. If she bolts again, I need to be able to keep up with her."

"Okay." I sit, pulling Victoria down to the ground with me, and unearth two passion fruits from my pocket. "While we wait, I'm sorry for accusing you of selling our marriage certificate to the tabloids."

"You did what?" Theo rasps. He lifts his head and stares at me in disbelief.

"Shut up!" Victoria snaps.

"I don't know why I said it! I shouldn't have."

"I said, be quiet!" she shrieks. "Do you hear that?" She looks up.

"What?"

"An airplane." She leaps to her feet, tugging me up with her. I stumble, but then I hear it. The unmistakable drone of an airplane; the sound of hope.

We all scream in unison.

The plane comes into view, thousands and thousands of feet up. Still, we have to try.

"HELP!!!" We scream and jump and wave our arms in the air, mine and Victoria's cuffed wrists frantically slamming into each other.

"HELP!" I scream the word over and over until my throat is raw, but it's no use. The plane disappears into a cloud, leaving nothing but a contrail and utter devastation in its wake.

Brooke and Henry join us, their eyes wide with hope, but Victoria fills them in on the bad news. Except in her words, it's not so bad. "It's going to turn around," she says confidently.

Brooke and I exchange an uneasy glance. The plane was so high up, and was going so fast, that I'm not confident of anything.

We sit on the rocky side of the volcano in shocked silence. Now that we're out of the forest, the mist has burned away. The sun beats hard on the back of my neck, and the only sound that breaks the silence is the continuous swatting of mosquitoes against skin. If things were bad before, they feel worse now. It's hard not to think of that plane as our last hope, and now that it's gone, it feels more and more like we'll be on this island for longer than any of us thought. And with each passing hour, Victoria is getting sicker. Not to mention Winston's broken leg and Naomi's blistered foot. I drop my head into my hands.

Victoria stands up suddenly. "Look for a boat," she says. But when I look at the ocean, it melts into the horizon on all sides, making it feel like we're the last people on earth. Something about the view nags at the back of my mind—it's wrong, some- how, but I'm too tired and hungry to figure out why.

"There's no one out there," I tell her.

"Then we need to pick up the pace," Victoria shoots back. She takes off at a jog, and thanks to the handcuffs, drags me behind her. Only Comet can keep up.

"I thought you said you were done running!" I gasp. Metal bites painfully into my skin. "Please, wait! I'm going to fall."

"Don't threaten me with a good time," she says.

"If I fall, you fall!"

"Play stupid games, win stupid prizes!"

"Stop quoting Taylor Swift!"

She stops abruptly and I slam into her back. "Ow!"

"I need to sit down. I don't feel good." She bends over to catch her breath. Comet sniffs around our feet, whining frantically.

"What's wrong, boy?" He clamps the leg of my pants be- tween his teeth and pulls hard. "What are you—"

The ground underneath our feet collapses.

CHAPTER 26

land hard on my back, and I can't breathe. I gasp for air, but there is none. Next to me, Comet springs to his feet and whines.

I'm going to die. I can't breathe.

Victoria's ashen face appears above me. "Relax. Breathe slowly. In and out. In and out."

"I can't!" I rasp, barely pushing the words out. I shake my head as tears stream sideways across my cheeks.

She holds my shoulders and moves so her face is the only thing I can see. "Breathe in, one two three, breathe out, one two three." Her eyes mirror my own panic, but her voice is low and calm.

I breathe in time with her until the pressure on my lungs finally eases. She releases my shoulders and sits back on her heels, the handcuffs dragging my wrist with her.

I glance around and see a hollow tunnel made of rough stone walls. The only light is coming from above, where the ground caved in at least ten feet above us. Comet scratches at the wall, his two front paws scrabbling uselessly against stone.

"The ground just fell in. I don't understand what happened," Victoria says.

"Have you felt any earthquakes today?"

"I mean, yeah. Small ones. Do you think an earthquake caused this?"

I press my hands to the cool stone. "If it did, we need to get out of here ASAP. The walls could cave in on us if another one hits."

"Wren! Victoria!" Theo yells from somewhere above us.

"Down here!" we call.

He crouches near the edge of the cave-in, and the unstable ground shifts, sending loose debris cascading into the tunnel.

"Not too close!" Brooke and Henry grab Theo's arms to keep him from sliding in. Dirt falls into my eyes and mouth, and Victoria pulls us away as I have a coughing fit.

"Are you all right?" Theo asks.

The air clears enough for me to crane my neck to see him, bright spots bursting in my vision from the sunlight overhead. "We're okay!"

"No, we're not!" Victoria yells. "We're stuck in this freaking underground tunnel . . . *thing*, and we need to get out before it collapses on top of us."

"It looks like a lava tube," Brooke says. "They're formed by flowing lava—"

"No need for a science lesson, Professor!" Victoria snaps.

"Wren, boost Victoria up and we'll reach down and pull her out," Henry says.

Brooke nods in agreement, and I wonder where her democratic ideals are now.

"The princess first? You sure we shouldn't vote on it?" I deadpan.

"Wren." Brooke's voice is exasperated.

"Okay, okay! I'm kidding."

"No you're not," Victoria mutters.

I lace my fingers to boost her up before realizing that the handcuffs are going to make this impossible. I reach into my pocket to get the key, but it's not there. "Hang on." I search my other pocket, but it's also empty. My stomach drops. "Uh-oh."

"Where's the key?"

I comb through each pocket again, and then again. It's not here. I finally meet Victoria's hard glare, alarm blaring in my chest. "I lost it."

"That's not funny."

"What makes you think I'm joking?"

"Theo! Your bloody *wife* lost the key to the handcuffs!" Victoria yells.

"Did it fall out of your pocket when you fell?" Theo asks.

Victoria and I drop to our knees and frantically search the ground. I run my hands over stone and dirt until my palms are raw.

"Where is it?" she snaps.

"Give me a minute!" I close my eyes and try to recall the last time I definitely had the key. I remember putting it into my pocket with the handcuffs and running after Victoria. When I found her, I gave her some passion fruit, also from my pocket.

Did I feel it then?

I don't know. I realize with a sinking feeling that it could have fallen out just about anywhere.

"I don't think it's down here," I call back, after several tense minutes of guilty silence from me and pointed huffs and puffs from Victoria.

"Do you have an idea where it might be?" Theo asks in a strained voice.

"I might have dropped it where Victoria and I were jumping when the plane flew by."

I hear whispers. They're probably all conferring about what an idiot I am. One by one, their faces disappear, leaving Victoria and me alone and giving her time to probably kill me.

"Should we look again?" I ask.

"All right," she says flatly.

We resume our search, and while it's obvious she wants to pretend I don't exist, it's nearly impossible since we're chained together. Every time I shift to the left, she yanks me hard to the right.

After a long, uncomfortable stretch of silence, she slumps against the wall of the lava tube and lets her head rest on her knees. I lean against the hardened lava and take slow, steadying breaths. *Don't panic, don't panic.* Comet settles next to me, nuzzling his head under my legs.

"I really am sorry I accused you of selling our marriage certificate to the tabloids," I say quietly. It feels like the others have been gone for an eternity.

She doesn't respond.

"Does Henry really want to be the king, or is it just an act?"

Nothing.

"The two of us could probably lift Comet and sort of toss him up. Do you want to try?"

I might as well be talking to the magma wall. I use my cuffed hand to scratch an itch on my nose, because my left arm is once again throbbing in pain. The red streaks have grown, and pus is oozing from the stitches. If I die chained to Victoria, I wonder how she'll react.

"This wouldn't have happened if you hadn't run off. *Twice*," I say.

"Are you joking?" She turns to me with fire in her eyes. "You are a *complete* blighter! None of this would have bloody well happened if you weren't here! You should have stayed in Chicago where you belong and out. Of. Our. Lives."

I bite back my smile. "And that's how you make a princess talk to you again."

She screams in frustration.

"I'm sorry, okay! I'm sorry about the handcuffs—I'm well aware this is all my fault, trust me. And I'm sorry I ruined your life."

She rolls her eyes with a huff. "Don't be dramatic."

"Sorry."

She drags a hand over her face. "Stop apologizing to me! I'm not the one who needs to hear it."

I jerk my head back. "What does that mean?"

She whirls on me, her eyes blazing. "I don't like you because Theo was utterly gutted when he came home! All I knew was that you spent a week with him, and he had your dog for some reason, and he tried not to talk about you, but he sucked at it, and every time he mentioned your name it was obvious that he's still bloody in love with you, but you were nowhere to be found!"

Defensiveness flares in my chest. "It's not that easy to get in contact with the King."

She looks unimpressed. "You should have tried harder. He was devastated about our mum's death, and what else?" She taps her mouth with her finger. "Oh right! There was this small thing about assuming the throne and planning a coronation he never wanted." She glares daggers at me. "You should have been there."

"How? By scaling the palace gates?" I shout, my annoyance with her reaching a boiling point.

She keeps talking like she didn't even hear me. "And you should have thanked me for taking care of Comet for three months."

"I might have if—"

"And now you and your stupid wedding are going to bring our family an astronomical amount of press at the worst possible moment. The entire world is just waiting for Theo to screw up because he's young, and people are going to use the fact that he married an American stranger as an excuse to call him a nutter, and when you leave, he's going to be heartbroken all over again, and I won't be able to help him!" She furiously blinks away the tears building at the corners of her eyes, and it finally hits me why she's so mad at me.

"I love him too," I say softly.

Her head snaps up. "What?"

"You're worried about him, and you love him. We have that in common."

She crosses her arms, letting my wrist hang painfully in front of her. "We'll see how much you love him when the tabloids are stalking you and printing lies about you and acting like your private life is their public business just because you're with Theo." She quickly swipes away an errant tear. "Mum always said we have to give the press something to talk about, but he'll never give them you, and that's why it won't work out."

"We know what we're up against, and we're not going to fight it."

Her brows knit together suspiciously. "I saw you two tangled up together this morning."

My heart surges, making it painfully obvious to myself how much I wish Theo and I could find a way to make this last. "It's only until we're rescued."

Red splotches appear on her cheeks. "So, you're not even going to try?"

I'm confused by her sudden outrage. "You *just* said that we're doomed!"

"And you proved me right." She sweeps her eyes over me in a way that makes me feel indescribably small. "He deserves better than you, anyway." She turns away. "And I would never, ever sell him out to the tabloids. If you don't know that, you don't know anything about our family."

I slump against the wall as we lapse into a strained silence. The longer we sit here, the more the walls feel like they're closing in. Victoria leans to the side and dry heaves, and I realize that she needs a distraction as badly as I do. "Will you tell me about your family, then?" I ask.

She throws me a sidelong glance. "What do you want to know?"

"What's Henry's deal?"

"With the monarchy or with Theo?"

"Both. And why has he been flirting with me?"

She sighs in exasperation. "How dense are you? I bet it drove Henry nuts to watch Theo pretend he's not in love with you. That's a major chip on his shoulder."

"What is?"

"The fact that Theo doesn't go after what he wants or appreciate what he has."

"Like what? His title?"

"What else? Mum never gave Henry the attention she gave Theo, so Henry made himself into the perfect little royalist. He learned everything there is to know in every boring English history book. He thought that she'd love him more that way."

"How'd that work out?" I ask, although I can already guess the answer.

Victoria slants me a look. "How do you think? She was a busy monarch and a widow with six kids. She had so little attention to give, and she gave it all to Theo. It didn't matter that she was critical of him most of the time, Henry was still jealous. And now he's frustrated that Theo doesn't even want to be the king. Henry wants him to appreciate it."

"'It'?"

She waves her unchained hand in the air. "The Crown. The title. The influence. All of it."

"Meanwhile, Theo thinks Henry would make a better king," I say.

"He would think that," she says with an exaggerated eye roll. After a beat, she adds, "They'd both be a lot bloody happier if that was the case."

"Would you want it?" I ask.

She crooks an eyebrow. "Does it matter?"

"I'm curious."

She considers this for a long time. "We're not strangers to the criticisms of the monarchy, and to be honest, I don't think it will last forever. It'd be brilliant to be involved in shaping the future of it, but . . ." She trails off with a shake of her head. "I don't know why I said that. What I really want is for my family to be happy again."

"I want that too," I say.

We fall into silence again. There must be a timeline out there where Theo and his siblings aren't royalty; where instead of going to state dinners and royal balls, the six of them spend their weekends playing "football" together before Theo bakes them a banoffee pie (football and banoffee pie being the two most British things I can imagine while stuck in a hole in the ground, with an arm throbbing in pain, chained to a princess with a grudge). If Theo and I met in that timeline, I think he'd have brought me home to meet them, and I bet Victoria and I could have been friends. She's pretty funny when she's not trying to make me cry.

"What did you do during Comet Week?" I finally ask.

"The same things as everyone else, probably."

Probably not, considering she had a bunker to hide in while the rest of us only had existential dread. "Humor me. If we're going to die in a freaking lava tube, I'd like to know something about you."

She closes her eyes and takes several shaky breaths. "I'll *127 Hours* your hand before I let us die down here."

I grab her hand. "Are you okay?"

She pulls her fingers from mine and opens her eyes. "You went a bit blurry there, but you're back now," she says, and it's obvious that she doesn't want me to press further.

"Okay, so you watch survival movies. That's something I didn't know before."

She sighs and picks at the fraying hem of her skirt. "I run a lot, but I hate it ninety-five percent of the time."

"When do you like it?"

"When I'm the fastest."

"That tracks."

I drum my fingernails against the ground until Victoria glares at me. I shiver and realize I'm covered in goose bumps. "Why is it so cold down here?"

"It's not that cold."

Untrue, but whatever. "Have you ever eaten banoffee pie?"

"Yeah. Theo makes a great one."

I *knew* it. "What's a banoffee?"

"You're painfully American," she says, but her eye roll is interrupted when the ground and walls begin to shake. I throw my arms over our heads as rocks crash into the lava tube. The sound is deafening. We crouch with our arms around each other and Comet until the earthquake stops.

A hush falls over us after the last rock falls, but I'm too afraid to move.

"I'm all right. Are you?" Victoria asks after an unsettling stretch of silence, her arms still pulling me tightly to her.

"I think so," I say, swallowing a tremor of fear. Now is not the time to be paralyzed. We need to get the hell out of here. "We can't be down here if that happens again. Hand me that rock." I point to a sharp rock by her foot. She releases her white-knuckled grip on my arm and hands it to me. I lift the rock and Victoria cries out.

"Blimey, Wren! I was joking about cutting your hand off."

"Cover your eyes." I hold the rock like a knife and slam it into the chain connecting the handcuffs. It barely leaves a scratch. I do it again. I'm lifting my injured arm to strike the metal a third time when a guttural roar like a jet engine rumbles through the earth beneath us. I freeze with my hand in the air, waiting for the world to fall apart. Comet tucks his head into his paws.

"What the bloody hell was that? Another earthquake?" Victoria asks.

"I don't think so." It felt like something worse.

Something bigger.

CHAPTER 27

Victoria! Wren! Comet!" Brooke's face appears at the mouth of the cave-in. "Can you hear me?" Comet barks at the sound of her voice.

"We're okay. You guys?" I call.

"Um. We're alive." Her voice is strained beyond anything I've heard before. I break out in a cold sweat.

"Where's Theo?" Victoria and I demand in unison.

"He's coming," Brooke says, her eyes now fixed on something we can't see.

"Did you find the key?" Victoria asks.

"No. Not yet . . ." Her attention drifts away from us again.

"Brooke!" I clap my hands. "What's going on? Where is everyone else?"

It's hard to tell from so far away, but she looks terrified.

"Just tell us what happened!" My mind races through a hundred horrible scenes, each one worse than the last.

"The earthquake triggered a . . . a . . ." She trails off, eyes wide with fear. I pick up the sharp rock with my slick palm and slam it into the handcuffs again. Pain radiates from my shoulder to my fingertips.

"Snap out of it, Brooke!" Victoria shrieks.

My sister breaks out of her trance and looks down at us. "The volcano is erupting."

Blood rushes in my ears. I blink to get the black spots out of my vision. I think I'm hallucinating a worst-case scenario, until I see the terror on Victoria's face and realize I heard correctly. We're trapped in a lava tube during a volcanic eruption.

I'm too horrified to move.

If I'm about to die, I don't want to be racked with guilt when I go.

"I lost your insulin," I tell Victoria.

Her face freezes in shock, but then her eyes keep roving the walls, looking for a way out. "Apologize later. We have to get out of here."

The rumble within the earth is growing; I can feel it in the soles of my feet, and I have to get this off my chest in case I don't get another chance. "I found your purse after the crash. I wrapped it around me, but it was too hard to swim. I felt like it was dragging me underwater, which doesn't make sense because it was so small, but that's just an excuse because I *did* bring it to shore, but then you made a snarky comment about sharks so . . . I let it sink."

Victoria wrenches the rock from my hand and slams it into the metal. On her sixth strike, the handcuffs break in half.

"Remind me to speak to Winston about his crap handcuffs," she says, tossing the rock to the side.

"Hurry!" Brooke shouts. "I'll grab your hand!" She leans into the tube and stretches her hands as far as they'll go.

I brace myself against the stone wall and lace my fingers together to give Victoria a boost. She puts her hands on my shoulders and brings her face close to mine. "Don't tell Theo about the bag." Her breath smells alarmingly fruity.

"Why not?"

"It won't change anything. It'll just be another fact he uses to torture himself, and your guilt isn't more important than his peace of mind." She places her foot in my palms and climbs onto my shoulders. She pushes onto her tiptoes and I think there's no way Brooke is going to be strong enough to pull her out, but then Henry and Theo appear, each stretching a long arm to haul Victoria up and out of the lava tube. The moment her feet hit solid ground, Theo jumps down next to me.

"What the hell are you doing?" I scream.

"Getting you out of here," he shouts. "On my shoulders, now!"

"What about you?"

"I swear to God, Wren, if you don't get on my shoulders, *now*—"

I place my foot in his laced fingers and he quickly lifts me up. Henry grabs my hands and drags me out of the lava tube, the rough stone wall scraping across my body, stitches stretching and tearing in my arm. I roll onto the ground and shield my eyes against falling ash and debris. Brooke throws her arms over me. A thick column of white steam spews from the volcano above us. The heat is unbearable, and if we were any closer to the top, the steam would be burning us alive. It still might, if we don't get out of here ASAP. The earth around the crater is cracking, and red-hot, bubbling lava is seeping through the fissures and sliding in our direction. Brooke may have told us that the volcano was erupting, but nothing could have prepared me for this. I choke on the rancid, sulfuric smell.

"Run!" Theo screams from down below.

"Run now," Henry agrees. "I'll stay with Theo."

Victoria hesitates.

"RUN!" I scream, and she listens, stumbling across the rocks as she sprints away from us.

"Wren!" Brooke grabs my hand and tries to tug me away.

"Go!"

"Not without you."

I glance back down in the lava tube, where Theo's trying to scale the wall. A tremor rolls through my body. He'll never make it. The stone is too smooth, and there are no footholds or rocks for him to grab. Next to him, Comet is on his hind legs with his paws extended toward me, his big, trusting eyes begging to be rescued.

"I can't." I blink away tears.

She glances down at Theo and then pulls me close. "Don't be a hero, and don't be an idiot."

"I'll never forgive myself if I don't try. Go without me." My eyes burn from the ash and steam, and my skin feels like it's on fire.

She takes my hand in hers and squeezes hard enough to bruise. "Promise me that you won't wait until it's too late."

"I can't—" My voice breaks off as fear claws its way up my throat. I don't know if that's a promise that I can keep.

Henry pulls Brooke aside and whispers something into her ear. She glances at me again and then nods. She gives my hand one final squeeze. "I'll meet you at the beach."

When she's gone, Henry and I stare up at the flowing lava.

It's moving quickly over the steep terrain, and I doubt we have more than a couple of minutes. I look back at Theo. His shoes slide against hardened magma as he drops back to the ground.

He growls in frustration. "You need to go, Wren."

I grind my molars. "No. We're getting you out." I look at Henry. "Hold my feet."

He digs his heels into the ground and braces himself, wrapping his wrists around my ankles and holding tightly to my calves. I crawl over the edge of the hole and dangle against the side of the wall, arms outstretched. My head swims.

I close my eyes. "Send him up!"

My hands close around two small, hairy paws. Comet thrashes against the wall, his back paws scrambling for impossible purchase. I look down. Theo has his hands under Comet's butt, pushing him up toward me.

"Got him?" Theo asks.

"I think so."

Henry starts to pull us up, but gravity immediately drags Comet back down. He's whining and twisting and so, so heavy in my arms. "Be still, boy. Please be still," I beg as his nails dig into my palms. My heart throbs painfully against my rib cage. "He's slipping."

Comet whines, his brown eyes wide with fear.

"You've got this," Theo says, but I don't feel like I do. I'm so tired, and everything hurts so bad.

"I don't," I sob. One of Comet's paws slips from my sweaty hands, and all ninety pounds of him transfer to my injured arm. My second hand gives out, and Comet falls into Theo's waiting grasp. Blood trickles out of my torn stitches.

"Listen to me, Wheeler," Theo yells as he secures my thrashing dog. The steam and ash are so thick in the air that I can barely see, and breathing feels impossible. "Can you hear me?"

"I'm sorry," I cry, and I can't believe it's come to this. All we've been through, and this is how it ends. Caught in a freaking volcano, and I'm not strong enough to save the person (and pup) I fell in love with. I was so stupid to ever even daydream a happy ending for us.

"What did you say in your wedding vows?" he asks.

The blood rushing to my head makes it hard to think. "All dogs are worth saving?" I sob harder.

"No. Well, yes, but no. You said you owe me one, and I'm cashing in the favor. And what did I say in *my* vows?"

This one is easy; the words are burned in my mind. "You said we were fate." I don't know if he even hears me over Henry screaming and Comet barking and the world ripping apart.

"I said I won't give up on you. You are the strongest person I know, and you *can* do this. Now save your dog."

His voice cuts through the chaos and I hear every word clearly. Theo pushes Comet up into my arms and with Henry pulling on my legs, I summon every ounce of strength left in my body and drag him over the edge. He flops on top of me, his weight knocking the breath from my chest, and licks the tears off my face.

"Ready to go again?" Henry asks. I nudge Comet off my belly and pull myself back over the edge. Theo's hands reach for mine, the tips of his fingers just barely grazing.

"I can't reach," he says.

"Try again," I insist.

"The lava is coming," Henry warns from above. "We're running out of time."

Theo freezes, and even through the ash and steam, I can see panic in his eyes. "You have to go." His voice is pure rasp.

"*Try again!*"

He walks back as far as he can in the cramped space and then runs forward, placing his foot on the wall. He scrambles up and I reach out, grabbing his hands like a flash of lightning. Gravity drags him down, pulling me with him and nearly dislocating my shoulder. Henry shouts as he slides forward, feet slamming into the dirt and stopping all three of us from crashing back into the lava tube. Slowly but surely, Theo uses my hands as an anchor as he walks his way up the wall.

I scream as my sutures tug against swollen skin. Theo releases my injured arm and grips the edge of the lava tube with his free hand. He pulls himself up, his biceps straining with the effort. We collapse next to each other on our backs, gasping for fresh air that doesn't exist. Theo looks at me and places a scratched and bloody hand on my cheek. He leans in and kisses me. I don't realize I'm crying until I taste salt on my tongue, but I don't care. I'll kiss him while the world burns around us.

Henry clears his throat. "We *really* don't have time for this."

Theo and I pull apart and stare at Henry, who looks at us like we've lost our minds.

"Lava, remember?" He nods in the direction of the crater.

Theo and I look up. A stream of lava as wide as the length of a semitruck gushes toward us, devouring everything in its path. Theo yanks me up and we run, Comet leading the way, down the side of the volcano and away from certain death.

I run until my vision blurs and my windpipe feels like it's collapsing. I've lost track of how many times I've fallen and scraped my knees, my shins, my palms, but we keep moving forward, and we're faster than the lava. We're outrunning it.

"Can we stop?" I gasp.

Theo and Henry slow down; I don't so much slow as I come to a crashing, fumbling stop. I trip over my own feet and land on my bad arm, a shock of pain reverberating all the way to my bones, and I realize *this* is how I'm going to die. Not from the volcano, but from the pain in my arm. "It was nice knowing you both. Theo a little more than Henry, no offense."

Theo kneels next to me. "You all right, Wheeler?"

Wheel-a. I'm obsessed with the way my name sounds in his mouth. He was right. I am half in love with my new nickname, and I'm fully in love with him.

I push his hair out of his eyes. "I can't move. I'm leaving this world Pompeii-style."

"It's hardly a Pompeii-level volcano."

"Donate my GoFundMe money to Comet, and make sure he knows it's from me and not Victoria."

Theo's sigh is long-suffering. "When we're rescued, you and Victoria are going to have to figure out this Comet issue on your own. Maybe work out shared custody."

"Between countries?"

He tucks an errant strand of hair behind my ear and trails his hand along my neck. "Sometimes I like to pretend it's possible."

I don't think we're talking about my dog anymore, and suddenly I can't move for completely different reasons. I'm paralyzed by fear. The closer we get to the bottom of the volcano, the closer we are to rescue.

Ahead of us, Comet barks, and a voice calls my name.

"That's Brooke," Theo says. His hand is in mine, and I don't know how long it's been there, but it strikes me as important that we keep reaching for each other. He helps me to my feet. "Just a little further."

"Do we have to?" I sag against his body. "We could build ourselves a tree house and learn how to fish."

He smiles sadly at me, and I wonder when I'll stop wanting things I can't have. "Victoria needs us to keep going," he says, and I know he's right. She's what matters right now.

At the bottom of the volcano, we enter a forest like the one on the other side of the island, where Naomi, Winston, and Reggie are hopefully safe from the eruption. The trees filter out some of the ash, and it's easier to breathe under their cover. We catch up to Brooke and Victoria, who are both covered in so much ash it's hard to see anything but the whites of their eyes.

"You look awful," I say, because it's the only thing that won't have me bawling on Brooke's shoulder.

"So do you," she agrees. She leads me away from the group so they can't hear us. "You're really in love with him, aren't you?"

I glance over her shoulder at Theo, who is almost strangling his siblings in a hug, and it's hard to breathe. "Yeah," I sigh.

It's gut-wrenching that the only part of my future that I'm sure about is the one thing I'll never have.

We find another stream and take a minute to scrub the ash off our faces in hopeful silence. We've almost made it. Rescue is imminent.

"How close are we to the beach?" Victoria asks, her eyes bright with anticipation.

"I can hear the waves again. I think we're close," Brooke says.

"Let's get moving," Theo says.

We're coughing, wheezing, and limping as we push through

the forest. The sun sets, but we don't stop. We get closer and closer to the water, the salty air providing a welcome relief from the oppressive smell of sulfur and ash as the volcano continues to emit a column of steam into the atmosphere.

We walk until we hit sand. This beach doesn't have the same cliffs that we left behind on the other side of the island, but otherwise, it looks the same.

No roads, no homes, no businesses, no cars, no people. I look left and right at the dark empty shoreline unfurling in both directions.

We're surrounded by nothing but salt, and sand, and an ash-blackened sky.

"How will we find the people who live here?" Victoria asks. It's the question I've been dreading in my bones.

Brooke gives me an uneasy look that says everything I've tried not to dwell on. It's what gave me pause looking over the island at our highest point.

There's no one here.

We trekked this entire island in two days, and if people lived here, we would have seen evidence of it.

The village Reggie promised us doesn't exist. We've made it as far as we can go, and we're alone.

CHAPTER 28

There's no one on this island," Theo says in disbelief. All the color has drained from his face.

In front of us, the black ocean stretches into eternity. Behind us, the volcano is still spewing ash. We're trapped, we're injured, we're sick, and we're no closer to being rescued.

"Look at the bright side, Your Majesty," Henry says, and even I can tell that he has nothing positive to say.

Theo stares blankly at his brother.

"Never mind," Henry mumbles.

"Say it," Theo challenges.

"You'll get to skive off your coronation." Henry runs a hand through his curls. "Sorry, bad joke. I was just trying to lighten the mood."

"Is the fact that we're stuck on a deserted island too depressing for you?" Victoria says, but it doesn't have her usual bite. She stumbles sideways.

"Whoa." I grab her arm. She shakes me off before walking several paces away. She wobbles again, then sinks to her knees in the sand while she throws up all the water she's consumed today. "No one look at me! I'm disgusting." She tucks her head between her knees and presses her shaking fists into the sand, the broken handcuff still hanging from her wrist. I close my eyes and force myself to think. We can still fix this.

There has to be a way to buy her more time.

"She needs to eat," I say finally. It's not groundbreaking, but it's true. Theo lost the backpack at some point during the cave-in/rescue/volcanic eruption, and none of us have eaten in hours.

"I'll look for food," Henry says. "You three split up and walk along the shore. Reggie was confident about our location. We can't give up yet."

"Not to be a downer, but Reggie didn't know shit," Brooke says.

"Henry's right. We'll split up." I'm surprised to hear myself agree with him, but we don't have any other choice. We either keep looking, or we give up, and Theo and I promised each other we wouldn't do that.

"You two go north, I'll go south," Brooke says, and the false optimism in her voice makes me nauseous.

"I'll stay with Tor and build a fire," Henry tells the rest of us. Theo tosses him the lighter from his pocket. "Look for the flames to find your way back to us."

Theo kneels in front of Victoria. "In case I don't get a chance to say it—"

She pushes him away. "Abso-bloody-lutely not. Get up."

Theo sputters, but Victoria doesn't have time for him. She motions between Brooke and me. "Uh-uh, break it up."

Brooke freezes, halfway toward hugging me.

"*Step. Away,*" Victoria orders. Brooke drops her arms. "We are not saying goodbye, and we are not crying." She turns to Theo. "This isn't a funeral; I turn eighteen in a few weeks, and I intend to be alive to celebrate. Do you understand?"

Silence. Awkward, uncomfortable silence.

"I said, *do you understand?*" She fixes me with her best glare.

"Yes, Your Highness," I say as I dip into an unplanned curtsy.

Victoria grins triumphantly. "Good. Now leave and don't come back without help, food, or a plan to get us rescued." She checks an imaginary watch. "You have one hour."

Theo and I hurry off before she can give more orders. We walk to the edge of the water, where we both slip off our shoes and walk in the soft, wet sand, the tide coming up over our toes, sinking a little with every step.

Theo throws me a sidelong glance, his eyes dancing with delight. "I cannot believe you curtsied to my little sister."

"I don't know what happened! It's like I was possessed by the spirit of your ancestors!"

He bites back a laugh and shakes his head. "I don't even know who you are anymore. You used to be so idealistic." He sighs wistfully.

"I wasn't so much anti-royalty as I was pro-getting-under-your-skin," I tease as I kick water into his face.

He tackles me in a bear hug, soaking us both in cold water, and before guilt or worry or fear can set back in, Theo gently tugs me into his side and wraps his arm around my shoulders. "Pretend with me."

"Pretend what?" I ask, though I already know I'll say yes.

He plants a kiss on my temple. "That we met on your senior trip to London, and I asked you on a date."

I close my eyes, letting the false memory wash over me. "What did we do?"

"We went to an animal shelter and signed up as dog walkers for the afternoon. We took them to the private palace gardens, along with a picnic basket filled with pie that I made specifically to impress you."

My chest burns. I can picture it so easily. It strikes me that even in his perfect reality, he's still him, a royal by birth, and I'm still me, an eighteen-year-old American who loves to play with dogs. But with a slight change in circumstances, we might have had a chance.

"You really pulled out all the stops."

"I didn't have much time to impress you, I had to do everything I could."

"What happened next?"

"The world was never ending, and we fell in love the way most people get to, without the threat of complete annihilation hanging over our heads."

I sigh. "Sounds too easy."

"You flew back home at the end of the week, but you were proper obsessed with me—"

"Bloody unlikely!" I tease, pulling out my dreadful British accent.

His mouth hitches up in an easy smile. "Fine, I was obsessed with you. You were all I thought about. But when I missed you so much that I thought I'd go mad, I picked up the phone, and I called you. When I scrolled through your social media, I commented on every single picture. I didn't haunt the palace hallways in the dead of night because I was crawling out of my own skin thinking about you."

"You didn't?"

"Not in this timeline. And when my mum died, you're the first person I called."

He has no idea how much I wish that's what happened. "I hated the thought of you going through that alone."

"That's the thing, though. I never really felt alone, even with you on the other side of the pond. In this scenario, we never went more than an hour without texting each other. Our friends took the piss out of us, but it didn't matter, because we were happy."

"Sounds delightfully uncomplicated for a long-distance relationship with a reigning monarch."

"It was, until you were about to start university, and I went mad with jealousy. I imagined you in a new place, surrounded by hundreds of smart and interesting blokes from all over the world. Guys who could walk you to class without bodyguards and take you on a date without the tabloids stalking you—"

"I thought we were pretending away the bad stuff."

He shakes his head. "You're right. Sorry. You were about to start school, so I invited you on vacation before you got swamped in your studies. A week on a tropical island in Portugal."

"Does Victoria hate me in this timeline, too?"

He laughs. "To retain some semblance of reality, I'll say she's skeptical of you. But my siblings didn't come, obviously, and neither did Brooke. They'd be at home, where they would be safe and healthy and not intruding on our romantic holiday."

His voice cracks at the mention of Victoria's health, and guilt burns my stomach like acid.

"Do you want to turn around and stay with her? I can keep going on my own," I say.

He furiously blinks back his tears. "No. *No*. We're avoiding reality by pretending everything is fine. Help me out here, Wheeler. I learned from the best."

I squeeze his hand in mine. "What happened when we saw each other again? In Portugal?"

He clears his throat. "Right. Our reunion. I was so bloody nervous. What if things were different?"

"And were they?"

He tilts his head back to the sky, considering this. I'm not sure if he's pondering a real answer or a fake one. "I'd started to wonder if I'd made you up. Like maybe in my head, you were a little bit prettier, quicker, funnier. I'd imagined that moment hundreds of times, and by the time it arrived, I was worried reality wouldn't live up to the you in my head, because how could it."

I slant him a look. "It's impossible to overestimate how funny I am."

Theo laughs. "True. But my imagination sucks arse, because it forgot the way your nose scrunches when you're pretending to be mad at me, and the way your eyes light up when I say your name, and the way I'm happiest when I'm with you, even when comets or airplanes are literally falling out of the sky."

My heart is beating too fast. This was supposed to be a game of pretend, but it's gotten way too real. He doesn't know that I let Victoria's purse sink because of a stupid grudge, and the sweeter he is, the guiltier I feel.

A strong wave sweeps over our legs, and I realize we've drifted deeper into the ocean than I thought. I stop in my tracks.

Theo rubs a hand over the back of his neck. "Was that too much?"

A breeze rolls through the trees and scatters goose bumps along my arms, and I can't pretend for another second.

"We have to go back and be with Victoria."

He furrows his brow. "We're looking for help."

"You know there's no help out here." I throw my arms wide in the black. "This is all there is. Either rescue comes or it doesn't, but either way, we need to be with your sister. She's putting on a brave face, but she's not okay."

He freezes for one heart-stopping second, and then he takes my hand. "You're right. Let's go be with her."

If possible, I feel even worse. "I'll feel so guilty if anything happens to her."

He silences me with a kiss. "I already told you not to worry about the phone call. C'mon."

He tugs us back down the beach. My calves burn from trekking through sand, but before long we find Victoria hauling an armful of firewood.

She stops to catch her breath. "Did you find anything?"

Theo shakes his head. "Nah. We're back to hang out with you."

She puts her hand on her hip and cocks it. "Why?"

"Wren was worried. Turns out she likes you, despite your best efforts." Theo unloads a handful of branches from Victoria's arms. She looks annoyed and relieved at the same time.

"He's lying," I say dryly. We can't go letting the princess know just how worried I am about her.

Theo chuckles. "Your conscience wouldn't be so guilty if you didn't like her at least a little bit."

"Guilty?" Victoria's eyes snap to mine. "You told him about my bag?"

"Told me what?" Theo frowns.

My heart sinks. "I . . . no . . . we weren't talking about that . . ." I say desperately.

Victoria's eyes widen as she realizes her mistake.

Theo turns to me. "What's she talking about?"

Ooops, Victoria mouths over Theo's shoulder as she backs away from us.

"Hey." Theo steps close to me. "What's wrong?"

"I found Victoria's bag and let it sink on purpose," I say in one rushed breath.

His gaze clouds as he steps away from me. "What the fuck?"

"I didn't know about the insulin, but I knew the bag was hers. I found it and brought it to shore, but then she made a joke about sharks attacking me, so I let it sink. If she—" My voice breaks off, and I can't bring myself to say the word. "If anything happens to her, it's my fault."

He shakes his head. "You told Victoria about this?"

I nod, and his face falls.

"Why didn't you tell me?"

"I didn't know how." I can barely push the words past the lump in my throat.

Theo rakes his hands through his hair, looking dazed. I step toward him, but he holds out his hand. "Please," he says. "I just need a minute to think." The flash of betrayal in his expression makes one thing crystal clear: he will never look at me the same way again.

I press my lips together as tears burn behind my eyes. "I'll find a way to fix this. I'll figure it out. I can do this," I promise as I back away from him. When my feet hit cold water, I turn and run.

"Wren—wait," he calls.

Don't follow me, I think, but I'm still devastated when he doesn't.

⚜   ⚜   ⚜

I run along the shore until my lungs give out, and then I walk until the sandy beach turns into volcanic rock. The rocks form a shallow tidepool, and I step over them and into the water. I shiver; this is the opposite of a hot spring, and I hate it. I pretend I'm in an ice bath, which is another thing health nuts do in the name of wellness; *Gwyneth Paltrow has definitely done a cold plunge,* I think. I sink until the water hits my belly button, and I know immediately that this isn't wellness. I feel violently *unwell.* My teeth chatter and my body spasms while I try to think of a way out of this.

I need a new plan, and this one has to be something I can do on my own. I don't have Naomi or Brooke or Theo to help me anymore.

I squint through the dark, and at first, my frozen mind has trouble separating the black sky from the black water, but then I blink, and a shape emerges that's just a little bit blacker than the sky *or* the water. I move toward it until I hit the volcanic rock barrier.

I squint harder, and it's small, but it's there. A big black blob in the middle of the horizon.

Land?

If rescue isn't coming for us, we'll have to get it ourselves. We need to find another island or a passing ship. Either way, we need to leave this island.

I've never felt as alone as when I finally drag myself out of the cold tidepool and up to where rocky sand meets the trees. I gather fallen shoots of bamboo and slowly pull them from the trees. My muscles are burning and my fingers blistered by the time I move on to gathering vines. The temperature must have dropped, because my feet are dry and I'm somehow colder than I was in the ice bath, and dizzy, too.

I can't remember the last time I drank water. My legs give out as I drop a heavy vine next to my collection of bamboo. I wrap it around the bamboo and tie it off. It's not going to win any awards, but I'm on the right track. I decide to take a five-minute rest, and then I'll get back to working on my raft.

Just five minutes. That's all I need, and then I'll be good as new.

I'm almost there.

I can do this.

I curl up on my side and close my eyes.

CHAPTER 29

I dream I'm floating.

Except . . . everything hurts. Nothing is supposed to hurt in a dream. Also, this is bumpier than my usual dream-floating.

I dream I'm being jostled?

Hmmm.

I open my eyes and scream.

I scramble out of the arms of the figure carrying me, spraying sand in every direction, including into my own eyes.

"*Ow!*" I press the heels of my hands against my eyes, pushing the grains of sand in deeper.

"Careful! You'll make it worse!" Henry's voice is in my ear.

"What are you doing here?" I demand. "You scared me!"

His fingers brush against my wrist. "Let me help."

"It hurts!" I flail around until my elbow slams into what can only be Henry's head.

He hisses in pain. "Hence the help!"

"I can't see!"

"Get your hands out of your bloody eyes!" he yells in exasperation.

I drop my hands and try again to pry open my eyes, but the sand and my tear ducts have fused together to form an unbreakable bond. "I can't open them!"

Henry gently circles my wrists with his hands. "Then let me bloody help you!"

"Fine!" I shout. I stop moving, and he leads me toward the sound of the waves lapping against the shore. I kneel in wet sand and tip my head back as he pours handful after handful of briny seawater over my eyes. The water spills down the sides of my cheeks as I blink out painful grains of sand until I can open my eyes again. I wait as my vision adjusts to the dark, and when I can finally see Henry kneeling next to me, I repeat my question. "What are you doing here?"

"You're welcome, happy to help," he mutters, rubbing the spot near his temple that my elbow struck.

I stand up and brush myself off. "If you'll excuse me, I have things to do."

"Such as?"

"I need to finish the raft I started."

"You mean that?"

He points to a pitiful bundle of sticks and bamboo with a flimsy vine looped loosely around it.

I scan the beach for the rest of my supplies. That *can't* be all I did. It took forever, and it was so hard. When I realize it is, in fact, all I did, my cheeks grow hot. The raft that I thought would save us all is roughly the size of my leg. To further humiliate me, Henry lifts his foot and shoves the "raft" into the water. The vine slips away as the planks quickly fall apart.

I clear the embarrassment from my throat. "It appears we need a new plan."

"You mean like that one?" He points a little ways up the

beach, where a fire illuminates a giant "SOS" spelled out of tree branches, rocks, and bamboo shoots. Is *that* what I spent the entire night working on? Am I some sort of survival sleepwalking genius? I was pretty out of it before I fell asleep.

The thought cheers me up and I wander toward the message. "Did I do this?"

"You sound mental," Victoria says. She's lying on the sand next to the second S. Her eyes are closed, and light from a flickering fire reveals dark purple shadows under her eyes. She looks sick, but she still sounds like herself, which must be a good sign.

"Where'd you come from?"

"There was a plane in the sky, see, and it crashed—"

"Did you do this?" I gesture to the message.

She finally opens her eyes. "I supervised."

"Where's Brooke?"

"Not back yet."

"Where's Theo?"

"In the forest."

"Doing what?"

"It's not proper to discuss."

"Did *he* do this?"

"Obviously."

"And the fire?" I point to the dancing flames in the dead center of the *O*. I turn to Henry for clarification.

"Also us," he confirms as Theo and Comet join us on the beach. Comet quickly makes a chew toy out of the large stick at the top of the *O,* so the message now reads "SUS."

Theo watches me carefully, his expression unreadable.

"But I thought—" I sputter, trying to remember exactly what happened before I fell asleep. "I gathered sticks and bamboo for my raft. I didn't tell anyone."

"You thought you were the only one with a rescue plan?" Victoria asks dryly.

"I thought I was *alone*."

The royals blink at me like I'm an utter idiot.

"You can't get rid of us that easily," Henry says.

"To be fair, she could probably bump me off pretty easily at this point," Victoria says. Henry nudges his sister with his foot. "Fine." She rolls her eyes. "This is not an ideal situation, but we're in it together."

I wish I could believe that. I turn to Theo. "You didn't follow me," I say quietly.

His expression darkens.

"Look!" Brooke's voice screams. I spin to find her in the dark. A swell of nausea rises in my stomach and I sway on my feet. Theo steadies me.

Henry shouts. Every muscle in my body winds tight, preparing for the worst, but when I look at him, he's jumping up and down, waving his arms in the air. "Over here!" he yells. "We're here!"

I glance up at the dark sky. Wind whips my hair across my face as a swirling tornado of sand and leaves and branches rises into the air. I choke on a mouthful of sand. Theo yells, his words drowned out by the thrum of helicopter blades. We run for cover behind the trees. Theo pulls me to the ground and shields my body with his just in time for us to watch as a trio of helicopters land on the beach.

The doors are thrown open, and people spill onto the sand.

Theo's eyes are wide as saucers as we share a glance. "It's over," he whispers.

We're hidden behind a thicket of trees, so the rescuers run immediately for Henry and Victoria. Henry points to his sister, and two people in emergency medic uniforms kneel next to her, ripping open a bag of medical supplies. The part of my brain that has been terrified about her health relaxes for the first time in days.

We survived. It's over.

Which means *we're* over. Theo and I are officially out of time.

I'm too in shock to move. All I should feel is relief and happiness, but fear grips me in a steel trap. It's too soon. At least in Greece, we had a countdown to the end of the world. I made a call to the Firm, and I knew they were coming. I had time to prepare myself for the emotional hand grenade.

"Is this goodbye?" I ask, suddenly realizing I don't know what happens after this. Will the Firm still take me to London, or is it too close to the coronation now to worry about the desperate American? Maybe they drafted our divorce papers after the plane went down. I'll sign them over the Atlantic and they'll hand me a parachute over Chicago.

Theo puts a hand on my cheek, then pulls back and looks at his palm. "Why are you so hot?"

"Are you hitting on me? Does this mean you forgive me?"

He nudges the torn fabric of my shirtsleeve to the side and curses. "Bloody hell. Your stitches are infected. Do you feel okay?" His eyes search my face, and his voice sounds like it's a million miles away. "You're not really looking at me."

I don't feel okay, actually. I need some of Gwyneth's healing Goop powers. Theo's face blurs in my vision.

"Wren?" His voice is sharp. "Look at me. Wren?"

He stands and pulls me up. I stumble over my own feet, struggling to stay upright. He sweeps his arms underneath my legs and lifts me in one fluid motion. I'm floating again, and once again, it feels awful.

"Apologies in advance if I puke on you," I mumble. My head falls to Theo's chest, and it's the most comfortable I've been in days. He's so warm.

"She needs help," Theo shouts as he runs. He sounds so scared it makes me wonder if I should be scared.

"We've got eyes on the King. His Majesty is alive," a voice says. Half a dozen people rush toward us, forcing Theo to set me down as they inspect the King for injuries.

"I'm fine! Wren needs help." He tries to shake them off, but they don't listen.

"Theo, I . . ." My vision tunnels.

He tears off the oxygen mask they've just placed on him as I collapse in his arms.

"WREN!"

His scream echoes in my head as everything goes dark.

PART III

CHAPTER 30

It's 2:00 A.M., and the hospital library is dead silent. Yes, a hospital *library*. I was confused too. Patients can also do Pilates in the basement gym or take a dip in the heated hydrotherapy pool. (Wellness junk!) Not me, though. I've been advised against strenuous exercise or swimming until my new stitches heal. And since I don't want to risk a *second* case of sepsis, I'm in the library, where my chances of contracting another infection are sufficiently low.

Like a lot of the building, this room looks nothing like a hospital. It has an empty fireplace, carpeted floors, and velvety red furniture covered in throw pillows. I'm lying on one of the sofas now, my eyes glued to a gold chandelier above me, wondering how many of Theo's ancestors have died in this institution.

It's morbid, but I need to focus on *something* to drown out the restless, anxious "do something" energy that has me wandering the halls in the middle of the night. When my nurses find out I'm missing again, they're going to be pissed. (American version.)

I thought the endless waiting would be over once we were rescued, but it turns out this hospital is just a different kind of limbo. I've been here for two days, and although I was mostly unconscious for the first several hours, it feels like I've been here for a month: waiting to be discharged, waiting to find out if I'm the accidental queen consort, waiting for Theo or Graves or the Firm to remember that I exist. But maybe Theo is still mad at me, and Graves is too busy fighting back against the news stories claiming Theo is unprepared for the throne, and the Firm is knee-deep in arrangements for the coronation.

I wonder how much of royal life is waiting for instructions from *the Firm*. Honestly, that doesn't sound so awful right now. If someone official showed up and gave me a list of royal duties and instructions, at least the limbo would be over. Not knowing what comes next is a special kind of hell.

A cold draft of air blows through my thin hospital gown. I rub the goose bumps on my arms and walk to the window, pulling back the heavy drapes. Despite the hour, there are paparazzi camped out on the street. Naomi was thrilled to report that they got pics of her and Brooke on their way to the hotel where they're now staying with my mom, and then equally devastated when the blurry shots were banished to a small corner on page 3 of the *London Echo*.

Mom, Brooke, and Naomi all have tickets to fly home in a couple of days, and it'd be nice to know if I'll be allowed to go with them. No one has told me anything, though. I still don't even know if Theo and I are married.

The door to the small room opens.

"I'm sorry I couldn't sleep and I was hungry and looking for food!" I blurt, wincing in preparation to face the mean nurse who yells at me when I get out of bed.

Instead, a head of dark, curly hair peeks in, and my heart spikes.

"Henry?" I'm shocked but surprisingly happy to see him, and I don't stop myself from throwing my arms around him.

"Oof!" He wraps his arms easily around me and lifts me off the floor in a big hug, and then I'm crying. I was starting to feel like the last week was a fever dream, and like the royal family and I had never crossed paths.

"Did someone say hungry?" Henry sets me down and displays a greasy take-out bag with a flourish. "I thought you might be getting sick of hospital food."

My mouth waters at the smell of hot french fries. I open the bag and shove three in my mouth at once. "Why are you here in the middle of the night?"

"It was the only time I could get away. They're keeping you under lock and key. Top secret. I had to sneak in the back door so the wankers with cameras wouldn't see me."

"Is that why no one else has been here?" I ask, my voice wavering on "no one else" in a way that makes it obvious I'm only talking about one person.

Henry doesn't make eye contact as he runs his fingers over the dusty spines on the bookshelf. "I reckon Theo's been pretty busy with coronation stuff."

My stomach sinks. Theo and I said we'd be together until we were rescued, but I didn't think he'd take it quite so literally. I flop backward on the red couch. "How'd you find the time at"—I check the clock on the wall—"two thirty A.M.?"

"Tragically, no one needs the spare at the coronation," Henry says, his head bent over the pages of a thick book with a throne on the cover. His tone makes it sound like a joke, but by this time I know him well enough to realize there's a fundamental sadness underneath his words. Even after his mom's death, he's trying to be the perfect son that she always wanted.

"Why are you really here?"

"I wanted to see how you're doing. Plus, you know, I have to get checked out, make sure everything looks good after my procedure."

I sit up straighter. "What procedure?" Brooke and Naomi told me that other than dehydration, Victoria's hyperglycemia, and Winston's broken leg, no one else from the crash had serious injuries.

"You didn't hear?" Henry crosses to the couch and brandishes his inner elbow in front of my face.

"What am I looking at?"

He points to a red dot the size of a pinprick, so I lift the sleeve of my hospital gown and show him my eight inches of sutures. "Again, what am I looking at?"

"The reason you're alive." He smirks.

I roll my eyes. "Explain."

"You needed a blood transfusion, and I was a willing pincushion. Theo was rather annoyed about that."

I raise my eyebrows in surprise. "Why?"

He gestures between us. "Because we have the same rare AB-negative blood type, and Theo's O-positive arse was useless."

"Another competition? Really?" I groan. If not even surviving a plane crash together can get them on the same page, I don't think anything ever will.

"If by competition you mean my jealousy and his self-loathing, then yes. Both are thriving." He cracks open the throne book while I stare at the side of his face in disbelief that he's the one who's here, in the middle of the night. I guess somewhere in the cracks of tragedy and his and Theo's sibling rivalry, we became friends.

I can tell he knows I'm watching him when the dimple makes an appearance. "Is there something else?" he asks, not taking his eyes off the page.

"What are you going to do after the coronation?"

He looks up at me with a grin. "I'm headed back to school in Scotland. I could pull some strings and get you in."

I slant him an annoyed look. "My life is in Chicago."

"I don't know if anyone's ever told you this, but your life is allowed to be whatever and wherever you want."

He's clearly underestimating the number of times American children are told they can do anything they set their minds to. But for some reason "anything" didn't ever seem like it was meant to be taken literally. In my family, I knew that "anything" was code for getting good grades, going to a good college, and starting a sensible career path. "What if I don't know what I want?"

"That's the beauty in being eighteen, darling," he says with a wink. "You've got all the time in the world to figure it out. Starting now." He looks pointedly around the empty room, and then goes back to reading while I let my mind wander through Northwestern's campus and down palace halls. Despite Henry's claim, I feel the pressure of time even more than I did on the island; classes have already started, and the coronation is in four days. Sand is falling so quickly through the hourglass that it reminds me of the days before the comet. Only this time, I know I'll have to live with the consequences of my actions.

I yawn, and my eyelids start to droop. "I should go back to my room before the nurses send out a search warrant."

"Want some company? I bet we can find a truly awful info-mercial to watch."

I feel a prickle behind my eyes that makes me worried I'm going to cry again. "You'd do that?"

He's still staring at the page as he clears his throat. "If you're anything like me, it's been hard to sleep since the crash."

"I traded nightmares of sinking boats for flaming airplanes."

He tucks the throne book under his arm. "For me it's the vol-cano, except instead of spewing ash and magma, it's an eruption of quicksand."

"How would that even work?"

Henry laughs and pushes his hair out of his eyes. "I don't know! I wake up in a cold sweat before it kills me." He reaches for the door, and I put my hand on his to stop him.

"Thanks for coming," I say, and I mean it. It's nice to have one royal who's still willing to talk to me.

Henry smiles, and the dimple really is overwhelming. "I do have one more surprise for you, if you can keep a secret." He motions for me to follow him, and we tiptoe past stained-glass windows and a sleepy receptionist wearing a waistcoat and tie, through empty corridors, and all the way to my room without being seen.

I glance up and down the empty hallway. "Where's the sur-prise?"

"Go in." He nods, and my heart beats double-time as I twist the handle with sweaty palms. I pull the door open, and Comet is waiting for me on the other side, his tail thumping excitedly.

I don't even bother fighting the tears as I kneel on the hard floor to hug my dog. I glance over my shoulder at Henry, who is watching me with a grin. "The nurses are going to kill you when they find him in here," I say.

He stuffs his hands into his pockets. "Do they not teach 'snitches get stitches' in America?"

Comet and I climb into the hospital bed, and Henry pulls a chair next to us, puts his feet up on the end of my bed, and flips on the TV. We settle on an old episode of *Doctor Who,* and after ten minutes I've never been more confused. I turn to Henry to demand an explanation, but he's already asleep with his head on his shoulder. Twenty minutes later, the mean nurse comes in to check on me and kicks Henry and Comet out with a nasty glare.

Stitches, Henry mouths as she ushers him into the hall. He lifts his fists and dances on his toes like we're facing off in a boxing match. The nurse slams the door in his face.

I slouch down into my bed and fall asleep with a smile.

CHAPTER 31

Despite telling me to use my alone time to think, Henry gives me almost no alone time. The day after he and Comet snuck in to see me, he stops by again, this time with his fifteen-year-old sister, Louise, in tow. Louise has the same fair hair and complexion as Victoria, but her dimples remind me of Henry. She enters the room shyly, half hidden behind her brother's back.

"We heard you're getting sprung loose this afternoon, and Louise had an idea." Henry nudges his sister toward me. In her hands, she's clutching a small suitcase.

For the first time in days, I feel a surge of adrenaline. I push myself up to my knees. "I'm leaving? Who told you that?"

"Uh . . . the doctor. Who else? Go on, Louise."

Louise's cheeks turn scarlet. "It's probably a silly idea."

"You were buzzing to get over here. Just ask," he says.

Louise's shoulders are nearly to her chin as she heaves her suitcase onto the foot of my bed. She opens the case to reveal enough makeup to make a beauty influencer swoon. "There are cameras swarming the hospital waiting to get the first photo of you, so I thought, if you want, I could maybe do your makeup? It's a hobby of mine."

I can't help but smile. If she didn't look just like Victoria, I'd have a hard time believing that they're related. "Oh my gosh, thank you!" I haven't felt pretty in days.

Louise beams and gets to work, picking out shades to match my skin tone while Henry settles in with the throne book that he borrowed from the library.

"Where's Brooke and Naomi?" Louise asks as she curls my eyelashes. "I saw the pictures in the *Echo* and was hoping to meet them, too."

I glance at the clock. It's still early, and my jetlagged mother might be sleeping in, but I wish I knew for sure. The first thing I'm doing when I get back to Chicago is buying a new phone. "They'll probably be here soon if you want to wait."

"Look up," Louise says. I do, and she swipes mascara over my lashes. "I have my last dress fitting for the coronation in an hour."

"How's that going? The coronation, I mean. The, um, planning of it. It's still happening?" A flush of heat sweeps over me, and I'm tongue-tied out of nowhere. If the coronation is still going forward, either Theo and I aren't really married, or I'm about to be crowned queen consort, and I won't have to spend any more sleepless nights staring at the ceiling, planning my future.

Theo would never *agree, but if he did* . . .

Louise waves her hand in the air. "Boring ceremony. Big hat. Stolen jewels. There's not much to talk about."

I burst into laughter. "Did you just refer to the Crown Jewels as a 'big hat'?"

"I saw it on TikTok and it made me laugh. It's not wrong," she admits with a smile.

"You are officially my favorite royal."

Her face positively sparkles. "Theo will be so jealous."

"What's he been up to since the crash?" I pretend like the question's not eating me alive.

"Skiving off his responsibilities, if you believe the press."

I jerk away from the mascara wand. "*Should* I believe the press?" He hasn't been photographed or seen in public once since the rescue. Some TV news stations have speculated that Theo is just busy preparing for the coronation (Graves's handiwork, I assume), but others claim he's missed a bunch of his scheduled meetings and isn't returning his "We're glad you're alive!" phone calls from foreign leaders.

Louise's eyes dart to Henry. "No, sorry. I was joking. I don't know what he's doing. I haven't seen him." She fixes the mascara I smudged with my sudden movement and holds up a mirror.

I'm disappointed she doesn't know more, but I can't deny that she's a magician with a makeup brush. "You're great at this. Thank you," I say as she repacks her mini suitcase.

"I hope I get to see you again, but if not, it was really nice to meet you, Wren. And I love your dog."

An alarm goes off on Henry's phone. He silences it and stands up. "Shift's over. Thanks for letting us keep you company."

They leave, and for the second time in two days, I'm nearly speechless as Henry walks out of my hospital room.

What shift?

Either I'm still delirious, or something strange is going on with these royals.

⚜   ⚜   ⚜

Brooke, Naomi, and my mom are the next to arrive in my parade of visitors.

"Whoa! You look gorgeous!" Naomi says when she sees my makeup.

"We're late because we bought you clothes," Mom explains. "We went to Camden Market, but it might not have been the best choice." She glances warily into the shopping bag hanging from her wrist.

"Nonsense," Brooke says. "Every girl wants to leave the hospital in knee-high boots." Naomi digs through the bag to reveal a pair of stacked lace-up combat boots.

"I don't know what happened," Mom admits. "My daughters almost die in a plane crash and suddenly I've forgotten how to say no."

"The Firm is going to hate this," I say in delight as I pull a Victorian-style corset out of the bag.

"But think how badass your stitches will look," Naomi tells me.

"And your boobs," Brooke adds.

Mom looks like she's going to faint. "We also bought normal clothes. There's a T-shirt and jeans in there."

"And where's the fun in that?" Naomi asks as the door opens once again and my doctor walks in with a smile on her face.

She inspects my sutures and my chart and then tells me she has good news. "Your vitals look great, your wound is healing beautifully, and the nurses tell me that you're doing laps around the halls when you're bored. Sounds like you're ready to get out of here, Wren."

Finally. I'm out of the bed and halfway to the door before realizing I'm still in a hospital gown. I grab the boots and the bag of clothes and shut myself in the bathroom.

"Is she healthy enough to fly home with us tomorrow?" I hear Mom ask. I know she feels guilty that they can't stay longer, but she has a trial starting and Naomi and Brooke are both desperate to get back to school. Brooke contacted Northwestern *immediately* upon being rescued, and they pulled some strings to let her start law school this semester.

I should tell the King that there are *some* perks to fame.

My stomach lurches at the thought of Theo, the MIA king of England. It seems weird that not even Theo's siblings know what he's up to. I don't understand why Graves hasn't kicked him in the ass and forced him to do a public appearance, especially since Henry's already been photographed doing charity work with orphans.

I can't help but wonder if something is wrong. Of course, as soon as I start to worry, I remember that we didn't promise each other anything, and then I feel silly for being worried, then mad at him for making me worry, then annoyed at myself for caring.

It's a whole cycle.

"She's safe to fly," the doctor says, and the knot in my stomach tightens. As eager as I am to get out of here, I didn't go through all of this just to be kicked off the continent without a definitive answer to the marriage question *or* a final conversation with Theo. The least he can do is say goodbye.

I trade my gown for the jeans, the boots, and the corset, because what the hell. If I'm going to be in the tabloids, I may as well make an impression. Brooke catcalls me as I strut around the hospital bed, and we're about to leave for good when a nurse stops me in the hall.

"Wait! We have something of yours." She rifles through a drawer behind the nurses' station and retrieves my ring. *Theo's* ring. My knees go wobbly as she drops it into my open palm. "The chain is broken, but I saved this for you."

"Thanks." I struggle to get the word out. I feel three pairs of eyes bore into me, so I clear my throat and push the ring into my pocket. "Ready to go?" I ask my mom.

"Have you heard from Theo at all?" she asks softly.

"Nope! Should we go? Let's go. How do we get out of here?" I turn to the nurse for help. If I don't stop this conversation now, I'll cry off all of Louise's hard work right before the paparazzi see me for the first time. If that happens, I could become a meme that will haunt me for the rest of my life.

"There's a decoy car waiting for you out front to trick the photographers, and two more cars waiting out back where you won't be seen," the nurse says as she leads us through a hallway.

"Who arranged for the cars?" I ask.

"I can't say, but they're waiting for you right out there." She props the door open with her foot and gestures to a blacked-out Bentley.

"Damn." Naomi looks at me sideways with a growing smile. "Do you think it's him?"

My stomach fills with butterflies.

I look back at the nurse with my eyebrows raised.

"It was nice to meet you, Your Highness," she says with a wink and a quick curtsy.

I'm suddenly dizzy. None of this feels like real life.

I walk on shaky legs to the car. Someone steps in front of me to open it, and I slide into the car with bated breath. I look up, and instead of Theo, I come face-to-face with Richard Graves.

CHAPTER 32

Right now, Richard Graves is my least favorite person in all of England. No, Great Britain. Scratch that, Theo's press secretary is my least favorite person in the entire United Kingdom. (And I'm definitely *not* confused about the difference between those three places . . . just don't quiz me on it.)

"What are you doing here?" I ask as the car door shuts behind Naomi. I turn to look out the rear window and see my mom and Brooke getting into the second car. Great. Maybe Naomi and I *are* about to be *Taken,* and the reason Theo is getting such negative press is because his secretary has been busy plotting our deaths instead of feeding puff pieces to the tabloids.

"I am always in service to the Crown," Graves says, and I'm reminded that the Crown and the monarch aren't necessarily the same thing. He could be here for a dozen different reasons, and Theo might not even know about it.

"Where are we going?"

"Don't worry about it. Everything has been arranged," Graves says.

"What if you're trying to kidnap us?" I ask dramatically, and I feel somewhat better when Graves scowls.

"Why would I want to do that?" he asks.

"Because you hate me!"

"I don't think we have to worry about our safety," Naomi says as her eyes grow wide.

"Why not?"

She nods out the window. I look up and see the gates of Buckingham Palace. "Because everything the light touches is your kingdom."

I elbow her in the stomach.

"I'm serious. Look." She points to the mounds of flowers and stuffed animals leaning against the wrought-iron gates. The piles are so deep and sprawling that they nearly spill into the street. I assume they're for the late queen, but then I see several posters with faces on them. Theo, Victoria, and Henry, obviously, but I'm *not* prepared to see posters with my face, at least one of which features a hand-drawn tiara on top of my senior yearbook photo.

"What the hell?" I blurt without thinking. *They couldn't have used a better picture?*

I crane my neck as the car cruises past the palace. Either I actually died on the island, or I'm trapped in a surreal daydream.

I press my palm to my forehead to check if my fever has returned. "How did I go from being called a gold digger and a crazy stalker to . . . this?" I direct Naomi's attention to a poster with my and Theo's faces superimposed over a picture of London. It reads MY KING AND QUEEN.

"People love a love story! Especially one with a wedding and a happy ending!" Naomi squeals.

Butterflies fill my stomach. I turn to Graves, who is still glaring at me. "Are Theo and I really married?"

"No," he says quickly, but before I can sort out how I feel about that, he adds, "Probably not."

"You don't know yet?" I gape at him.

"We've been a bit busy," he says tightly.

Naomi leans forward in her seat to get a better look at him. "But if they *are* married, she's about to become the queen consort."

"We are figuring it out, and you will stay in London until we do," he says.

"When can I see Theo?" I ask.

"The King does what he wants," Graves says acidly.

I flinch. So, it's entirely Theo's choice not to see me. *Cool. Cool cool cool. That's fine.*

The ring in my pocket digs uncomfortably into my hip.

We pull to a stop, and a set of solid black gates opens, allowing the car to pass through the throngs of reporters waiting on the street.

"We've arrived." Graves steps out of the car on the driver's side, and the door swings shut behind him. When Naomi's door opens, she yells "One minute!" and closes it firmly.

She turns to me. "Don't listen to him. I'm sure there's a reason why Theo hasn't seen you yet."

"Like what?" I ask doubtfully.

"Maybe there's some sort of national emergency we don't know about?"

I flop back into my seat, a nagging feeling eating at my stomach. "Isn't it weird that the press is writing negative stuff about the King just a couple of days after he came back from the dead

and less than a week before his coronation? He should be un-
touchable!"

"I'm telling you, the press here is bizarre."

"Okay, but like, why does Henry get a ten-minute news seg-
ment about playing soccer—sorry, 'football'—with orphans,
while Theo gets dragged for missing a phone call from the
queen of Norway?"

"The press always goes easy on Henry."

"Because of the dimple?" I ask.

Naomi laughs. "What else could it be?"

"The curls?"

"The combination of the two *is* lethal," she confirms as the
car door swings open. She looks at me over her shoulder before
climbing out. "Don't tell Levi I said that."

"I would never."

I follow Naomi out of the car and into the gray humidity.
I can practically feel my red-orange hair frizz around me as
my eyes lift to a three-story white stucco Regency-style town
house. It's not quite a palace, but it *is* stunning.

"No way," Naomi says in a hushed voice.

"Where are we?"

Graves clears his throat. "Welcome to Clarence House. This
is where you'll be staying."

⁂

Clarence House is a property owned by the Crown Estate that
sits empty eleven months of the year and is only used for guided
tours in the month of August. It is beautiful, full of history, and,
as far as I can tell, a massive waste of resources.

It's also my temporary home, so I can't complain too much.

I hold my breath as the four of us walk through the columned entrance of the house and into the ground floor and its maze of formal rooms. Knickknacks on every surface have been swept to the side to make room for gift baskets and bouquets. I open the first few Get Well Soon cards I see and don't recognize any of the names, so I stop reading the messages and instead pick out nuts and chocolate as I pass through rooms full of fancy antique furniture. There are golden candelabras on the walls, a dizzying number of clocks, heavy busts on side tables, lamps *everywhere*, moody paintings of trees and geese, and shelves filled with books whose pages have probably never seen the light of day.

"I bet Theo wants you to move in permanently," Naomi whispers as we climb the steps to the second floor.

I feel a brief shock to my system. "I doubt he even knows I'm here."

"Don't pretend like you haven't thought about what it'd be like," she continues after my mom claims a small room on the second floor and closes the door behind her, announcing that she needs a nap.

Ignoring my best friend, I poke my head into another small room, at the end of the hall. I'm about to call dibs on it when Brooke hollers down to us from the third floor. "Wren, your room is up here!"

Naomi and I race up the stairs, and I stop short at a closed door with a piece of paper taped to it. Written on the paper is my name in familiar script: *Wren Wheeler.*

After months of staring at my marriage certificate, this handwriting is seared into my brain.

At the very least, Theo knows where to find me.

CHAPTER 33

It's been twenty-four hours since Graves dropped us unceremoniously on the doorstep. My mom, Brooke, and Naomi are leaving for the airport any minute, and I still haven't heard from Theo, but I can't bring myself to leave London.

Not until I know why he taped that paper to my door.

Naomi and I are watching TV in my bed when Brooke pushes the door open and plucks a bottle of wine and a wheel of cheese out of the nearest basket. "I'm taking these."

"Knock yourself out." I pick up the TV remote and turn the volume down. Theo would be mortified by how much royal press coverage I've been consuming, but I can't stop thinking that there's something off about all of it.

Brooke picks up a corkscrew and opens the bottle of wine. "Wait. They're talking about you!"

"What?"

"They showed a picture of you! Turn it up!"

I turn the volume back up as my picture is replaced with one of Henry.

". . . life-saving blood transfusion . . ." an anchor is saying as the screen zooms in on a small, colorful bandage on Henry's left arm.

"Quite a heroic thing to do, innit?" the other anchor chimes in.

"We've always known he's a cracking lad . . ."

"Theo saved me from a freaking volcano! Why aren't they talking about that?" I'm indignant on his behalf.

"Henry's going to be so smug about this. He'll never let Theo hear the end of it," Naomi says.

Brooke props her hip against the wall and takes a swig from the bottle. "If Theo wanted to be a hero, *he* could have donated."

"He volunteered, but his blood type didn't match mine. Henry and I are both AB negative."

Brooke tilts her head, studying the picture of Henry on the screen. "What blood type does Theo have?"

"O positive."

She frowns at me. "Are you sure?"

"That's what Henry said."

"But that means . . ." She shakes her head. "I need a piece of paper." She rifles through one of the gift baskets until she finds a pen and uses the back of a Get Well Soon card to sketch a rough table. She stares at it for a minute, chewing on the back of the pen. Finally, she looks at me and blows her overgrown crisis bangs out of her face. "Theo and Henry don't have the same parents."

Naomi's eyes widen with shock.

"That can't be right," I say.

Brooke hands me her Punnett square. "It's impossible for the same two people to have an AB-negative child *and* an O-positive child."

I glance up at the TV, where the news anchors are still singing Henry's praises, two days before his brother's coronation. A chill runs up my spine.

I turn to the royal expert in the room. "Theo told me there were cheating rumors in his parents' marriage. Do you know about that?" I ask Naomi.

"Of course. There are cheating rumors in every royal marriage."

"Was it his mom?"

She slowly nods. "There were whispers that right after the wedding, the Queen had an affair with one of her advisers. Do you think . . ."

She trails off as we turn our attention to the news, which has finally switched from the story about Henry to a quick coronation countdown update.

"Holy shit," Brooke says, echoing my thoughts perfectly. She looks at me, her eyebrows sky-high. "I don't think your boyfriend is the rightful heir to the throne."

My entire world flips upside down.

Naomi grips my hand. "What are you going to do?"

I turn to Brooke. "How did you know law school was the right choice?"

She shrugs. "I just felt it in my gut."

"There wasn't a sign?"

She must hear something desperate in my voice, because she studies me for a long moment. "Wanting a sign *is* your sign, Wren."

Well, that was not as helpful as I hoped it would be. I give her two sarcastic thumbs-up.

Before I have a chance to process any of this, it's time for them to leave for the airport. I spend so long hugging everyone goodbye that the Uber honks three times.

"Don't forget to call," Mom says. (Once she realized I wasn't getting on the plane with her, she bought me a new phone.)

"I won't," I promise.

"And come home soon."

"I will."

"Remember that your dad and I love you," she says as Brooke drags her toward the door.

I follow them to the front porch. "I know."

"And call me if you need a divorce lawyer. I know a good one." She kisses me on the head.

"We're going to miss our flight," Brooke says, and Mom gives me one last wave as Brooke forces her into the back of the car.

An uneasy silence settles over Clarence House when they're gone, punctuated by the ticking of a large grandfather clock in the corner. "What now?" I say out loud, because I'm procrastinating the inevitable. I do another lap of the ground floor, skipping the fruit baskets (I'll never eat another passion fruit again) and stopping by a box filled with cheese and crackers. I tuck the whole thing under my arm and am climbing the stairs when the doorbell rings, and my heart stops.

I open the door, and my hopes crash.

"Victoria." She's the last person I ever expected to visit.

The princess is wearing boyfriend jeans and a beige crew-neck sweater that looks like fall. "Careful. Your excitement is overwhelming," she says with a straight face.

"Why are you here?"

"I was bored," she says with a shrug.

"If you feel guilty, you can tell me."

Her eyes slowly narrow. "Why would I feel guilty?"

"For being bitchy when I was dying of sepsis."

"You threw out my insulin, so let's call it even. Besides, I'm bitchy to everyone; you're not special."

Now that I know her better (and I'm not about to collapse from hunger), Victoria's insults sting less than they did on the island. "Can I help you with something?"

She whistles, and Comet darts out from behind a low hedge. She holds up a leash. "Want to go for a walk with us?"

I'm tempted to make a snarky remark about returning my dog, but I'm too distracted by her offer of fresh air and a chance to get some answers about Theo. "Am I allowed to leave?"

She arches an eyebrow and looks around the empty court-yard. "Who's going to stop us?"

CHAPTER 34

Victoria's bodyguard probably could have stopped us from leaving Clarence House, but instead he walks ten feet behind as the princess and I stroll through the private gardens at Buckingham Palace. I feel just like a character from a Jane Austen novel, minus my sweatpants, my (eventual) economic independence, and my access to indoor plumbing. Other than that, I may as well be an Austen heroine, right down to the chaperone and the way I'm pining for the guy who lives in the massive palace towering over us.

My nineteenth-century daydreams are shattered by the stressed and sweaty vendors who keep getting lost on their way to set up for a pre-coronation garden party. Victoria wordlessly points them in the right direction as we take turns throwing a tennis ball for Comet to chase while we walk down a tree-lined path.

"I keep expecting to run into Mr. Darcy out here," I say as a man wheeling a hand truck piled high with table linens nearly veers into the lake.

"As if you need to," Victoria says with an eye roll. "Sorry to disappoint, but I've yet to meet a single eligible bachelor in these gardens, unless you count the garden party where Mum made me dance with the prince of Denmark and he spent the whole time sniffing my hair."

"Ew! Why?"

"It remains a mystery."

Comet's ball bounces into the lake, and he hesitates at the shore before abandoning it in favor of chasing birds across the sprawling lawn. He's obviously been spoiled living here, and he's going to be in for a culture shock when I bring him back to the city.

I glance sideways at Victoria, and I can't help but wonder again why she's bothering to spend time with me. I don't think she actively hates me anymore, but she's not tripping over herself to make conversation, either.

"Shouldn't you be busy with coronation prep right now?"

"What do you think I'm going to do, clean the church?"

"It takes place in a church?"

She pulls down her sunglasses to gawk at me. "It's a religious ceremony."

"You learn something new every day," I say.

"It concerns me that I can't tell if you're taking the piss," she mutters. "But no. No one wants my opinion or trusts me with anything important. I told the planners that we should return the Koh-i-Noor diamond to India and the rest of the stolen Crown Jewels to their rightful owners before the coronation in an act of goodwill, but they laughed me out of the room."

"That's actually a good idea."

"I know." She looks at me like I'm a moron, then softens. "Thanks."

"I'm sorry that no one takes you seriously. They're idiots not to."

Her mouth drops in surprise, but she quickly shakes it off

with an exaggerated hair flip. "I was hoping things would change when Theo took the throne, but he's too resentful of the whole institution to know how to change it for the better."

My eyes stray to Buckingham Palace, and it might be my imagination, but I swear I see a curtain move in one of the windows. My self-restraint finally snaps.

"Can I ask you about Theo, or are we still pretending he doesn't exist?"

"Yes," Victoria says.

"To which question?"

"Yes you can ask, and yes I reserve the right to ignore you and pretend my brother doesn't exist."

I'll take what I can get. "Why did your mom treat Theo differently than the rest of your siblings?"

She laughs. "Blimey, I thought you were going to ask why he's been avoiding you—"

"Why *is* he avoiding me?"

She raises her eyebrows, and I know immediately *that's* a question she'll be ignoring. "It's simple. He was the heir."

"Theo seems to be under the impression that your mom thought Henry would have made a better monarch."

"Who hasn't thought that? Theo's made it clear how little he wants the job, even now . . ." She trails off, seemingly lost in her own thoughts, before cutting me a sidelong glance. "Sorry, what was the question?"

"Do you think your mother wanted Henry to be king?"

She stops in her tracks. "Maybe . . . but that's not what happened, is it?" She gives me a strange look.

My chest feels tight. I can't shake the feeling that something bad is going to happen if I keep pulling at this thread, but I can't stop myself. I glance up at the palace again, and all the curtains in the windows are still. I pick up a smooth stone from the garden and toss it back and forth between my hands. My arms aren't strong enough, and my aim isn't that good, but I wonder what would happen if I tapped on Theo's window. *Would he even answer?*

Victoria grabs the stone out of my hand. "Don't be desperate. It's cringey. C'mon, I'm getting sweaty."

On our way back to the car we pass a pile of fireworks the size of a small home. "Looks like a fun party," I say pointedly, but either Victoria doesn't pick up on the hint, or she doesn't care.

"It won't be" is all she says before ushering Comet and me back into the car.

Back at Clarence House, there's a large bookcase next to the grandfather clock in the sitting room, and I approach it with a plan. I move a vase of flowers sent to me by the prime minister's office (a weird move, unless they think I really *am* going to be the queen consort), grab a book about the history of the kings and queens of England, and take it up to my bedroom on the third floor. I toss it onto the four-poster bed and settle in for an afternoon of reading. I don't actually open the book, though, because who needs six-hundred-page tomes when the internet exists. I do all my research online, alternating between twenty-year-old tabloid stories, royal-gossip message boards, and Wikipedia pages about lines of succession.

The Wikipedia articles confirm what I remember from history class about illegitimate royal babies (they have no claim to the throne), and the gossip threads unearth dozens of insane royal conspiracy theories, from Moonbumps (don't look it up) to the late Queen Alice's suspected affairs.

It's a lot of information to take in all at once, and I still don't know what I'm going to do with it, or how to confirm my suspicions that Theo is the product of an affair—and therefore not eligible to sit on the throne.

This could change literally everything for Theo, Henry, and me. I could go back home, and Theo could come with me. He wouldn't be stuck in a life he resents, and Henry could have everything he ever wanted.

On the other hand, that's a lot to assume, considering Theo hasn't spoken to me in days.

A firework explodes in the distance, pulling me out of my online rabbit hole.

I slide off the bed and step over a sleeping Comet on my way to the en-suite bathroom. I brush my teeth, strip off my clothes, turn the shower water to scalding, and sit under the spray until my eyelids are heavy.

I dry off, put on a clean pair of sweats, and cross the room to the window, where the fireworks are going crazy. I picture Theo, Victoria, and Henry sitting on the grass under the colorful explosion, and my stomach twists sourly. Our last night on the beach, they told me I wasn't alone. *That I couldn't get rid of them.* I guess people will say anything when they're starving and dehydrated and struggling to survive on a deserted island, because now I'm alone in a house down the street while they celebrate at a royal party that I couldn't even score a pity invite to. I'm starting to lose hope that I'm ever going to see Theo before the coronation.

I should stop kidding myself and fly home tomorrow.

I'm grabbing the drapes to pull them closed when a large shadow moves outside the window.

I gasp and scramble back, but then my eyes adjust, and I realize that someone is perched on a tree branch.

My heart shifts into another gear as Theo reaches out and knocks on the glass.

CHAPTER 35

I haven't seen the King in almost a week, and now that he's waiting outside my window in the pitch black, all I can think is: *It's about damn time.*

He motions for me to unlock the window, but I'm still frustrated by the days of silence.

I shrug and put a hand on my hip.

He freezes, looking unsure, then points to himself and mimes climbing down the tree. Finally, he cocks an eyebrow in question.

I shake my head too quickly, giving myself away. I unlatch the window and tug, but it doesn't budge. "Good luck getting in, because it's stuck," I call, still trying to pretend the way his eyelashes brush against his cheekbones doesn't tie me in fucking knots.

"You think that's going to stop me?" Theo's voice is muffled by glass, but I can hear the smirk in his tone. He reveals a crowbar and jams it under the window, slowly prying the old glass a few inches open. "Stand back." He tosses the crowbar onto the carpet and wrenches the window the rest of the way up. A cool burst of earthy, rain-scented air whooshes into the room.

I cross my arms. "What if I'd already been asleep? Would you have pried your way in anyway?"

"That'd be a bit dodgy, Wheeler. I wouldn't sneak into your room without your consent."

"Oh, really?"

"Of course not. I would, however, request that you be given this exact room for this exact purpose." He's perched on an overgrown tree branch, wearing sneakers, dark jeans, and a black jacket. His hair is falling over his forehead, his cheeks rough with stubble, and I wonder if it's possible to get used to the way I can't breathe when he looks at me. Every time feels like the first time.

"Victoria says it's cringey to knock on someone's window," I tell him.

He grins. "I embrace the cringe."

"A brave and noble cause that will definitely get you roasted by a teenage princess."

He grabs the window frame and leans in slightly like he's dying to come inside. "Has she been terrorizing you?"

"I can handle her, but it's confusing the way your siblings won't leave me alone."

He cocks an eyebrow. "Almost like someone told them not to?"

I think back to Henry showing up in the middle of the night, bringing me Comet, watching *Doctor Who* with me when I couldn't sleep. "Henry too? And *Louise*?"

He shrugs. "There was a schedule."

I imagine Theo gathering his siblings and forcing them to sign up for "Wren duty" and don't know how to process it. "But I thought you were mad at me."

He blinks at me in surprise. "Why?"

"Because when you found out about Victoria's insulin, you let me wander into the dark without following me!"

"In my defense, you told me not to, and we could see you the whole time," he says.

I don't remember saying that out loud, but I *was* feverish and delirious. I also thought I walked alone for miles, and it was only a few hundred feet.

"Not this again. You really thought I abandoned you out there?" He sounds royally annoyed, and I'm even more confused than I was five minutes ago.

"I thought you'd never forgive me."

His head jerks back in surprise. "I never blamed you! There's no way you could have known what was in her bag."

"Then why have you been avoiding me? You never even called the hospital to see how I was doing."

"I called every day to get updates. *Three times* a day! And I did my best to make sure you didn't feel like you'd been abandoned." He looks pained as he closes his eyes. "If you let me in, I'll do my best to explain."

I hesitate, torn between needing to blurt out my suspicions about his parents and wanting to protect him from it all, but I can't pretend I don't want him here. When I nod, he climbs through the open window and sits on the sill. "I'm sorry I didn't call you, and that I haven't been clearer about what's been going on. I wanted to see you, but I was afraid that if I did, I wouldn't be able to stop myself."

Every nerve ending in my body is on high alert, but I hardly dare to hope. "From what?"

With a deep breath, he stands up and steps toward me. "I let you walk out of my life once without knowing how I truly felt about you, and I won't let that happen again."

I feel like we're balancing on a precipice, but I don't know which way we'll fall.

"I love you, Wren. End of sentence, no conditions. It's not 'I love you *if*' or 'I love you *but*.'"

It sounds so perfect, but it's not the truth. Our relationship is the definition of conditional. We agreed that it's "I love you until." That was the deal: together until we're rescued, and not a moment more.

He crosses the room and lifts me up in one fluid motion. The button of his jeans presses against the inside of my thigh, and if I lean in even a fraction, I know he'll kiss me.

"What happened to ending this on the island?" I ask.

He lifts me up higher, his breaths turning jagged. "I've said a lot of stupid things in my life, but none as daft as that," he says in a low voice. "When they loaded you into that helicopter, I knew I'd never be able to say goodbye to you."

"But nothing has changed," I whisper as he presses a slow kiss to the underside of my jaw.

"Not yet, but I'm working on it." His voice is as raspy as the stubble scraping across my skin.

I jerk back as my pulse hammers. "What do you mean?"

He slowly releases his hold on me. "If I could find a way out of this for us, would you want me to?"

I blink in surprise, wondering if he already found out what I did, but I don't want to say anything until I'm one hundred percent sure. "How?"

"I can't explain it yet, but I've spent every minute since your doctors told me that you'd be okay trying to figure this out, and I think I've found something."

Hope is a dangerous emotion, because it makes me believe in impossible things. Theo and me together in Chicago. Him waiting for me after class with a maple latte in his hand, and no one from the Firm controlling either of us. I didn't think it would ever be possible, but maybe I was wrong, and all the things I wished for in the middle of the night *can* come true. Maybe we can still spin our tragedies into happy endings.

"How soon will you know?"

"Before the coronation," he says.

"That's in less than forty-eight hours." It doesn't feel like enough time.

"I'll make it work." Theo grins. "Now let's get out of here."

"Where are we going?"

"On our first date, Wheeler." He winks, and his smile is brighter than I've ever seen it.

I feel dizzy with hope as I swipe on mascara and lip gloss and change into a miniskirt and a tight turtleneck sweater in the bathroom. When I come out, Theo groans and drags a hand over his face.

"Not good?" I raise an eyebrow, baiting him, because I know I look good. For maybe the first time ever in all the time we've spent together, I'm not a mess.

"Too good, and you know it."

He climbs back out onto the tree branch, I follow him, and soon we're shimmying down the tree and running like criminals across the garden, pretending that two bodyguards aren't waiting patiently for us outside the gate. He could easily open it, but instead he hoists me over the metal bars, and thankfully this time I don't twist my ankle when I land on the damp sidewalk next to a cream-colored Vespa. Theo buckles a helmet strap under my chin, and then puts one on himself. I take a seat behind him and wrap my arms snugly around his torso, and he kicks the moped to life. My arms tighten as a surge of adrenaline shoots through me, and I feel a sickening lurch as I flash back to the plane plummeting into water.

"You all right back there?"

"Yes. Maybe. I don't know." We haven't moved yet. "I'm just remembering the crash."

"We don't have to do this."

"Just don't go too fast, okay?"

He laughs. "This thing is incapable of going fast. Hold on, and yell in my ear if you want to stop." The Vespa lurches forward and I squeeze all the air out of his lungs. After a few seconds my stomach settles, and I open my eyes.

"Oh." I exhale softly.

At night, London sparkles. Theo points out buildings and landmarks as we cruise past, and it feels both magical and impossibly real at the same time. A perfect date with the boy I haven't been able to stop thinking about since we met.

There were so many moments—*all* the moments we've spent together until tonight—when I didn't think a night like this was in the stars for us. I press my cheek against his shoulder and memorize the feel of my heartbeat against his back. Fate might have us in her crosshairs, but in this moment, everything feels possible.

Theo stops the Vespa on a wharf by the bank of the Thames, in front of the glittering Tower Bridge. I unbuckle my helmet and wipe the tears from my cheeks, unsure if they're the product of windburn or the cacophony of emotions in my chest.

Theo catches a wayward tear with his thumb. "Was this a bad idea?"

I shake my head, the emotion in my throat making it difficult to speak. "It almost made me feel like we could be normal." I push myself onto my toes to kiss him but stop short. I look around the dark wharf. "Are we going to be seen?"

Theo removes his helmet and replaces it with a baseball hat from his back pocket. "Everyone thinks I'm at the party right now, but if anyone gets too close, my guards will take care of it."

We watch lights dance on the water and talk until our bodies are stiff from sitting on pavement, and then I get on the driver's seat of the Vespa and make a few jerky trips up and down the empty boardwalk while Theo tries (and fails) not to laugh at me.

When I give up and admit defeat, he kisses me for a long time and whispers, "Do you want to get out of here?" and I've never agreed to anything faster. We drive back to Clarence House and climb back up the tree and to the open window. He hesitates, but I grab him by the lapels and pull him in through the open window.

"Tonight's been my favorite night in a very, very long time," I say.

He draws back, his eyes lit with excitement. "I forgot to tell you the news. I got the final, official word today: we're not married."

My hands drop from his jacket. "Oh." There's a sudden pit in my stomach. "Are you sure?"

"We triple-checked. There's a process to getting legally married in Greece that includes a bunch of paperwork and fees and registering the marriage within forty days at one of their offices. You're officially free to make all your own choices without worrying about me or the Firm or anyone else."

"Well, that's . . . that's, um, obviously that's—" My stomach is in knots, and not the good kind. I reach for the missing chain around my neck that I got so used to wearing.

This is good news, I tell myself.

This *should* be good news.

I imagine Mom, Dad, and Brooke exchanging a triple high five across the pond as Brooke makes a crack about not starting freshman year as a divorcée.

I've been waiting for this answer for weeks, but it doesn't feel like I thought it would.

"What does this mean for us?"

Theo nudges my chin up. "Do you trust me?" he asks.

I don't hesitate. "I always have."

"We're going to make our future on our own terms, Wheeler," he promises with a light in his ocean-blue eyes that I've never, ever seen. Not when we washed up on the shores of Amorgos, and not when we stood under the stars and said *I do*.

Whatever he's doing, whenever he's ready to tell me, it's going to work.

"What are you thinking?" Theo asks as he runs his fingers through my hair, his hand cupping the back of my neck.

It's hard to think about *anything* when he's this close, but I go with the simplest truth. "That I love you, and I'm so glad the world didn't end."

He laughs, and I cut him off with a slow kiss, pushing his jacket off his arms and letting it fall to the floor. He presses his body to mine, and I shiver as he walks us through the room until the backs of my knees hit the bed and I fall back onto it. He falls on top of me, careful not to land on my sore arm, brushing a featherlight kiss over my shoulder. I nudge his arms over his head and pull his shirt off and then he does the same, staring at me like he can't believe I'm real.

"I never thought I'd be this lucky twice," he whispers in the dark. The rest of our clothes come off one piece at a time, and then I'm caught in his eyes and tangled in his arms, and life has never felt so exactly, perfectly right.

CHAPTER 36

Theo slips out of bed just as the hazy dawn light is spilling across the rug.

I roll over with a tired groan. "Not yet," I mumble, snuggling deeper under the covers.

"Not yet," he agrees. He pulls on his shirt and bends to kiss me on the head. "But soon. Meet me at Buckingham this afternoon? I have good news."

"I can just walk in the front door?"

"Not for long, but today it should be okay," he says with a wink.

The next time I open my eyes he's gone, leaving the window slightly open and a breeze blowing through the drapes.

I do everything slowly, appreciating what might be my last day in this museum of a house. I take Comet out for his morning walk in the courtyard and let him coerce me into an hour-long game of fetch, because why not? Then I stay in the shower until the water runs cold and sample every kind of weird British candy from a box that was delivered to the house last night. I even sit on a couch that looks like it hasn't been touched this century and Google my name, where I see that Theo's press people have released a statement confirming we're not married.

When my stomach does a weird little somersault, I tell myself it's because I ate something called "wine gums."

I use my new phone to text Victoria and ask for a ride to the palace. She sends me a car in the early afternoon, and I load it up with all of the untouched gift baskets that will go to waste if they sit around this house. When I ask Comet if he wants to go to the palace, he barks in excitement and hops into the back of the car.

"Buckingham Palace, please," I tell the driver. It feels *ridiculous*, and I half expect him to laugh at me, but instead he drives me right past the crowds on the steps of the Victoria Memorial, through a set of black gates adorned with gold accents, all the way to the front door, where Louise is waiting for me.

I try not to think about the cameras pointed at me on the other side of the gate.

"You brought gifts!" Louise exclaims. "Andrew and Charlotte will be excited. Let me get them!" She runs into the house and returns minutes later with the two youngest royals and their nanny, Penny.

"You must be the infamous Wren. I've been badgering Teddy to bring you around." Penny folds me into a warm hug, her mom energy so strong that tears pool in the corners of my eyes. Penny has been the royal nanny since Theo was a baby. She's one of the people he cares about most in the world and the woman he tried to save by refusing to get in the bunker. I love her for loving him unconditionally when no one else did.

"I didn't know you called him Teddy," I tell her.

"I'm the only one who's allowed," she says with a chuckle

and a wink, before looking at me seriously. "We've got a lot of catching up to do, but for now, let Andrew and Charlotte help you unload the car." Penny loads the kids' arms with gift baskets bigger than themselves, to their extreme delight.

The Buckingham Palace Grand Entrance Hall is darker than I expected; the windowless space makes me feel like I've stepped into something that belongs in a fairy tale. Red-carpeted staircases branch in every direction. Goose bumps trail up my arms as I take in dozens of marble columns and Greek sculptures displayed in golden niches. I mentally take notes on everything, including the scent of the thousands of bouquets at the palace gates, so I can describe it in perfect detail to Naomi.

"I'll give you a tour!" Louise says as she leads me to the Grand Staircase, and Andrew and Charlotte challenge me to a race up one side and down the other. Andrew wins (and does a victory dab at the top) and then Louise shows me half a dozen rooms, each with its own name: the White Drawing Room, the Green Drawing Room, the Music Room, the State Dining Room. Everything is blending together into a haze of gold and opulence when I stop dead in my tracks in front of an open door.

"Is this . . ."

"The Throne Room, yeah," Louise says.

You hear the word "king," you see the paparazzi, you walk through the palace, but nothing can prepare you to see a red-carpeted dais holding two honest-to-goodness *thrones*.

I swear under my breath. "He really is a *king*. Weird."

"And here I thought I was hiding it so well."

I turn at the sound of Theo's voice, and my stomach floods with heat to see him leaning against the open door of the Throne Room. "I'll meet you in here in ten minutes?" he says.

"In the Throne Room?"

He rubs a hand self-consciously over the back of his neck. "Why not?" He then turns to Louise. "We need to talk." He motions for her to follow him down the hall.

I hesitate at the entrance to the Throne Room, not sure what to do in his absence. Andrew and Charlotte come cruising past me, balancing one of the largest fruit baskets between them. "Go on now," Penny says, ushering them along. "Theo called a family meeting." She takes the basket from them and hands it off to me. "Find somewhere to put this? I overheard the kids plotting to drop a pineapple from the top of the Grand Staircase." She shakes her head in exasperation as she follows the youngest royals down the hall.

My stomach flutters with excitement as I wait for Theo to come back, and when I see Richard Graves walking briskly toward me, even that's not enough to ruin my good mood. "What are you doing here?" he demands.

I smile blandly at him. "Theo invited me."

"Where is he?" He looks over my shoulder into the empty Throne Room.

"I don't know."

His brows narrow in suspicion. "When are you leaving? You can't be seen here so close to the coronation. Especially not looking like that."

I smooth my hand over my messy ponytail and cross my arms. "Or what?"

His scowl deepens. "If you see His Majesty, tell him that I'm looking for him."

"Okay." I probably won't, and to make up for it, I hold out the gift basket. "Are you hungry? Do you want some pineapple?"

He looks at me dismissively. "I'm allergic to pineapple," he says as he brushes past me down the hall.

"Wait!" I call out, before I even know why I'm doing it. My brain trips over itself trying to remember something important, and then it hits me in the chest like a crashing plane.

I get a flash of Victoria dismissively rolling her eyes—not at me, but at Henry, poison-testing passion fruit on the island. *"Pineapple gives you an itchy tongue."*

Graves looks at me over his shoulder. "What?" he asks impatiently.

"I saw the articles about Henry playing football for charity. He looked great," I say quickly, hoping that I'm wrong.

Graves smiles, his dimples flashing. "He always looks brilliant, doesn't he?" He nods proudly and walks away, and all the jumbled pieces in my brain fall into place.

All at once, everything makes sense. No wonder Graves is constantly throwing Theo under the bus in favor of his younger brother. It's not because Henry is "more authentic" or "works harder."

Henry gets special treatment from the media because his biological father is the press secretary.

I pull out my phone and quickly Google old pictures of Richard Graves. Hidden in the depths of an old royal message board is his high school photo, complete with a mop of black curly hair.

I close my eyes as I'm hit with another memory, this one excruciating: Theo told me that his mom leaked the news of her own divorce in order to bury a story she didn't want out. Theo's dad died as a result of trying to cover up that story, and I'd bet anything that it had to do with Alice, Graves, and the child they had together.

I step into the Throne Room and close the door behind me, fighting to keep my breathing steady. My theory was right in all the wrong ways: it's not Theo who's ineligible for the throne, but Henry, the only sibling who ever really wanted it.

The door clicks open, and I jump. Theo and Henry walk into the room wearing matching smiles. Henry's nearly vibrating with excitement. Dread seeps into my veins as he slowly approaches the thrones on the dais.

"Has Theo told you the good news?" he asks in an unsteady voice.

I shake my head, too afraid to ask.

Theo crosses the distance between us, takes the fruit basket from my hands, and places it on the floor. Then he looks at me, relief and excitement written in his eyes and his smile and his easy posture.

"I've spent the last several days with my political advisers and every constitutional expert I could get ahold of, and now it's official." He grins at me expectantly, but I feel like I'm falling into quicksand. "Before the coronation tomorrow, I'm going to abdicate the throne, and Henry is going to become the king."

Henry pushes his hair out of his eyes, and with a deep breath that he's been waiting all his life to take, he sits on the throne.

CHAPTER 37

Henry, leave," I say. There's not enough air in the Throne Room.

He blinks in surprise. "I mean, I will this time, but you won't get away with talking to me like that when I'm the king." He smirks playfully.

I feel like I might pass out. I rub my sweaty palms on my thighs.

Henry slowly stands up. "Whoa. Weird energy in here."

"Go," Theo barks at his brother.

Henry throws me an odd look as I pace across the carpet. When the door shuts behind him, I can't bring myself to look at Theo. I feel sick. I don't want to have to be the one to tell him about Henry.

My legs shake and I feel dizzy. My fingertips and lips go numb. Theo's talking to me, but his voice sounds far away. I think I'm having a panic attack.

I fall into a chair, realizing only after I've sat down that it's one of the thrones. Eighteen-year-old American Wren Wheeler on a throne.

Impossible.

Unless . . .

I feel like I'm going to throw up. *What the hell am I supposed to do now?*

I look down at the throne, and the answer to all of our problems pops into my head. It might be crazy, but when have Theo and I ever done anything that wasn't?

I close my eyes and wish for a sign. Brooke's words ring clearly in my mind.

Wanting a sign is *your sign, Wren.*

My vision from last night shifts from Chicago to Buckingham, and I see it all. Theo and me planning royal tours together. Working together to make positive changes for the future of the monarchy. Ball gowns and tiaras and a happily-ever-after.

"Wren, what's wrong?" Theo's voice is urgent. He kneels in front of the throne, his eyes wide with fear. It snaps me out of my panic attack, and I take my sign and run with it. I kneel on the bloodred carpet in front of the throne and say the only thing that makes sense.

"Theodore Geoffrey Edward George, will you marry me?"

His brows crease. "Did you hear what I said? Henry is going to be king. We get to be together, away from all of this."

I don't want to ruin his fantasy, but I'll never be able to look him in the eye again if I don't say something. "I think Richard Graves is Henry's father; he's not a legitimate heir."

Theo blinks in shock. "What are you talking about?"

"Your blood types are different. It means that you don't have the same two parents."

The color drains from his face. "Are you sure?"

"Yes. I'm not a hundred percent positive about Graves, but doesn't him being Henry's dad just make sense?"

I can see his mind racing until he comes to the same conclusion that I did. His eyes fill with betrayal, and it looks like falling backward off a cliff, so I give him something to hold on to.

"We're out of options. You're going to be the king no matter what, and I want to be with you without any of the Firm's bullshit trying to separate us. What do you say?"

He pulls his teeth over his lower lip. "If we get married tonight, you'll become the queen tomorrow . . ."

No matter the circumstances, I think somehow Theo and I were always going to find ourselves here. "I'm not interested in a path that doesn't involve you."

He tears his eyes away from mine and runs a hand over his face. "Even if I do everything I can to protect you, the press and public scrutiny and loss of freedom might ruin your life. Nothing has changed."

I close the final inches between us. "We love each other, and if we let it, that changes everything."

"I don't want to lose you," he says, sliding his fingers down my neck until I feel my pulse in the palm of his hand.

"Do you remember what you said in your wedding vows?" I ask.

"I said we were fate," he whispers.

"Maybe it's true, maybe it's not. But I choose you anyway, every day, forever."

He kisses me once, so soft I might have imagined it. "Tonight. Under the stars."

"Is there any other way?"

He kisses me harder, and I've never felt so sure of anything.

The first time Theo and I got married, it was because the universe was holding a gun to our heads. This time, it'll be because we want to.

⁂

We split up and agree to meet in the gardens after sundown. When I ask if we have enough time to make *this* wedding legal, Theo assures me that he'll take care of it, that he'll call in favors and pull strings if he has to. ("Perks of being the king" followed by "Shite. Henry's going to be miffed" followed by a wide-eyed "How do I explain any of this?")

I'm dazed as I walk out of the Throne Room. I don't know where to go, or what to do, but I somehow wind up at the foot of the Grand Staircase. I slowly glide my hand over the bronze casting and look up to see an etched-glass dome filtering in soft gray light, and it hits me that this is going to be my *home*. Not the dorm room in Northwestern with my new Target bedsheets, but the three-hundred-year-old palace that Theo grew up hating.

I sit on the bottom step and close my eyes. For the first time since the comet, I see my future in perfect clarity. Theo and I will live here. He'll be king; I'll be queen consort. I'll take classes at Oxford, figure out if photography is still my passion, and spend long afternoons playing fetch with Comet in the palace gardens. We'll find a way to move the monarchy into the future, to make Theo hate it less. No more guesswork. No more stressing over what to do with my second chance. No more hazy, uncertain daydreams. Just Theo and me together, finally, without any catastrophes to tear us apart.

I call the only person who might understand what I'm about

to do, and I swear I hear my heartbeat echoing off the glass ceiling as the phone rings.

"Hey, what's up?" Naomi's voice is hushed.

"Is this a bad time?"

"No, hang on." The line goes quiet for several seconds. I hear her say goodbye to someone, and then she's back. "Sorry, I was in my room, but I can talk on my way to class."

"What class?"

"Calc. But oh my gosh, I have to tell you about my English Comp professor. He's old, so I thought it would be boring, right? But no. He's actually hilarious and so cool. He's covered in tattoos and swears all the time and treats us like adults. He doesn't even take attendance. Not that I'm going to skip class—I would never—but still. I *love* it here." She sighs dreamily, and it makes me want to cry. Suddenly, I feel sick with envy. She's exactly where she's supposed to be, and she *knows* it. "Hang on, I'm cutting through Sarge, it's going to get loud."

I wait until the noise around her subsides, and it gives me time to remember how to breathe. "What's Sarge?"

"Sargent. It's what everyone calls the dining hall."

"Oh." I realize with a start that I could be with her right now, using student slang like "Sarge." It feels unthinkable. If I were there, I don't know what I'd be doing with my life, or what it would mean for Theo and me.

"Have you talked to Theo yet? What's going on with the coronation? And when are you coming home?"

My blood pressure spikes, until I remember that I finally have answers. "Theo and I are going to get married," I say quickly.

She doesn't respond for so long that I check to see if the call dropped. "Naomi?"

"Yeah, sorry, I just . . . I don't know what to say. Obviously you and Theo are soulmates, but is it going to be a long engagement type of thing?"

"We're getting married tonight."

"What?!" I hear a door slam behind her, and she lowers her voice again. "That's *crazy*."

"I want to be with him, and this is the only future for us that makes sense."

She's quiet for a long moment. "You can't even wait for me to be a bridesmaid?"

I don't want her to think about that. I want her to be excited for me. "You have a room at Buckingham anytime you want. Hell, you can have a dozen rooms! Come for your birthday in December!"

"I'll be studying for finals," she says flatly.

"Oh yeah." My stomach drops. "Well, I'll come visit you! You can show me all the best places to hang out on campus."

"Will you be allowed to do that?"

I remember Theo's endless warnings about stalkers and bodyguards and paparazzi, and the hairs on the back of my neck stand up. *My life will never be normal again.*

"Wren—" I hear muffled voices in the background. "I have to go. Class is starting. Just . . . don't do anything until you've really thought about it, okay?"

I assure her I won't, but I'm dazed as we hang up. If my best friend and the biggest royal fanatic I know thinks this is too much too soon, should I reconsider? My stomach squirms uncomfortably, and I realize quickly that I can't. Despite Naomi's lack of enthusiasm, I'm relieved to finally have a life plan again, even if that plan is to secretly marry the king of England the night before his coronation.

I pace in front of the staircase as I mentally make a list of everything I'll need for tonight, starting with paperwork. I text Brooke and ask her to scan me a copy of my birth certificate—along with an ominous Don't ask questions! (After Naomi's reaction, I don't want anyone else to second-guess me.)

I also need my ring, a dress, Comet, witnesses—

"Oof!" I run smack into Victoria.

"There you are." She smooths her skirt. "Has Theo told you the news yet?"

"Do you want to be my maid of honor at our wedding tonight?" I blurt.

She looks gobsmacked. "You're joking."

"I'm really not."

"Explain everything," she demands as she grabs me by the arm and drags me to her bedroom.

I tell her about Henry and Graves, and she takes a lot longer to process it than Theo did. Comet and I play with a pile of dog toys on the floor of her room while she paces and Googles and occasionally swears under her breath. After nearly an hour, she walks out the door.

I bop Comet on the nose with a stuffed teddy bear he's nearly ripped to shreds. "Do you think she's coming back?"

He cocks his head as if he's thinking about it.

Five minutes later the princess returns with a bottle of champagne in hand. "I'll do it. I'll be your chief bridesmaid." She pops the top, takes a small sip, and disappears into her closet.

"Should I tie the ring to Comet's collar?" I ask as she discards dress after dress. Comet is on his dog bed with his head in my lap, and I'm gripping the ring Theo gave me tightly in my palm. My stomach is a riot of butterflies.

"What if he swallows it?" She emerges with an armful of dresses.

I look at the pool of dog slobber in my lap. She has a point. "He really sleeps here every night?" I ask, even though it's obvious from the dog bed to the toys that Comet is fully at home in Victoria's room.

"I have trouble falling asleep unless he's here," she says from behind a pile of fabric. "Since Mum died."

I glance at my rescue dog, who was only mine for a few chaotic days, and finally say what I should have said days ago. "Thanks for taking care of Comet."

Victoria lays the dresses on the bed and cocks her hip. "I did it for him, not you."

I'm too excited and overwhelmed to be fazed by her prickliness. Or maybe I'm just getting used to her. "He can stay here with you, as long as I can still hang out with him."

She wrinkles her nose. "Shared custody?"

"We *are* going to be sisters."

She suppresses a smile as she focuses on the dresses. "I've never worn half of these. If you find something you like, I can get a tailor in here to make quick alterations. We'll tell them it's for the coronation tomorrow."

I run my fingers across the expensive fabric, unexpected tears burning my eyes. This isn't exactly how I would have wanted my wedding to go—no family and no Naomi—but I have Theo, and that's more than enough.

Victoria cocks her head and surveys me seriously. "Are you sure this is what you want? Because you're about to lose complete control of your life."

I'm tired of getting the same warning. I know palace life is going to be different than what I'm used to, but if Theo and

I can be happy together on a deserted island, we can make it work anywhere. "The *only* thing I'm sure of is that I want him."

"Is this what Theo wants?" she asks, and my stomach twists anxiously. No future in which Theo is king is a future he wants, but it's the one he's got, and because we live in a world where a comet could hit or a plane could fall from the sky or the earth could open up and swallow us whole, why not do what makes us happy?

"I really do love him," I say.

"I know you do." She looks up at the ceiling and blows out a breath. "And I guess I'm sorry that I've been an utter git," she mumbles quickly. "It won't suck having you as my big sister."

I gasp. "What did you say?"

"Don't make me say it again or I'm taking back the dresses," she threatens.

"I don't believe you," I gloat, a smile growing on my face. "You don't hate me. In fact, you kind of like me."

"Ugh." She groans, tossing a tulle dress at my head. "We don't have time for this. We need to turn you into a bride." When I push the fabric aside and glance at her, she's smothering another smile as she turns away.

CHAPTER 38

I'm going to marry Theodore Geoffrey Edward George, again (for *real* this time), in a floral-embroidered tulle gown. The pink, purple, and orange flowers remind me of a certain Greek sunset from several months ago, and if I thought my life felt surreal *then*, nothing could have prepared me for the moment my apocalypse dog dragged me through the starry gardens at Buckingham Palace, on my way to marry a king.

Last time, I told myself that it didn't matter, that it wasn't real because it wasn't legal, but I couldn't shake the inescapable feeling that marrying Theo on that beach meant *something*. This time, marrying Theo is probably the most life-altering decision I'll ever make, but it feels more like crossing the t's and dotting the i's on the paperwork for a choice we already made.

"Did you know that Theo left me at the altar the first time we tried to do this?" I whisper to Victoria as we sneak through the darkened gardens. The palace was buzzing all day in antici-pation of the coronation, and it took until hours past sunset for the halls to quiet down enough for us to sneak out. There will be a lot of angry people in Buckingham Palace tomorrow, but that's a problem for daylight. Tonight is for making our own destiny.

"He's not skiving off this time." Victoria points toward the rose garden, where three figures wait in the dark.

My pulse thrums in anticipation.

Henry meets us on the path to the rose garden with a hand-picked bunch of roses held loosely in his fist. "Heard you're the reason I've been kicked off the throne." His voice cracks with suppressed emotion, and my stomach pitches in guilt.

I've been so focused on how this news affected Theo and me, but Henry's the one whose entire life was blown up. "I'm so sorry."

"It's fine. I'm fine. It's completely fine." He says the least believable thing in the history of man and forces a fake smile.

"Do you want to leave?"

He slants me a pained look. "And go where? Inside, to confront the father who's been lying to me for my entire bloody life? I can't emphasize enough how much I don't want to do that, so even though I feel like I'm dying inside, I'm here to support my brother. And you, because you're going to be my sister." He must see the guilt on my face, because when I open my mouth to apologize again, he holds up his hands. "I'm serious. I'll deal with my looming existential dread in the morning."

"Theo's lucky to have you," I tell him.

"Damn right. And I'm about to steal his title as the saddest, moodiest, most miserable bastard in the palace."

I can't help but laugh. "Does everything have to be a competition?"

"Yes," he says seriously as he offers me the roses. "Careful where you hold them. I'm bleeding in three places."

I cautiously pinch the flowers between my fingertips and tell myself that it's not at all a bad sign that my bouquet can double as a weapon.

"Did you see anyone on your way here?" Henry asks Victoria.

"No. Why? Did you?"

His eyes scan the palace grounds, lit only by stars and moonlight. "No . . . I don't think so, anyway." He looks around a final time.

A shiver runs up my spine and I clutch the flowers on instinct. "Ow!" I draw in a breath as blood drips onto my ivory gown. "Crap!"

Victoria quickly unties a ribbon from her hair and wraps my palm. "You didn't let Comet have the ring, did you?"

"No. Why?" I touch the chain around my neck for reassurance and take a deep breath.

"Just making sure nothing else can go wrong."

"Don't take too long. Theo's losing his mind waiting for you, and the archbishop just wants to go to bed." Henry salutes as he jogs backward away from us.

Victoria straightens the back of my gown, and I start to walk toward Theo, but stop after a few steps. I turn to her. "Should there be music?"

"How would I know?"

It's weirdly quiet out here, now that I think about it. There's a reason that brides don't walk down the aisle in silence; the eye-contact situation would be awkward for everyone. "I think there should be music."

Victoria raises her eyebrows. "I didn't bring my phone. Did you?"

"No." I glance back at the rose garden. *Was it always this far away?* "Can you sing?" I ask suddenly.

She puts a hand on her hip. "What song?"

"Something romantic?"

"'My milkshake brings all the boys to the yard—'"

"Stop!" I brandish my weapon-bouquet at her. "Don't ever do that again."

She rolls her eyes. "Will you just walk?"

I do, but Comet gets bored or distracted on the way and dashes in the wrong direction across the dark grass.

"I'll get him. You keep going," Victoria calls as she runs into the dark. Which is how I finally make it to the rose garden with a bloodstained dress, humming a twenty-year-old meme song under my breath, without my maid of honor or chief bridesdog. When I lock eyes with Theo, however, none of those things matter.

"Hi," I say.

"Hi," he says back. Even in the starlight, I can see his cheeks turn a shade of pink that makes my stomach flutter. "You look beautiful."

"So do you," I tell him as my own face heats. "I mean, good. You look good. Perfect?" I swallow the lump in my throat. "I'm nervous."

"Wren, this is the Archbishop of Canterbury." He nods to an old man in gold robes, and it's a credit to how good Theo looks in his dark suit and tie that I didn't notice an *old man in gold robes* until now. "Your Grace, this is Wren Wheeler."

"Your Grace! Wow, that's . . . um . . . fancy titles for every-one over here." Sweat drips down my back.

Henry smothers a laugh while I cringe at my own rambling.

I appreciate the archbishop doing this for us, but I weirdly miss having our wedding officiated by an old Greek fisherman with cake crumbs in his mustache.

Victoria is out of breath when she finally leads Comet into the rose garden by his collar. Our dog has half a tree branch in his mouth. "What did I miss? Are you two married yet?"

"The archbishop was just telling me he would like us to move the ceremony to Westminster," Theo explains. "I know it's not what we pictured." He passes a hand over the back of his neck, and I realize I'm not the only one who's nervous.

"You're right. I've changed my mind." I turn and pretend to run.

Theo grabs my hand and yanks me into his chest. A flush of heat rushes through me as his gaze burns into mine. "If you're going to leave, tell me now and put me out of my misery."

I tilt my chin up and run my fingers through the hair on the nape of his neck. He shivers and presses a soft kiss to my lips, and I realize I'd choose him anywhere. On a beach in Greece, an island in Portugal, or an old church in London. My chest almost hurts with how much I'm feeling, and I pull away as tears prick my eyes. "Westminster it is."

Theo's eyes flash. He looks like he has a hundred things he wants to say, but before he can, Henry claps his hands together, breaking the spell. "I'll drive."

⁎   ⁎   ⁎

Buckingham Palace is less than a mile from Westminster Abbey, and the archbishop decides he wants to walk. (I'm sure it has nothing to do with Victoria saying she's going to play "Milkshake" on top volume, or Henry laughing chaotically when Theo asks which car he's going to take.) I slip off my shoes and Theo, Comet, Victoria, and I walk across the grounds and meet Henry on a side street, where he's rolled up in a classic convertible Aston Martin with the top down.

Theo cocks an eyebrow. "How is this more discreet than just walking to the church?"

"Relax. It's almost midnight," Henry says as he reaches across the front seats and opens the door. Theo, Comet, and I climb into the (cramped) back seat while Victoria takes the passenger seat next to Henry. He peels away from the curb and floors the gas pedal. I hit the back of my seat hard as Victoria turns the radio all the way up.

I glance sideways at Theo as the car races down the sleepy London street, and my stomach bottoms out. I try not to think about sinking ferries and falling planes. "Does he know what he's doing?"

"Slow down," Theo says to his brother.

"Hang on." Henry readjusts the rearview mirror. "I think someone's following us."

Victoria, Theo, and I all whip around to see a car tailgating us. A camera flashes and spots of light burst across my vision.

"Is your seat belt on?" Theo asks. I nod and try to slouch down in my seat, but there's no room that isn't already being taken up by Comet.

"Should I try to lose them?" Henry yells.

"No!" Theo growls. "Just take us to Westminster."

"They'll follow us to the church," Henry says. "I'm going to try to lose them up here." He makes a sharp turn that throws me against Theo's side. The panicky feeling in my chest grows. I look back at the car and my lips go numb when I see that it's still following us. I close my eyes, throw one arm around Comet, and grasp Theo's hand.

"Stop the car!" Theo barks.

"Just give me a second. I know I can lose them," Henry protests. He turns up another narrow side street, weaving around parked cars. Victoria screams at Henry and throws her hands over her head. The tingling numbness extends to my hands. I draw in a jagged breath.

"Slow down!" Theo orders, and Henry finally lets off the gas and flips a U-turn to take us to the church. I crane my neck to see the car, and my pulse hammers when I see how close it still is; its bumper nearly touches ours as Henry slows to a stop at an intersection. I make eye contact with the driver, and goose bumps race across my arms.

"It won't back off," I say as a sick feeling of dread washes through me. I try to take a deep breath but can't get enough air. There's a pressure slowly crushing my chest, cutting off my airway, and I'm shaking all over. Henry rolls our car forward, and another series of camera flashes blind me. I tear my eyes off our stalkers, spin around in my seat, and barely have time to register the second car that appears from a side street before it slams into us.

The crunch of metal on metal makes my stomach pitch. Victoria screams. The Aston Martin spins across the road, crashing over the curb and into a tree. By the time I look up, choking on a cloud of smoke, the other cars have peeled away from the scene.

"Is everyone okay?" I blink through the smoke and check Comet for signs of injury. My hands are shaking so violently that it's painful.

"I think so."

"I'm good."

"Not hurt."

My knees tremble as I unbuckle my seat belt and hike up my dress to climb out over the side of the car. My bare feet hit cold sidewalk, and I walk around to look at the smoking, crumpled front corner of the car. My stomach drops, and I can't breathe. *I'm back in the water after the plane crash, plunging toward the ocean floor.*

"What do we do now?" Victoria rubs her neck. Behind her, the pointed arches of Westminster reach into the starry sky.

My gaze rises to meet Theo's. His face is ghostly pale.

"This is still happening, right? I didn't cock up the wedding, did I?" Henry looks between Theo and me.

"You and Tor go in. Wren and I need a minute."

My panic rises as they leave. I close my eyes and breathe slowly through my nose, fighting off the familiar warning sirens in my head that scream to untangle myself before I run out of air.

It's the dress, I decide. The dress is too tight.

When I open my eyes, Theo is crouched in front of the damaged car. "Someone could have been killed."

I remember thinking the same thing after being chased in Toronto, and the wedding dress and fancy car don't make this time any less awful. "Almost dying is what we do best," I quip to cover my anxious energy.

Theo looks wordlessly at me, his expression pained. "Wren," he says softly, and I realize too late that joking about this isn't going to make it any less terrifying.

"I know," I say. We both look wordlessly up at Westminster, and I see our future as clear as the illuminated church. If Theo and I get married tonight, we'll spend the rest of our lives hiding from the press and fighting with the Firm. And the craziest part of all? I still think it might be worth it.

"Wren—"

I cut him off, because my name sounds all wrong. "Call me Wheeler," I say, grabbing his hand. "Better yet, call me American girl. I always loved when you did that." He pulls his hand out of mine, and tears burn behind my eyes.

"Wren—" he says again, and this time his voice breaks on my name. "I love you more now than I did at our first wedding, which is why I can't let you stay. You won't be happy here."

I feel like I'm climbing up sand, scrabbling for purchase as the ground caves beneath my feet. "Does it matter what I want?"

His eyes search mine. "Why do you want to marry me?"

"Because I love you."

He looks like he's in pain. "And why do you want to be queen?"

What kind of question is that? "Because you're the king."

His expression crumples, and he looks like he's pleading with me. "If that's all you've got, then you're going to regret giving up your choices. You deserve a future made on your own terms."

"What terms?" I cry. "I don't know what I'm doing, Theo! I've never felt so lost in my life. If I go back home, everyone else has their life figured out, and I can't even pick a major! All I know is that I love you, and if I'm the queen, I'll have plans and a purpose again. I *want* that. I'm *excited* for it." I push the words out in a desperate plea, and only realize they're a lie once I've said them.

I want to be with Theo, but neither one of us wants it like this.

Immediately, it's easier to breathe. "Leave with me," I say quickly.

Theo's eyes widen in shock. "What?"

"Tonight. Right now. Let's go. You've run away once; you can do it again." The pressure on my chest eases, each word bringing me closer to the surface.

Theo glances around the empty street, his mind calculating. After a long moment, I see the instant he gives up on us. He straightens his spine, a note of bitterness in his voice. "And what would that future look like for us?"

I close my eyes and see nothing but black. I can't even conjure a hazy daydream of Theo and me in this impossible, hypothetical future, but I don't care if it's easy or clear or makes immediate sense. I want it anyway.

"I'm leaving tonight. Are you coming with me or not?"

His mouth twists as he blinks away unshed tears, and his silence is my answer. I pull my eyes away from his, so he won't see me fall apart.

"You said I won't be happy here, but are *you* happy?" I ask.

"Being royal has very little to do with happiness, Wheeler."

Wheeler. It strikes me right in the heart. "Don't call me that."

Pain flashes across his features, and I can feel the weight of a backpack strap pulling me to the ocean floor. My lungs burn for air, and I realize he's right. If I stay, I'll drown.

I yank the chain from my neck and let it slip through my fingers. "You deserve to be happy too, Your Highness."

Tears blur the sight of Theo's ring landing on the ground, and I take off running into the black.

CHAPTER 39

It turns out that the "too long; didn't read" version of almost marrying the king of England is just the word "almost." It could have happened, but it didn't. Close but no cigar. The happily-ever-after-that-wasn't.

And just like Princess Louise predicted, the tl;dr version of King Theodore Geoffrey Edward George's coronation ceremony is: *Boring ceremony, big hat, stolen jewels.* (Now with a side of heartbreak.)

I've never felt so helpless as when I watched the live stream of the event and saw the desperation in his eyes. I wanted to be the one to make him happy, but I couldn't. Theo and I were impossible from the very beginning; we fell in love in between life and death, the sea and the stars, reality and make-believe. It was *never* going to work, but I still feel mystified that it didn't.

After the coronation, I quickly deleted my Google Alert for "Comet, dog," and then blocked everything royal from my social media feeds, but it didn't help. It's the irony of my life that fate wasn't enough to keep Theo and me together, while the plane crash has made sure it's all anyone wants to talk about. Everywhere I go, I'm "one of the plane-crash girls." At the library and the dining hall and freshman movie night in the dorm, I'm bombarded with royal news.

"Did you date King Theo?"

"Did you hear about Prince Henry's real father?"

"Princess Victoria's having a blowout eighteenth-birthday party. Were you invited?"

Kind of, yes, and *obviously not.*

I'd pay a hundred bucks just to have someone ask what my major is instead. (Still undeclared, but I'm trying every day to embrace the uncertainty instead of stressing over it.)

I'm packing up my things after the end of a Psych 101 lecture when my phone buzzes. It's a message from Naomi. She texts about two hundred times a day to check on me, which is equal parts thoughtful and emotionally draining. I'm never sure how to explain that even though leaving was the right thing, I still sometimes feel like I'm trying to breathe from the bottom of a muddy river.

I step out of Swift Hall, and my eyes are drawn to the water. Northwestern's campus is located on the shores of Lake Michigan, and not a day goes by that I don't think about the way the Eiffel Tower lights reflect off the Seine or how the sunset burns over a beach in Amorgos. Sometimes when I close my eyes, I can still smell passion fruit on an imaginary breeze and feel the sticky sweet juice on my fingers.

All of that is great, but there's something special about Chicago in October. The photography club met yesterday afternoon and we drank maple lattes and took pictures of each other crunching orange and red leaves underfoot. It turns out "the future" is an overwhelming concept, but that's not reason enough to latch on to something that promises easy answers, and going to college and joining clubs and figuring things out one day at a time isn't as scary as I thought it'd be.

My phone buzzes again. I open the texts from Naomi as I wander down Campus Drive.

Get your ass to Wrigley.

Dad scored tickets to the game.

Levi and I are waiting for you.

I blink at my phone in surprise. The Cubs have a home play-offs game today, but Naomi never said anything about wanting to go.

My thumb hovers over my phone as I debate what to say. My classes are done for the week, but I have homework. I could go, but what if someone recognizes me?

Stop thinking of excuses and just come.

Don't be sad and alone when you can be sad with me, a hot dog, and hot guys in tight pants!

I can't help but smile, and even though the air smells like rain that reminds me of London, I agree to meet up with her at the game.

I quickly swing by my dorm to drop off my bag, and then I run to catch the Purple Line from Evanston to Wrigley Field. The platform is so crowded with baseball fans in white and blue that I miss the first train and am forced to wait for the next one. I shoot a text to Naomi.

Ugh. Missed the purple line

She responds instantly. NOT THE PURPLE!!!

The second train is wall-to-wall with bodies. I squeeze toward the end of the car, put my headphones on, and zone out until my phone buzzes in my pocket. It's Naomi, checking on my location. I'm typing my response when the train slows to a halt.

I pop out my headphones in time to hear most of the announcement. "Unexpected delay . . . obstruction on the track . . . please be patient . . . we'll be moving again as quickly as possible."

Train delay. Might be late, I tell Naomi.

Don't be!

The air in the crowded car is sticky and humid, and every minute feels like a hundred. I'm questioning how much I even like baseball by the time the train starts moving again. The energy among the Cubs fans amps up, and they make room in this overcrowded sweat lodge to accommodate a trio of bucket drummers that block me from getting off when I try to make my transfer.

I have to get off at the next stop, and I just squeeze through, narrowly avoiding being smashed. I check the time and see four new texts from Naomi. I glance at the arrivals board and debate waiting for the next train or running the last half mile to the stadium.

A fat raindrop falls on my phone screen. I glance miserably

at the sky and decide to cut my losses. Fate clearly does not want me at this game.

It's about to rain and I'm exhausted. Have fun without me!

Her response is lightning fast. Just come!

The rain falls harder, soaking through my shoes. I'm heading back to campus. Sorry. Rain check!

Naomi's next text arrives as I hit send. Don't make me ruin the surprise, Wheeler.

The train pulls in. I pause half in and half out of the train, my heart in my throat.

Wheeler? There's only one person on earth who calls me that.

I'm slightly dazed as I take a seat on the vacant train car. My phone buzzes again, but it's not Naomi. It's from a ten-digit number, the kind that belong to people who live in the UK.

Keep an eye on him for us, okay?

P.S. You owe me a dress.

All at once I understand what's happening, even if I don't understand how. My heart is in my throat as the train leaves the station. I'm the first one out the door at the next stop, and I sprint toward Wrigley Field in the pouring rain, where I run into Naomi and Levi outside the stadium.

"What are you doing here?" she asks, looking alarmed.

"Where is he?" I grip her arms as I double over to catch my breath.

"On his way to campus!"

"He's on the train?" I'm already backing away from them,

toward the nearest crosswalk. I weave around people and someone yells at me to slow down. Finally, I reach the train stop
and elbow my way through the crowd, looking under umbrel-
las and rain ponchos. Every face is a stranger's, and my heart
begins a hummingbird rhythm.

He's not here.

The platform is crowded with game-day crowds, and I'm
quickly swept into the fray and onto the train, stuck between
a woman with a stroller and two men loudly arguing over the
Cubs' chances of going all the way this year.

"Are you looking for someone?" The woman with the stroller
frowns at me as I crane my neck, still searching. "What do they
look like?"

"He's . . . tall," I say unhelpfully.

The train stops and I slip out to transfer back to the Purple
Line. I find an empty seat at the back of the car and sit down
in sopping-wet clothes. I glance at my reflection in the window.
My hair (brown again) is hanging in clumps around my face,
and my eyes are wide with shock. I drop my head against the
window. This rapid fluctuation between wild excitement and
crushing disappointment can't be good for my heart.

I slump back in my seat as my phone vibrates again with a
new message from Naomi.

He's lost. Says he's coming back to Wrigley.

"Wait! I need to get off the train!" I yell. A young guy sticks
his foot between the closing doors and helps me pry them apart.

"Thank you!" I yell over my shoulder as I spill back onto the
platform. The train whooshes away, and I shield my eyes from
the drizzle to check when the next one is coming.

TRAIN DELAY.

I wail in frustration. "I'm just trying to get to Wrigley!"

"If you wanted to see me so badly, Wheeler, you could have called."

The hairs on the back of my neck stand up, and for a single, perfect breath, time stops.

Theo is waiting on the opposite platform, wearing a Cubs hat and a grin. Comet is by his side. We stare at each other for a moment that erases four weeks of hurt in one effortless heartbeat.

"Wait there!" we both shout at the same time and start racing down the steps to the street. He's faster than I am, and before I can breathe, he's crushing me into a hug that transforms into a kiss as he lifts me up and I wrap my legs around his waist. I taste salt on our lips and realize I'm crying.

I pull back, and he sets my feet on the ground, keeping his arms locked around me. I lean into him, too scared to hope. "How are you here?" I search the street for his royal entourage.

He brushes wet hair out of my face with one hand as the other slips into the back pocket of my jeans. "My plane didn't crash."

I'm trembling with anticipation. "You know what I mean."

"You made me brave enough to imagine a different ending." He pulls a lighter from his pocket and flips it open. The flame flickers to life as chills race across my skin. "Do you remember what we did the first time we met?" Fire reflects in his eyes.

"We burned my plans for the future." It felt so symbolic at the time, turning my itinerary to ash.

He pins me under his gaze until I can't breathe. "And now I've burned mine." He leans in with a whisper, his breath sending shivers across my neck and down my spine. "It's over, American girl."

My heart is in my throat and I'm crying again. Even on the nights I let myself hope for our future, I never dreamed of this, because wanting it was too painful. "What do you mean?"

"The minute you left, Victoria begged me to abdicate and let her take the throne. I said no over and over again because I didn't think it'd be fair to her. But then she came to me with plans and ideas and a way forward. She *wants* it, and I think the country deserves a leader who does. Plus, there's no denying she'll be bloody good at it."

Queen Victoria. It feels right. Say what you will about royalty, if anyone in that family can do it right, it's her.

"We decided to wait until her eighteenth birthday, but Parliament passed an official declaration of abdication today."

My eyes blur with tears, and I'm too stunned to speak. Theo holds me until Comet nudges his way through our legs, and I finally find my words again. "What about Comet?" I bend to give him a scratch behind the ears.

"Tor told me to tell you that he still lives at Buckingham, but we're free to visit him whenever we like."

My heart squeezes painfully; I don't know how to deal with all this news at once. It's too much like my impossible daydreams, too good to be true. "'We'?"

"The disgraced former king of England can't exactly stay in the palace, Wheeler."

"Where will you live?"

Theo's mouth twists wryly as he runs his fingers through my hair and rests his hand on the back of my neck. "I think that depends on you."

"Stay in Chicago. With me," I say quickly. I don't know what our future will look like tomorrow, or next month, or next year, but there's no one I'd rather be with as we figure it out. "I mean, not in my dorm. My roommate would freak out. But there are places close to campus. You could apply and start in January! Or not, if you need time to figure out what you want. But you should definitely stay here. In the city. With me."

Theo's lip twitches at my rambling. "If you insist."

Tears blur my vision as my world turns upside down again.

I spent the last month telling myself that fate didn't want us together, but I've never been so relieved to be wrong. "*Fate*," I whisper, almost to myself. I tip my head back and lock watery eyes with Theo. "You were right the whole time."

He shakes his head with a grin. "Nah. This isn't fate, Wheeler."

I blink in surprise. "It's not?"

"Fate can piss off."

"Shh! It'll hear you."

Theo cups his hands around his mouth. "Piss off—"

I cover his mouth with my hands, his shoulders shaking with laughter. I check the sky for falling bombs and then put my hands on my hips. "Don't tempt it! I don't want to deal with a disaster today."

"I'm not bothered, because we're stronger than fate," Theo says as he pulls his ring out of his pocket, turning it thoughtfully between his fingers. "What we have is better, because we chose it ourselves." He holds the ring up, his eyebrow cocked. I nod, and with steady hands, he slips the ring back on my fourth finger.

With Theo's other hand on the back of my neck and a promise in his eyes, I've never felt so rooted to a moment or this city or this boy who has always believed in us.

We kiss as cars honk and pedestrians dodge around us on a busy street corner, not unlike the first day we met. We probably don't have long until he's recognized, but we stand in the middle of my city anyway and kiss until drizzling rain turns to whisper-soft mist. When we finally break apart, he threads his fingers through mine.

"What do we do now, Wheeler?"

I take his hand and we start the long walk home. "Whatever we want."

Acknowledgments

One of the most exciting writing days of my career was the day I finished writing *The Prince & The Apocalypse*. The epilogue was exactly everything I wanted it to be—on one condition. I knew in my heart that Wren and Theo's story demanded a sequel, but I also knew that sequels are never guaranteed, especially when you write rom-coms. Thankfully, this is where my amazing editor, Sarah Grill, enters the picture. Sarah, I cannot thank you enough for making this book happen. Without your guidance and support and belief in me, Wren and Theo wouldn't have their happy ending.

A massive thank-you to everyone at Wednesday Books who had a hand in bringing Wren and Theo's story to readers, including Sara Goodman, Eileen Rothschild, Jen Edwards, Olga Grlic, Eric Meyer, Cassie Gutman, Diane Dilluvio, Terry McGarry, Devan Norman, Soleil Paz, Meghan Harrington, Alexis Neuville, and Brant Janeway, among others.

Thank you to my brilliant agent, Katelyn Detweiler, for everything you do and for always knowing exactly what I need to hear. And to Sam Farkas and everyone at Jill Grinberg Literary Management, for the endless support.

Thank you to the readers who reached out to let me know

how much you liked *The Prince & The Apocalypse* and how badly you needed a sequel. Those messages brought light to some of my roughest writing days.

Getting through this duology would have been a lot harder without the support and encouragement of Joanna Ruth Meyer, Nicole Adair, Kimberly Gabriel, and Gretchen Schreiber. Thank you!

Most of all, thanks to Scott, Owen, Graham, and Emmett for flying across the pond with me so we could stand in front of The World's End and Buckingham Palace and the Eiffel Tower, just like Wren and Theo. Thank you for taking that adventure with me. I can't wait for all the adventures still to come.

ABOUT THE AUTHOR

Kendyl Hawkins

Kara McDowell is the author of *The Prince & The Apocalypse, One Way or Another, This Might Get Awkward,* and *Just for Clicks.* She lives with her husband and a trio of rowdy boys in Mesa, Arizona, where she divides her time between writing, baking, and wishing for rain.